LAND OF
10,000 THRILLS

BOUCHERCON ANTHOLOGIES

Murder at the Beach (Long Beach CA, 2014)
Murder Under the Oaks (Raleigh NC, 2015)
Blood on the Bayou (New Orleans LA, 2016)
Passport to Murder (Toronto ON, 2017)
Florida Happens (St. Petersburg FL, 2018)
Denim, Diamonds and Death (Dallas TX, 2019)
Where Murder is a Capital Crime (Sacramento CA, 2020)
This Time For Sure (New Orleans LA, 2021)
Land of 10,000 Thrills (Minneapolis MN, 2022)

GREG HERREN, EDITOR

LAND OF
10,000 THRILLS

BOUCHERCON ANTHOLOGY 2022

DOWN&OUT
BOOKS

Down & Out Books
3959 Van Dyke Road, Suite 265
Lutz, FL 33558
DownAndOutBooks.com

Cover design by Maegan Beaumont

ISBN: 1-64396-290-6
ISBN-13: 978-1-64396-290-0

TABLE OF CONTENTS

TWO WOMEN AND A TARP

Susanna Calkins and Erica Ruth Neubauer

On the interstate
Milwaukee, Wisconsin
9:15 a.m.

"Can you smell it?" Dana asked, clutching the inside handle of the passenger door. "I think I can."

Em tightened her hands on the black steering wheel of the Prius and took a deep breath. "I don't think so." She pointed toward the disappearing Milwaukee skyline. "Maybe you're smelling the Miller brewery. The wind carries that yeasty smell pretty far."

"Could be." Dana sniffed again. "When do bodies start to smell anyway?"

"I don't know. We should Google it."

"Seriously, Em?" Dana stared at her friend's profile. "Weren't you a cop? I feel like that's something you should know. Something you would have had *training* around?"

Em shrugged. "It's been a long time since I served. I don't remember anymore." She checked the odometer. Still at sixty, just under the speed limit. "Come to think of it, we should look up when rigor mortis sets in, too."

"Right. We need to know that." Dana pulled out her phone and began to type into the search engine. "When do dead bodies start to—?"

She stopped, her index finger hovering over the tiny keyboard. "Wait! What if someone looks at my search history later?"

Em's eyes darted from the road, taking in her shaking form. "Deep breaths, Dana."

"I know, I know. I'm trying." She gulped for air. "What if someone saw me?" She tugged at her seat belt where it was cutting into her chest. "Maybe one of the neighbors. Everyone has a camera."

"No one saw you, Dana."

"Maybe they did!" A note of hysteria crept into her voice. "They could be searching for me right now. Ugh. I should just turn myself in."

Em kept her eyes fixed on the banana-yellow VW in front of her. "I'm telling you, Dana. Once we cross into Minnesota, everything will be fine. We'll find a good forest to bury the body. Some secluded woodsy area, with lots of good cover."

"You're sure about that crossing state lines thing? Did you learn that when you were a cop?"

"No. I saw a documentary once. This truck driver deliberately crossed a state line after he committed a crime. He knew state cops would be hard-pressed to track him down once he left their jurisdiction. That's why I wanted to cross *two* state lines."

For the next few minutes, they were silent. Then Dana read one of the green directional signs out loud as they whizzed by. "Madison. Seventy miles." Her fingernails dug into her palms. "How long until the Minnesota state line?"

Em glanced at the digital display on her dashboard. "Four hours, maybe?"

Dana put her hand to her forehead, resting her elbow on the door. "How the hell did we get here?"

***

Earlier that morning
Outside Chicago
6:00 a.m.

"*Em. I think I k-killed someone. With my car,*" Dana whispered, her voice hoarse and strained over the cell phone. "*Can you h-help me? I need to hide the body.*"
    "*Hide the body? Of course. I'll bring a tarp. And some shovels.*"
    "*Just like that? Don't you want to know who it is?*"
    A long pause.
    "*All right, Dana, who did you kill? Someone you know?*"
    "*Samuel.*"
    "*Samuel? Sam, you mean Sam? The guy who owns that restaurant?*"
    "*Yeah.*"
    "*The one you—?*"
    "*Yeah.*"
    Another long silence. "*Okay. Where are you now?*"
    "*Just outside Chicago.*" Dana gave her the directions. "*He...it...is in my garage.*"
    "*I'll be there in an hour.*"

On the interstate, just past Madison
10:33 a.m.

A Winnebago pressed by them on their right, two canoes tethered to the top of the rusty and weather-worn vehicle. A cheery bumper sticker drew Dana's attention. "Life is Better on the River." She snapped her fingers. "How about we just throw the body in a canoe? Float it down a river?"
    Em raised an eyebrow. "As in a Viking funeral? Should we shoot a flaming arrow too?"
    "Um, no. People might notice a canoe on fire—oh, you were

3

kidding." She snorted nervously. "I just meant, hide it in a canoe and send it down a river. Someone might think he, uh, died while fishing or something. Then we could just be done with this whole thing."

Em rolled her eyes. "Do you *want* to be on the world's most stupid criminals list?" He has tire tracks all over him. No one is going to believe he died fishing." She glanced at Dana. "So, you never said. How did you come to kill—run over him anyway?"

Dana slumped back in the seat, staring out at the stretches of farmland. "I don't know. It just happened."

At Dana's house
Highland Park, Illinois
5:05 a.m.

Dana pulled into her driveway, tears streaming down her face. A dark figure stepped out from the shadows of the garage, causing her to slam on the brakes.

"What the hell?" She lowered her car window. "Samuel! What are you doing here?"

"You wouldn't answer my calls." His voice sounded a bit slurred. Drunk as always. "I just had to tell you—it was all a mistake! I don't care about that woman. You're the one I love. The one I want to be with—"

She flicked on her high beams, suffusing his body in light. He was in head-to-toe black, the logo of his restaurant embroidered in red over his left breast pocket. "I'm tired, Sam. Get out of my way. I want to go to bed."

"Can we just talk?" He came over to her passenger door but she had pressed the lock before he could open it. "Oh, come on, Dana. Don't be like that. I swear, sometimes you can be so immature."

"You need to leave, Sam. I'm done. We're done." She began to inch the car forward.

4

"I'm not leaving until we talk."

"Fine, then I'm leaving." She began to turn the car around so she could drive back down the driveway. "I'm not in the mood."

He darted down the driveway and spread out his arms in a playful way. "Gosh, your jealousy is so cute. I'm not going to let you leave."

Dana took her foot off the brake, her eyes intent on his body. "Get out my way, Sam."

"I'm telling you—she didn't mean...Hey! What are you doing?"

Dana stamped down on the gas pedal like she was stamping on his cheating face.

On the interstate, Wisconsin Dells
11:36 a.m.

"Blood red," Dana murmured, her eyes half closed as she lolled back against the headrest.

"You dreaming, hon?"

This was the first time either woman had spoken in the last half hour.

Dana gestured vaguely toward the majestic foliage that lined the interstate, the leaves of the great oaks and maple trees scalding orange and crimson. "Glad it stopped raining. I hate when all the leaves are downed during a single storm."

"Agreed," Em replied. She peered up at the gray sky above to see a streak of sun cutting through the nebula. "Looks like it's clearing up a bit."

Dana jerked up in her seat then, the seat belt furiously snapping her back into place. "Oh my God."

"What is it?" Em asked.

"It's been *raining!* It could have rained in Minnesota too. What if the ground is all *wet?*" She clapped her hands to her mouth. "We'll be leaving footprints all over the place, won't we?"

Em patted her knee. "We'll figure it out. We won't leave any footprints. Don't worry, Dana. We've got this."

Dana swallowed. "If you say so."

"I know so."

On the interstate, outside Mauston, Wisconsin
11:58 a.m.

Em glanced in her rearview window and then blanched. "Oh. My. God."

The car swerved abruptly as she whipped off her red sunglasses and pivoted in her seat to stare at the back of the car.

"What are you doing?" Dana exclaimed, grabbing the wheel to straighten the car. A convertible to their right honked before blasting past them. "What happened? What's wrong?"

"His hand! I see it." Her voice sounded strangled, as her eyes kept flicking toward the rearview mirror. "My God. Is he *waving?*"

"What?" Dana pivoted to stare into the back.

A hand was touching the glass of the hatchback's rear window with curled fingers, swinging back and forth.

"Dana," Em whispered. "Are you *absolutely certain* that Sam was dead?"

"Are you kidding? *Of course* I'm sure. I ran over him, didn't I?"

"Then why the hell is he waving?" Em's calm demeanor was cracking.

A hysterical giggle burst from Dana's lips as realization set in. "I don't think he's *waving*. I mean, not on purpose. He's definitely dead. His hand must have just, I don't know, popped up."

"Stupid rigor mortis," Em muttered.

Dana couldn't stop another strained giggle from escaping as she craned her neck to look out at the passing cars. "What if someone sees the hand? All we need is one of these truck drivers to get a good look and then we're toast. They'll call the police on the CB radio or whatever the hell they use these days."

"Calm down, Dana," Em replied, having regained her original calm. "Let me just pull over. We'll fix it before anyone sees." She put on her turn signal and merged into the right lane. "I see a Festival Foods up ahead. They'll have a nice big parking lot and we can take care of this mess."

"It's pointing like—" Dana began to convulse into deep gales of uncontrollable laughter, tears streaming down her cheeks.

"Like what?"

It took a full moment before Dana could compose herself enough to speak. "A corpse's pointing finger. You know, l-like in medieval times, when the corpse would point to its murderer!"

"Jesus, Dana. Pull it together. Do I need to slap you?"

In the Festival Foods parking lot
Mauston, Wisconsin
12:03 p.m.

After forcing the hand back under the blanket, Em slid back into the driver's seat. Though she turned the car back on, she just sat there for a moment, letting the engine idle.

"Why aren't we leaving?" Dana asked. "What's wrong?"

"I was just thinking about what you said before. About the rain and leaving footprints. You're right. We need to figure out what to do."

Dana began to gnaw at her thumbnail. "Okay, so, do you have an idea?"

"We need men's shoes. *Giant* men's shoes." She smirked. "Even if we leave footprints, they won't be from *our* shoes."

"Hmm. That makes sense." Dana clucked her teeth. "But how will we buy them? We can't use our credit cards."

"I have some cash."

"Okay. That's good." Dana rubbed her nose. "Is he starting to smell now? I think he's starting to smell."

Em sniffed again. "I don't think so. But let's open the windows just in case."

They rolled their windows down and gulped in the fresh air. Em started to drive out of the parking lot, easing back to the on-ramp.

"So, we'll use the shoes," Dana said. "Then we'll need to dump them somewhere, right?"

Em tapped on the steering wheel, deep in thought. "A dumpster is best," she decided. "It can go straight into a landfill. A dumpster by a restaurant would be perfect." She pointed at the sign of a cheese emporium looming ahead of them. "Like that one."

On the interstate
Outside Black River Falls, Wisconsin
3:00 p.m.

"This traffic jam sucks," Em said, eating another cheese curd. Groaning, she dropped her head on the steering wheel. "We haven't moved in ten minutes. Must be an accident up ahead."

"If only we hadn't stopped to buy the shoes. And the *cheese.*" Dana looked accusingly at the half-eaten bag of cheese between them. "Maybe we'd have missed this mess."

Em shrugged. "I needed to eat. Relax. It will clear soon, I'm sure."

"People are looking at us. Don't you think they're looking at us? Can they see him?"

"Jeez, Dana. I told you! He's completely covered up. Besides, everyone is just trying to move along. No one is concerned about what's in our car." Em glanced sharply at her friend. "Girl, you have to *try* to look natural. People are going to notice if you keep staring at the other drivers like that. Quit with the crazy eyes already."

"I'm sorry. It's hard to act natural when, you know, there's a body back there."

She rubbed her eyes. A truck with an oversize load inched by, carefully balancing a prefab home across the flatbed. A gigantic banner strung across the home depicted a wholesome-looking family about to cross the threshold. "Your Dreams Start Here!"

"Too bad we can't just throw the body in there," she muttered. "We're going slow enough. How much longer until we get to Minnesota?"

"I'm guessing about two hours."

"Two hours? Shit." Dana tapped her foot on gray carpeted floor. "Although, Em, do we need to go this route? I thought there was a state line near La Crosse?"

Em slapped her head. "Sheesh. I think you're right. I've been driving like we're heading to Minneapolis. But let's keep this route. If someone asks us, we could just say we wanted to check out the Mall of America or something."

On the interstate
Outside Eau Claire, Wisconsin
4:15 pm

The billboard on the hillside captured both women's attention at once. "Join us out here," it proclaimed, with the word "Leinenkugel's" scrawled in fancy script over the image of two campers clustered around a campfire, drinking bottles of beer.

"Ah, Leinies," Em said, switching back into the faster lane. Traffic was moving briskly again, and they were back to pushing seventy. "I could use a lager right now."

"Same." Dana paused. "I've been thinking about my car."

"What about it?

"The whole front is dented. There's blood all over the front too. Even though it's tucked away in my garage right now, at some point, I'll need to drive it again. Someone may notice the damage, right? Ask me why I have blood on my car? Maybe I should just sell it."

"Don't sell it! At least not for a while," Em said sharply. She tapped her fingers on the steering wheel. "As for the blood, I've got it figured out. When we get back, we'll smear deer's blood and fur all over the front. The fenders, the grill, the headlights. All of it. Then you take it to a garage, give them a sob story about a deer crossing your path on Sheridan, and they'll take care of it." She smirked. "Easy-peasy."

Her eyes flicked over at her friend, waiting for her to reply. "Don't give me that skeptical look! I'm telling you, people hit deer all the time in Wisconsin and no one ever calls the police to sort it out."

Dana was quiet for a moment. "Where are we going to get deer fur?"

Em shrugged. "There's been a deer corpse about every hundred yards along this whole trip. We'll stop on the way back and get one." She frowned. "I wonder if I have a second tarp."

Dana swallowed. "That's disgusting."

Em rolled her eyes.

"So, we'll bring back this deer carcass, and then you'll just smear blood on my car when we get back?"

"No, *I* won't. *You* will."

"But I'm a vegetarian," Dana whined.

On the interstate, crossing the Saint Croix River
Wisconsin-Minnesota state line
5:30 p.m.

"Em, I think someone is following us."

"Get out of here. No one is following us." Em stared into the rearview mirror. "I don't see anyone."

"I think there is! That black car. I'm sure I've seen it before."

"Dana. You're getting paranoid." Still, Em changed lanes. "Shit. They changed lanes too. Who could be following us?"

"Someone who saw what I did?"

"No. That can't be right."

"Why do you say that?"

"Think about it rationally. If someone saw you run over that jerk, they would have called the police back when it happened. Back in *Chicago*. Right?"

Dana chewed her bottom lip. "Right. I suppose." She peered into the side window again. "Still, that car looks familiar." She sucked in her breath. "If I didn't know better, I would have thought it was Sam's."

"Sam's car? For God's sake. Before you make me completely paranoid too, let's figure out the place to hide the body." Em cracked her neck. "Once we cross this bridge, we'll be in Minnesota, and closing in on nightfall. Now, we'll just need to find a remote area with a lot of tree cover."

"An area with lots of tree cover, got it. We can't Google this either." Dana rummaged through the glove box. "Do you have an atlas?"

"An atlas? I imagine my husband gave me one when I first bought the car. Fifteen years ago."

"Found it." Dana spread the atlas across her lap and perused the Minneapolis-St. Paul area. "Fifteen years. Hmmm. How outdated could it be?"

Woodbury Golf Course
Woodbury, Minnesota
5:45 p.m.

"You've taken us to a golf course," Em said flatly, after they'd exited the highway and navigated a set of stops and turns. "I think someone will notice if we try to bury a dead body here." She pointed to a blue area slightly north of their current location. "How about here? Lake Elmo Park Preserve. It's just a few minutes away."

"Let's do it."

Lake Elmo Park Reserve
Minnesota
5:55 p.m.

Ten minutes later, Em pulled into a visitor's parking lot on the edge of a lake preserve that had not been taken over by McMansions and over-eager developers. A sign read "Park Closes at 6pm, Oct-Mar." A long chain hung between two poles, effectively barring them from entry.

"What do you think?" she asked.

"No other cars around. That's a good sign," Dana replied, pressing her hands together. "I think this will work. We can do this."

Em drove the length of the parking lot, looking for a place to enter. "We can't just drag this guy into the woods though. He'll be too heavy. We need to get deeper into the forest."

Dana pointed at a sign leading to a gravel road. A sign read "Service Vehicles Only."

"What about there?" she asked.

"Perfect," Em said, maneuvering the car through the service entrance.

They climbed out, standing in the shine of the headlights while they examined the little gate in front of the entrance to a dirt road.

"Huh. It's not even locked." Em swung the gate open. "Can you close it after I pull the car through?"

Dana nodded, pushing the metal gate closed again behind the car and hurrying to get back in the passenger's side. They bumped slowly along the dirt and gravel path, deep ruts having been carved by heavier vehicles.

"Here, do you think?" Dana asked.

"Not yet. I think we need to get a little further in."

6:05 p.m.

Em finally stopped the car. "This looks like a good spot," she said, unbuckling her seat belt.

Dana handed her a pair of the men's shoes. "Don't forget these."

A few moments later, they exited the car, breaking into hysterical giggles as they flopped along in their ridiculous clown-like shoes.

Peering over the steep embankment, they grew sober again.

"If we roll him down this hill," Em said, pointing downward, "it will be easier to drag him into those trees to bury him."

Using the dim light from Dana's cell phone to see, they pulled Sam's body out of the trunk and duct-taped the tarp around his head and feet. Still flop-walking in their men's shoes, they managed to get him to the edge of the road.

They looked at each other. "On the count of three?" Dana asked and Em nodded.

"One..." Dana said. "Two..."

"Three!" They shouted together and heaved the body down the embankment.

The body rolled several times before coming to an abrupt stop about twenty feet down.

"Shit," Em said. "He's stuck."

Grabbing the shovels, the women slid down the small hill to where the tarp-wrapped body was half curled around a tree stump.

"Jeez! I can't believe we didn't see the stupid stump," Dana said, kicking at it. "This is a lot harder than I thought it would be."

Grunting, they managed to push the body off the stump and send it on its way once again. Finally, they got to the bottom of the embankment.

"We'll need to drag him from here. You grab the top," Em said. "I've got his feet."

"Ugh, that's his head. Why do I have to hold that part?"

"Because you ran him over. And honestly, you can't even see it with the tarp. Just think of this thing as...something else."

"What else could it possibly be?" Dana muttered, but she grabbed the top end of the body without further comment.

Together, they dragged the body deeper into the stand of pines, grunting and gasping for air the whole while.

About two hundred yards in, Em stopped, trying to catch her breath. "Far enough," she managed. "We can dig here. In a minute."

Dana crouched over in relief, grasping her sides. When she'd regained her breath, she grabbed her shovel and began to dig.

6:45 pm

It had only taken a few minutes before the digging became tedious.

"How deep does this need to be? I don't think six feet is going to happen." Dana leaned against her shovel. "I'm going to get blisters through my gloves."

Em surveyed the ground. "I think three or four feet should be fine."

"Don't stop digging on my account," a man's voice came from behind them.

They whirled around.

A man in maybe his late twenties, dressed in a brown coat, gray cap, and jeans was standing there, holding a gun. "I'll need that hole for the two of you."

"Who the fuck are you?" Em demanded, lowering her shovel.

The man pointed to the tarp-covered body. "Samuel's nephew."

Dana squinted at him. "Jason."

"That's right. I know who you are too. And, more importantly, I saw what you did."

"What? How could you have? No one was there."

"Oh, but I was," Jason replied. "My dear Uncle Sam was giving me a ride home from the restaurant. When you didn't pick up his calls, he decided he needed to see you." He grinned spitefully at her. "We were parked in front of your next-door neighbor's house. I saw the whole thing go down."

"Shit. I didn't even think about his car," Em muttered.

"It was an accident! I swear!" Dana cried, starting to tremble.

"*Was* it an accident? Really?" Jason scoffed. "From what I saw, you had him in your sights and ran him down. Pissed you off, did he?"

"No, er,—"

"It was an accident!" Em declared stoutly, although there was a question in her eyes when she glanced at her friend.

"Then why did you and your friend load his body into her trunk?" Jason asked. "Explain *that*."

"I p-panicked," Dana said. "Truly."

Jason laughed. "Don't get me wrong, lady. I don't care if you wanted to kill him. In fact, it helps me out a lot, because I've been wanting to kill my uncle for years."

"Why? Oh, for his money? He always said you were a good-for-nothing lowlife."

"Guilty, I suppose. Why work, when you can inherit?"

"So let me get this straight," Em said, running her fingers along the shovel. "You saw him get run over. Why didn't you just call the police?"

"Well, now, that's where it gets tricky. He had something in his pocket that would ruin my plans. So, I needed it back." He frowned. "I thought I'd retrieve it after Miss Dana here left. I never expected her to call someone and for you to drive off with the body! I was forced to follow you."

"So you *followed* us this whole time?" Em asked. "From Chicago to Minnesota?"

"I couldn't figure out what you were doing—I didn't expect you to drive across two states to bury the body." Jason glanced at their feet. "Or to buy men's shoes. What was that for anyway—to disguise your shoe prints? Impressive, truly." He waved his gun toward them. "Thing is, I'm also going to need his body."

"What?" Em exclaimed. "That's gross."

"For the insurance. My uncle was *rich* and I'm his only beneficiary. Or at least, I thought I was. Turns out he hired a private investigator to look into an old girlfriend. Appears that Uncle Sam had a son twenty years ago. He just told me about him. Hadn't told anyone else it seemed, and I intend to keep it that way."

"Ah, so that was what was in his pocket. The P.I.'s report about his son—his *lawful* beneficiary?" Dana's giggle was tight. "I see that scumbag quality runs in the family."

"I just need to destroy the report. And then I need the body. Without evidence that he's dead, he'll just be a missing person and I'll never collect.'"

"I'm not sure that's how it works," Em replied, tightening her grip on the shovel.

Jason stepped closer. "I don't care what you think. Keep digging."

Still shaking, Dana began to dig again, continuing her prattle as she shoveled earth into a pile. "So, you're going to drag the body back up the embankment and then leave it somewhere? They'll just think you're the one who killed him."

"What? No, that's not right—" He started to say but was cut off by Em swinging her shovel, knocking the gun out of his hand.

Before he could shout, she swung her shovel again, striking him hard across his head. As he started to slump to his knees, Dana landed another glancing blow. Em struck him one more time, so that he fell directly in the freshly dug hole.

The women lowered their shovels and stared down at his still form. Blood was pooling around his head, and his eyes stared sightlessly upward.

"Do you think he's dead?" Dana whispered.

"I think so," Em replied. Still, she kneeled down beside the body, warily watching for any movement. She plucked the gun from his lifeless fingers. "Amateur," she said, shaking her head. "You never get that close to someone when you're holding a gun on them."

Dana regarded the man's body where it sprawled next to his tarp-enclosed uncle. "We're gonna need a bigger hole."

Lakeview Tavern
Minneapolis, Minnesota
9 p.m.

Dana took a long sip of her beer. "Just what I needed."

"Likewise." Em dipped another cheese curd into the ranch and popped it into her mouth. "I'm so glad they still have Oktoberfest on tap. It gets harder to find this time of year."

For a moment they leaned back, taking in the old oak tables, deer heads mounted on the walls, the pool table in the back. Next to them, some locals were joshing about curling and hot dish.

Finally, Dana spoke. "How long do you think that man's car will sit in the rest stop parking lot?"

After they had buried nephew and uncle side by side, Em pitched the shoes in a restaurant dumpster covered with Vikings stickers, while Dana drove Sam's car to a truck stop off the highway. They had met up again and driven into Minneapolis, stopping at the Lakeview Tavern, which had all local brews on tap.

Em shrugged. "Probably a month or so. As rest stops go, I think that place stays pretty busy. Who's going to notice his car? By the time they do, we'll be long gone."

Dana tossed back the last swig of her beer. "Speaking of which, should we head out?"

Em popped the last tater tot in her mouth and stood up. "You betcha."

THE ONE-THOUSANDTH LAKE

Eric Beckstrom

Minnesota, land of seventeen thousand lakes. Never let anyone tell you it's fewer. License plates lie.

All of those lakes, each one of them, contain dead things.

Some of those dead things are people.

I know because I put some of them there. One by accident—my twin brother, when we were nine and didn't understand ice—and others on purpose—after I grew up and did understand ice.

Never let anyone tell you there are only ten thousand lakes in Minnesota, not even—especially not even—on a state-issued license plate. And never let anyone tell you, not even facetiously, that there are two seasons in Minnesota and that those two seasons are (snicker snicker) winter and road construction.

There's only one season in Minnesota: it's always winter.

February is the two a.m. of a Minnesota winter. Who would you put under the ice, in February? Tell the truth. Don't say "No one." You don't have to hate someone to want them where hydrogen and oxygen aren't the only things that slow to a crawl, or to a stop. You just have to need them gone from the world above the two a.m. lake. In fact, you don't even have to need them gone. You only have to want them gone. Sometimes you can even just wish them gone when the two of you are ice skating on the lake too close to the rotted tree trunk thrust up from beneath the surface where the ice is always thinner, the hand of a drowning swimmer reaching for air. It doesn't even have to be a serious wish. Just a second of childish jealousy or envy. A parent's hug lasted a second longer or a second shorter than it should have. A brother's ice skating was always more straight or more crooked.

Sometimes it's someone else who needs them, wants them, wishes them gone, and sometimes they ask you to make their wish come true.

I didn't know I was going to write all of this until I sat down to make out my shopping list. I was heading into town to ask some questions, figured I might as well pick up some stuff, too. The kind of stuff that always runs out, breaks, or dulls with use.

Baked beans
Bread
Coffee
Peanut butter
Fishing line
Nylon rope
Ice saw blades

Then, items became paragraphs. Paragraphs with questions like, where is Jason Westcraft? And, who wants him there and why?

In my mind he's like Schrödinger's cat, both alive and dead while he remains unfound and unlooked upon. That's what I'm tasked with. Finding him. Will I kill him or give him life when I observe him? Why has it become *my* thing, to set his state in the universe?

Well, I already said. I was asked to. Tommy the Curb from Out East—Out East always said like a proper noun, as though Out East were a proper place—it isn't—Tommy the Curb directs traffic all over the country. You'd be surprised how heavy the traffic is up here, moving stuff from one place to another that's not supposed to move across state lines, or at all. The Twin Cities (fraternal at best), Duluth, Saint Cloud. Lots of traffic. If the mapping apps tracked that particular kind of movement, the highways and the county roads up here, in the country's attic, would be all red, all the time.

This was the only time Curby ever tasked me with finding someone. Usually, it's the opposite. Making someone not able to be found. Unlocatable. He knew I'd only unfind someone if that someone deserved it. It was an understanding we had. How that understanding came about, and how Curby and I met in Monowi, Nebraska—freaking Nebraska—a town of one resident—not even a one-horse town, but a one-person town—freaking Nebraska—how that happened is another story. The point is, Tommy the Curb and I bonded over the Freaking Nebraska Debacle. We go back a ways and so he asked me to find a guy instead of unfind a guy.

Jason Westcraft. I didn't think there could be two of them, not up here, so I did what everyone does and Googled the name. As far as I can tell there's not another one in the entire country. Which means it's the one and only Jason Westcraft, the same one who was my best friend throughout most of grade school and into middle school. Thinking about that, contemplating it—the odds and the oddness—was like pulling dry leather from a wet brain. It hurt.

Jason Westcraft went from my life decades ago for no reason besides the reason most people go from your life. Everyone has their own beneath and their own above, and people are always disappearing from our lives into their own beneath, or we're always disappearing into ours. I don't know how else to say it. People come and go, often for no other reason than that: people come and go.

But now Jason might be gone from life itself, and not just from mine. Up here in the cold attic, when people disappear they're almost always gone from the world. Or at least the part of them that matters is gone. You might not think a guy in my line believes in that stuff—God and the soul, which must exist if God does—but it's been my experience that almost everyone in my line believes in God. That's why we all walk around more afraid than most people. We're never nervous—can't afford to be, not in our line—but we're always afraid.

Beneath. Most people who disappear are beneath *something*. They're not just lying out in the open or on top of other things. A lot of them are beneath water. If Jason is one of them he could be in any one of seventeen thousand places, and that's only counting lakes.

I met Jason when we were nine, our birthdays two days apart, his October 30, mine November 1. When I first saw him, or first saw the bottoms of his feet, he was in one of the five thousand ice fishing houses covering roughly half the two hundred square miles of Lake Mille Lacs. Mille Lacs is two and a half hours north of the Cities, an hour and a half southwest of Duluth, and an hour northeast of Saint Cloud, if you're keeping track. Every year about two dozen of the temporary dwellings burn or sink through the ice beneath them because drunk or sleepy fishermen—it's always men who do the sinking because women are wiser—don't tend properly to their little propane heaters. Every year at least one poor idiot immolates himself because he uses wood to heat a ten-by-ten room...a room itself made of wood. More than once such a person has even hauled a wood burning stove onto the lake and plunged into the depths along with the cast iron as it melts through the ice like Minnesota's version of the China Syndrome.

Jason's dad had his fishing house on giant wooden sled runners to make it easier to haul around on the ice and through the constantly accumulating snow. I was out with my pole, heading toward a fishing house I knew wasn't locked and wasn't being used, it being the first week of March when people were getting ready to haul their huts off the lakes. It had snowed seven inches and was still snowing, so the surface of Mille Lacs looked deceptively solid despite the preceding week of warmer than usual weather.

Through the dense fog of snow—flakes the size of acorns—I heard wood sliding over frozen water. I could tell it was moving vertically, not horizontally, and something sliding downward was never good on the eve of spring on a softening lake.

I dropped my pole and tackle and ran toward what I knew had to be a hole in the ice, moving as fast as I could in my heavy snowmobile boots. Even with no wind against me it was like that nightmare everyone has had, trying to get someplace and being held back in slow motion, running through a thick slurry of cement.

Two horns reared up from the ice in front of me, and between them wriggled two proboscises, all of it indistinct through the white filter behind which the world lay, blurred and half disappeared.

After a moment the image resolved. The back ends of two sled runners were slipping over the lip of a hole and into the lake at a forty-five-degree angle. By then the rear side of the icehouse was even with the surface of the frigid water, and from a small square window, now missing its plexiglass, the legs of a kid kicked, booted feet trying to gain leverage against snow and desperation. Water was bubbling and erupting up through the window, which meant the kid's head and torso were underwater.

I jumped onto the back of the icehouse, grabbed the squirming legs, and pulled straight up. My weight had accelerated the sinking, but his buoyancy helped and a second later he popped up like a bobber and was out. He coughed and choked, exhaling water and inhaling snow as I stepped us both across the gap between the wood of the house and the dubious solidity of the snow and ice surrounding it. We trudged away from the hole toward my tackle, which in my mind seemed like base camp, like safety.

So, Jason Westcraft and I became friends. Not because he owed me his life—that kind of talk never came up—but because we'd shared an adventure. Because we were two third-grade loners who'd been out fishing by ourselves when we shouldn't have been.

Our friendship didn't end. It just slid beneath the surface of life because that's what happens. It was there, it just could no longer be seen or gotten to. Forty years later Tommy the Curb called from Out East, not knowing he was hiring me to find my old friend. Coincidence is coincidental with life. I never believed in providence, and I stopped believing in serendipity a long time ago. I no longer try to assign meaning to coincidence, but that doesn't make it any less striking when it happens. Jason and I, from the same lightly populated part of central Minnesota, bonded over a life-changing experience, lost track of each other, but, someplace in the back of the universe, had reconnected through Tommy the Curb. What were the odds? There are four casinos on West Mille Lacs. I thought about making the rounds.

The best way to locate people is through other people. I was born at Split Rock Lighthouse—literally, in the parking lot, near the cliff's edge—but grew up near Agate Bay, on the east side of Mille Lacs, before settling in Big Lake to be near the Cities. Through kindergarten Jason lived between Mille Lacs and Round Lake, which resembles a falcon or a terrier more than a circle, and moved to Agate Bay the same year I did. It was a few more years before we met on the ice. It's not always the case that everyone knows everyone around small towns, like the ones anchored to the edges of every body of water on Earth. That idea is either a truism with very limited application or it's a cliché. Lots of people live in isolated, low population areas precisely because they don't want to know or be known to a lot of people.

The Curb told me Jason was still around Agate Bay. It is *not* a cliché that if you're trying to find someone around a small town you start with the bars and the one or two locally owned restaurants. I dropped into Jim's Northern Bar 'n' Grill, just an old local stopping by looking for an old friend. Nothing. I stopped by the Taconite Teetotaler. Too alliterative, but they at least knew who Jason was. They hadn't seen him in weeks, though. Nothing helpful there.

I still had an ace in the hole. If you're looking for someone around here and you don't check the local bait shop, you're not really wanting to find them. In Agate Bay that's Agate Supply and Bayt, which is not clever and seems more like a pair of copywritten typos. But I know the owner, as everyone in Agate does. He's ninety-eight years old and has no hint of the Minnesota lilt. You'd expect him to be named Olaf and have an accent out of a Coen brothers movie, but his name is Anthony and he sounds like he's from nowhere.

That day it was cold enough for spit to freeze before it hit the ground. The entire internet seems to be wrong on this point. Anyone who lives up here has heard frozen spit hit the ground and bounce like a pebble. Jason and I used to have contests to see who could make their spit bounce the highest.

When I entered the shop Anthony looked up from his Minneapolis *Star-Tribune* the same way he had for decades, like he knew just who it was and had been expecting them, even if they hadn't been around for years.

"Well," he said, "let me guess. Beans. Coffee. Bread. Peanut butter."

Like I'd been in the week before, when I hadn't been in that shop since high school.

I shook my head in false wonderment—I was unsurprised—and then took off my mittens and shook his hand.

"Anthony. I knew you'd be here."

"Where else?" Not "Who else," but "Where else," as though I'd been looking for him and this had been the first stop on a long list of possibilities.

He put down his newspaper and I handed him my list. That's generally how it goes at Agate Supplay and Bayt. He's always moving everything around and no item ever seems to be in the same place twice. It's quicker for all concerned if Anthony assembles your items for you.

I got right to the point because he was a right to the point kind of guy.

"Anthony, have you seen Jason Westcraft lately? We lost touch and I'm trying to reconnect."

He didn't say anything for a full ten seconds, which is a long pause in a short conversation, especially with Anthony. In fact, it was unique in my experience. Normally, he was a talker.

A can of beans dropped from his hand and landed expiration date up on the concrete floor between us. I'd have three years to eat those beans before they'd become tainted. I noticed his hand was shaking and felt bad that he was doing my shopping for me like it was a half a century ago.

But then I saw that he was not infirm and not simply aged. He was scared.

He seemed to make a decision. He spoke almost inaudibly, as though he might be overheard, like maybe the cold would freeze not just spit but also words, and that someone watching from the little stand of trees between the parking lot and the lake could read those words and know that he was talking about something out of bounds and forbidden.

That was the kind of fear I saw in those century-eyes.

"Haven't seen Jason in a month, not since the middle of January. He comes in once a week, every week, never fails."

He paused again, the beat adding weight to his next words. Lead sinkers making the line taught.

"Not even if he's been visiting those friends of his Out East."

I picked up the can of beans, gently took the little shopping basket from his right hand, and continued gathering the rest of my items. He still held the list in his shaking left hand, but it wasn't long and I didn't need it. I let him keep it because having someone's list in his hand would feel familiar to him and that's what he needed just then.

"How did he seem when you saw him last?" I didn't bother trying to sound casual.

"They."

"Pardon?"

"It was him and some other guy, except the other guy never came in. Not from around here. Dressed like he didn't know winter. Like he only knew big city winter. Warm clothes, but too pretty. He just sat in the SUV. Not Jason's. Had to be the other guy's, but Jason was driving. Too new. A rental."

I didn't say anything. He was getting there just fine all by himself.

"Scared. Not nervous, you know? Jason was scared."

To my left, stacked to the bottom of the store's picture window, and in front me halfway to the ceiling, he had stacked hundreds of cases of Granite Glacier bottled water, something I'd never seen around here. I assumed it was the same trend as most other places. People paying a lot of money for bottled water when they could just turn on the tap. I dropped a two-pack of ice saw blades into the basket and waited for Anthony to share what was on his mind. I was a local who had once known him for fifteen years, so it didn't matter that it'd been a lifetime since we'd last spoken.

He'd seen my eyes sweep the bottled water.

"People started asking for that last year. I couldn't keep it stocked so I finally went all in."

I nodded and hung a fifty-foot coil of nylon rope around my left shoulder, made my way over to the till with him leading the way. It turned out the walk to the till wasn't just a walk to the till. It was Anthony making another decision.

"You know, Jason contracted—contracts—himself out. Not many people know that. Gathering soil and water samples. Testing 'em. Fertilizer companies. Herbicide companies. Chicken factories."

"Does he, now."

"I think it's just one thing he does," Anthony said, but he wasn't surmising. He knew Jason Westcraft had another line even if he didn't know what it was. There's always someone from somewhere taking vials of water or dipping sticks in water or dunking lab-labeled buckets in water around here. Testing water in the Land of Seventeen Thousand Lakes would have been the perfect cover for Jason Westcraft, a guy with business Out East.

And all that water Anthony had stocked and stacked. Water,

water everywhere. Another coincidence.

"That's not all he bought."

"Pardon?"

"Jason. What he bought last time I saw him. A case of water. Nylon rope. Ice saw blades. Like you. He shopped while that other guy sat in the truck, watching through the picture window. The other guy never seemed to blink."

I paid for my stuff and the till expectorated a curled receipt, the ink dark purple. Bruises shaped like numbers and words.

Anthony sat down on his stool and picked up the *Trib*, which was probably full of bad news. More ink, more bruises.

He said, "I looked out that window, too. The strangest thing."

I waited while he read without reading. His eyes moved back and forth across the columns like he was in open-eyed REM.

"When Jason went back out the guy said something and nodded to the back of the SUV. Jason handed the guy a bottle of water from the case and then stashed the rest. He got behind the wheel and it looked like the guy handed him something. Jason just stared at him. He was scared. Shook his head 'No' but the other guy opened his shiny city jacket like he was showing Jason something else. Like maybe something tucked into his waistband. Then Jason took a sip from a plastic jug, like a milk jug, except it just looked like water. That must be what the guy handed him. Then the guy looked, I don't know, gleeful. Determined. He said something else to Jason and Jason took another long swallow.

"Why would he make him drink water? The guy kept staring at him. Like he was shoving him with his eyes. Then Jason looked straight ahead through the glass of that windshield and through the glass of my picture window and right into my own eyes. He looked straight into my eyes and drank half that jug while the other guy nursed his own bottle of Granite Glacier and stared at the side of Jason's head like he was daring him to stop drinking."

"Then they drove away and you haven't seen either of them since," I finished for him.

Out of words, he nodded.

I made one more purchase, a role of fifty "Lucky 10,000 Lakes" dollar scratch 'n' wins. I looked at the receipt.

"Your till is computerized. It remembers transaction dates and times."

He nodded again, put down the paper again, and began tapping the till screen again. A few seconds later he handed me a copy of Jason's receipt.

"Cameras?"

He shook his head. No cameras.

He was tapped out. I thanked him and left him with his *Trib*, which he continued to not read.

Just fifteen minutes had passed, but outside it was less cold and more cloudy. More snow was on the way.

Boat rentals on a lake are one thing, car rentals another. People bring their own cars, so there were only a few places to check. I could only hope to get lucky.

I did. You might not believe it, but it's true. It's easier to bribe an hourly employee with fifty dollars' worth of scratch 'n' win tickets than with five twenty-dollar bills. The tickets seem to hold so much more promise of greater riches, even if the person could just turn around and buy twice as many chances with a hundred bucks. The thing is, most hourlies can't bring themselves to spend that much on gas station lotteries, but it's okay if someone else does it for them.

The truck Jason drove, and in which he was forced to drink God knows what from a milk jug, was rented by some guy whose name doesn't matter just now. I don't know yet what was in the water that was in that jug, or where exactly it came from. Nor do I know why the guy wanted to create a fresh human tissue sample out of Jason Westcraft. At first I thought it was all a cosmic red herring. Jason's water testing. Granite Glacier water in never-before-seen quantities. Childhood lakes. Present lakes. Snow. Ice. Too much water imagery to amount to anything.

I was wrong. Sometimes things are just what they seem, even

if you don't know quite what they are. I'll know soon enough, because I know that'll be my next task, courtesy of Tommy the Curb.

Extortion. Human tissue samples sent to someone doing illegal dumping would bring more credibility and leverage to bear than just a jug of water, as to the lengths the extortionist would go.

Revenge. Jason helped cover something up, and the SUV guy was really an avenging angel.

Just the opposite. Jason uncovers something and can't be bought. His fate is a message to others who might interfere.

A means to an end. Law firm planning to cash in on gigantic class action suit hires a guy to create evidence.

Something like that or something different. I'll know soon enough.

For a roll of instant-win tickets I not only bought the guy's info, but the rental's GPS log. My guess is he arrived in the area with a two-wheel drive vehicle only to realize he'd need something for off-road. Something that could be driven across a frozen lake.

I said before that Jason could be in any one of seventeen thousand places. But I knew he could really only be in one. You can find people through people, but in my experience finding them through poetics happens just about as often. You look where they've been, you imagine the tragedies and coincidences of their life. Everyone ends up beneath something—that is to say, everyone has a tragic life; and tragedy, in one classical sense, is born of events and people that shouldn't exist in close proximity to each other, but do. Jason never really made if off the lake. Not when we were kids, and not ever.

So now I know that's where I will find Jason Westcraft. All lakes contain dead things, and some of those dead things are people. Lakes are fractals; they cover a finite area, but have infinite perimeters. They can hold and keep infinite secrets, along with the finite motives and infinite emotions beneath those secrets.

Lake Mille Lacs is famous as the location of one of Houdini's most audacious stunts, reported at the time in the Minneapolis *Trib*. In the dead of winter he had a Houdini-sized hole chopped through the ice and a large hook submerged at the edge so he could find his way back. Eight minutes after he jumped in the men holding the hook felt a tug—"like a giant pike on the line," one of them reported—and Houdini emerged, having supposedly held his breath and endured the frigid water the whole time. It was later surmised that he survived by finding pockets of air just beneath the ice.

Mille Lacs translates from the French as "thousand lakes," which makes its full name—Lake Mille Lacs—a bit of overkill. Legend has it that Mille Lacs was the one-thousandth lake to be named in the Minnesota Territory. Naturally, the legend is myopically white, ignoring the history of the native peoples who thrived there for millennia before the French and other Europeans showed up.

So, I will find Jason Westcraft in the lake whose name is a lie. He will not be like Schrödinger's cat, both dead and alive until observed. I know without looking that he's just dead, with no uncertainty principle to save him. The rope around him. The sawed ice. The guy that made him drink tainted water by the gallon also made him buy the supplies he would use to hide and preserve Jason's own body. He will be tied with nylon rope beneath a block of ice that has been cut downward and inward, beveled at a thirty-degree angle to prevent it from falling through the frozen surface. The rope will be secured both beneath his shoulders and his crotch, and tied to the bottom of a T-handled ice auger protruding into the water like Houdini's hook. The auger handle will have been screwed down to the surface of the ice to make it invisible beneath the latest snowfall.

Everything, beneath.

I will turn the T-handle counter-clockwise. Doing so won't move time backwards and change the past, but it will reveal something of it. In physics, T is the symbol for time. I think of this whenever I'm on the ice, which, in Minnesota, is both eternal and ephemeral.

I'll work my ice saw with the shiny new blade around the edge of the block to free the slow-motion water. I will be a winter grave robber. The handle, newly raised, will provide leverage as I pry the lid from my dead friend's coffin. I will loop the nylon rope a couple of times around my mittened hands—every Minnesotan knows mittens keep your fingers warmer than gloves—and haul him back onto the surface adjacent to the hole, which my movements will have cleared of snow. His body, not frozen solid, will nonetheless clatter on the ice. That will be his clothes, which will be hard frozen. I'll have to wait until they thaw before I can check his pockets, but I won't find anything in them, except maybe a shopping list. I'll look, because that's what you do, but the body wasn't buried or destroyed, it was hidden; and you don't hide a whole body just to keep the contents of its pockets safe.

I will cut him free of the nylon rope and haul his body five backwards paces into the icehouse, inside of which the fishing hole will have long-since frozen shut. It will never have been used. The icehouse itself and the hole it contains will be lies. The house will have kept others distant, because etiquette compels that you don't put your fishing shelter near another person's claim. Or corpse. To thaw Jason Westcraft I will warm the house with the propane heater I will have brought along, not knowing in advance whether the ten-by-ten lie includes one or not.

I've read the weather reports and know that by then heavy snow will be accumulating. My footprints and the corpse track will soon afterwards be another secret beneath the storm, as will the re-lidded ice coffin.

Coffins are never really empty; so, for the moment, before I replace the lid, while I wait for the body and its pockets to thaw, I will drop a line or thrust a spear into the hole to see if my supper is down there. While its foremost purpose will have been fulfilled, there's no sense in wasting a perfectly good fishing hole.

Only then will I reseal it. It will eventually thaw and disappear into the wider hole that is Lake Mille Lacs.

I will remove the T-handle from the lid, as I'm sure the auger will yet come in handy this winter, when I find the SUV guy with the shiny jacket.

Not next winter. There is never a "next" winter.

It's always winter in Minnesota.

FAMILY REUNION
Sandra SG Wong

Is there anything quite as sad as a forwarded invitation, shuffled along to you, someone not on the list, by somebody who *thought you should know...*?

Drea understood the request, behind the sarcasm. For a few moments, she even let herself have an opinion about it. But she knew her place in the scheme of things. Opinions were ephemeral, unimportant.

So here she was. Three days since the demand dropped on her. Five days 'til her next scheduled deadline. Squeezing in this...in-between thing, last minute.

But just because she'd hauled ass to make it in time didn't mean she was just gonna waltz up to the cabin door and barge in. There were protocols to be observed. She needed to feel comfortable about her approach. She needed to know where she'd stand.

At least the unexpected email had included all the details. Hook Mouth Lake Resort, MN. A three-day weekend of family activities. Bring your trunks, your boats, and your tackle. Inner tubes and life jackets for the kids. Water skis and jet-skis if you got 'em. Family cabin assignments all diagrammed on a Google Maps satellite image.

Resort. She smirked. Is this what counted these days? A scattering of fourteen prefab houses, made more from plastic and vinyl than actual wood? She was no carpenter, but she guessed there were more particles than boards involved. Not that she was complaining. She'd managed to snag a good "cabin" for herself, a tiny thing that was supposed to go to a family of three. Still on the lake, set a little ways south from the rest of the rentals. An enormous poplar shaded the cabin from the worst of the summer sun. The unshaded cabins likely rented for more. But Drea had sensitive skin. She'd hate to burn.

Drea sighed, setting down her binoculars on the gritty arm of the Adirondack chair. She stretched her neck, releasing the tension in her shoulders. Tired after the long drive and then settling in, she'd barely moved all night on the bed.

In the distance, the lake shifted fluidly beneath the growing colors of the sunrise. There was even mist drifting moodily across parts of its surface. She couldn't decide if it looked like a horror movie set or a tourist ad.

"Oh, hello."

Drea whipped her attention around at the greeting. She eyed the interloper silently, assessing the woman from white flip-flops to pastel blue culottes to streaky-blond braids.

"Who are you?" The woman took a step toward the back door of the cabin. "Does Sadie know you're out here? Are you with the resort or something? The cleaning crew?"

"Dunno anyone named Sadie." Drea tilted her head. "I got here last night. And you are?"

"Oh." Disappointment flickered across her narrow face before she wrestled a plastic smile on instead. "I'm Dot McAllister. We rent number seven, just next to...here, behind that bit of shrubs." She gestured vaguely over her left shoulder. "Jet, my husband, and my four kids. We vacation here every summer and we always see Sadie and Beck and Juniper, that's the Thompsons. We've been in these same cabins for years now. Every July. It's kind of a tradition."

Drea nodded, noncommittal.

"I just don't understand how you got Sadie's cabin. Are you

36

with that family reunion going on?" Dot barreled on, sliding her hands into her back pockets. "They seem to have taken over the five best cabins out right. I mean, you don't look much like them, no offense, though I suppose it's impossible to know these days with all the mixing and matching going on."

"Not exactly with them, no," replied Drea blandly. People like Dot always showed who they were. Still, Drea found herself curious where Dot would take the conversation next.

"What does that mean?" Dot's gaze seemed to focus more sharply on Drea. "Who did you say you are again?"

"I didn't," said Drea easily. Dot was sharper than her first impression. "You thought I was a cleaner, remember? Because I'm brown." Drea paused. "I was trying to figure out how I wanted to handle your microaggression."

Dot's tanned face flushed a sort of dusky rose. So she did know what she was doing. Drea perked up. This might be fun after all. "Then you said the thing about mix-n-matching," she continued. "So my name seemed irrelevant."

Dot crossed her arms over her chest with a tight little scowl. "Well, I'm sorry it came out the wrong way. I was expecting my friend Sadie and found a stranger instead. I spoke a little more sharply than I normally would. I'm sure you can understand my surprise."

"Sure," replied Drea, still easy-breezy. "And I understand all that other stuff, too. But since you asked, my name is Shanti."

Dot's scowl faded with confusion. "That doesn't sound like Spanish."

Drea laughed, surprised. This really was too good. "You think I'm Latina?"

Dot flushed pinkish again.

"It's a Hindu name, if it matters," said Drea. "Means *peace.*" She still had a lot to do this morning, so she picked up the binoculars and started toward the cabin. "Sorry about your friends. I'm sure they'll turn up."

Dot's expression fell. "I know..." She looked away for a

moment, at the brightening lake in the distance, before turning back to Drea. "I'm sure you're right. It's weird, I know, but I don't have any way to contact her. Sadie. We...this is a lake friendship, you know?"

Drea wrapped the binocular strap around and around her knuckles as she considered Dot. "I don't know what that means." She squeezed her fist, testing the bind of the strap, hearing the leather creak. She should probably have gone with the nylon, but she hated the rasping feel of it against her skin.

"Oh, just that we know all about one another's business, but we only see each other once a year, for a week in July." Dot's laugh sounded brittle in the crisp morning air. "There's a lot to catch up on."

Drea let the silence stretch out, then gestured toward the cabin. "Like I said, I'm sure they'll turn up. Excuse me."

Dot flinched. "Right. Of course." Uncertainty painted her fine-boned features for a second before she turned away.

Drea watched Dot disappear past the shrubs between their cabins before going inside.

Around midday, Drea returned from her hike, dusty, thirsty—and limping from a moment of inattention on the far side of the lake. She peeled her small pack from her sweaty back, dumping it onto the lumpy rocker-recliner in the small living room. She moved to unlace her hiking boots, then reconsidered. Probably best to wait 'til she was ready to get off her feet.

Shaking her head at her clumsiness, she washed her hands and splashed her face with water from the kitchen tap. Next was a bottle of water and a pack of ice from the freezer compartment up top. She mentally inventoried her med kit as she gulped water cold enough to hit right between the eyes. Perfect.

Behind her, a scrape on gravel, then a light tread on the three stairs up to the front door. "Yoohoo, Shanti? It's Dot. Dot McAllister."

Drea smiled to herself. Dot must've been watching for Drea's return, to show up so quickly. *Yoohoo*, indeed.

"Hi, Dot, come on in." Drea shuffled to the round table in the eating nook. She plopped the half-empty bottle on the table and started unlacing the shoe on her injured foot.

Dot's bright smile preceded her into the shaded cabin. "So I know you're no Sadie, but that doesn't mean I can't be neighborly. Have you had lunch yet?" She came up short as she caught sight of Drea carefully pushing off her boots. Her cheer dimmed. "That looks bad."

"Oh yeah?" Drea decided not to bother hiding her amusement. "You can diagnose that from a glance, huh?"

"I'm a nurse," replied Dot simply. "But even if I wasn't, it doesn't take a genius to know ankles shouldn't be the size of softballs. Plus, I have four kids, seven to seventeen, all big and athletic like Jet. Plenty of sprains and scrapes, not to mention a few breaks to boot." She grabbed a plaid cushion from the plaid loveseat, set it on the chair she pulled out from the table, and angled the chair for Drea's foot. "Do you have a tensor bandage or something? To keep this ice pack on?"

"I've got duct tape." Drea chuckled despite herself.

"I'll bind this up properly for you." Dot slanted a look at Drea. "But only if you answer my question from earlier."

Drea raised her brows. "Blackmail already? I thought we were being neighborly."

"I've been called a busybody and with good reason." Dot shoved her hands into her back pockets with a shrug. "I like to know what's going on around me. Ignorance isn't a good policy. We women have to pay attention to our surroundings. You should know that."

"Should I?"

Another firm nod. "You're not exactly big and brawny."

Drea laughed outright. Dot lifted one corner of her mouth, then said, "Let me get that tensor bandage for you. Then you can tell me how you *don't exactly* know the family reunion people while I help you wrap that softball for you."

Drea had enough time for a trip to the bathroom before Dot returned, bustling through the door with an honest-to-God picnic basket in her hands and a first aid kit slung across her like a messenger bag. She set the basket on the table, washed up at the kitchen sink, then opened cabinets and drawers with swift efficiency. Placing plates and cutlery down, she jerked her chin at the dishcloth tied around Drea's raised ankle. "Nice."

"I'm good at improvising." Drea sniffed in appreciation. Apple pie. Was Dot for real? She lifted the basket lid and released the savory aromas of something fried, mingling with the heady smell of baked cinnamon. "So what are you expecting in exchange for lunch?"

Dot opened the freezer, peering inside suspiciously. "You hoarding ice packs for a reason or...?"

"I run hot."

"Where are you from?" Dot brought a new ice pack with her and laid her first aid kit on the table within reach. She squatted down to untie the dishcloth around Drea's ankle.

Drea waited 'til Dot looked up, into her waiting expression. "Did you seriously just ask me that?"

Dot flushed yet again. "I meant, are you from up north? Like, Canada. Is that why you run hot? It must feel extra muggy for you here. I'm originally from Tennessee, this is nothin'." She folded the dishcloth into a neat square, placed the melting pack on top, and set it all on the floor.

Drea shrugged, kept her smile inside. Dot was an easy target. "Genetics, I suppose. Who can say." She gestured at the basket. "May I?"

"Help yourself." Dot's hands slowed. "Oh, uh, you're not vegetarian, are you? Like, a religious thing?"

Drea raised her brows. "And what religion would that be?"

"Um, whatever yoga people are. Hindu? Is that right? You said your name was Hindu?" Despite the deepening flush on her face, Dot added, "Like Gandhi, right?"

40

"The religion is called Hinduism," replied Drea, "in case you need to file that away for a future awkward conversation." She paused to let Dot reply. The other woman kept her eyes down. "But no, I'm not a vegetarian."

"Okay, good." Dot let out a huff of laughter. "There's fried chicken, rolls, and a green salad. That apple pie pocket saves okay at room temp, if you don't have room for it now."

Drea hissed as Dot maneuvered the swollen ankle, expecting an apology from her impromptu nurse. But Dot only nodded, as if to herself, and continued manipulating Drea's foot in a cautious circle. "Sprained, not broken. Thought so, but always pays to be certain." She opened up her kit.

Drea made herself a plate from the offerings within Dot's various Tupperwares, smirking at the bottle of ranch dressing. Good Lord, the woman had even supplied cloth napkins. Drea pulled apart one of the small white rolls, popped the bite into her mouth. "Did you bake these, too? 'Sreally good."

Dot ducked her chin as she finished wrapping Drea's ankle with a few confident tugs. She stood, tidying up the melting ice and detritus. She set a small bottle of Advil on the table, fetched ice and glasses, then sat down across from Drea. "Yeah, Jet likes fresh rolls with his fried chicken. We've been married eighteen years. I can bake 'em in my sleep. You okay with sweet tea?" Dot poured them two full glasses from the pitcher in her magic basket. "Okay, time to pay up."

Drea took a drink first. "I wasn't invited to the family reunion, but…" She thought of who'd forwarded the email. "I needed to come."

"Why? If you don't even know them?" Dot frowned slightly.

"It's more that *they* don't know *me*." Drea shrugged. "I'm trying to decide how to introduce myself." She bit into a piece of chicken, the crispy skin giving way between her teeth with a satisfying crunch. "Especially to one of them. I'm sure you've noticed him. The man with the silver hair and handlebar mustache. The other adults are his kids and in-laws, the teens and little ones are his grandkids. He's like...the patriarch."

Dot's brown eyes widened. She looked like a cartoon character. "Is he...your dad? Wait. Or your granddad? How old are you, anyway? I can never tell."

Drea let the comment go, watching Dot over the rim of her glass as she took another drink. "Maybe my dad."

"Wow, that's like...it's like a TV show or something." Impossibly, Dot's eyes got even bigger. "What are you going to say? Did you just find out? How did your mother and him...get together? Does she still love him?"

"Well, aren't you just the romantic?" Drea sandwiched some chicken inside a torn roll, adding some of the salad. "Those are really personal questions, Dot," she said drily. "I'm feeling pretty vulnerable here."

"Oh my gosh, I'm sorry. It's just...this is so dramatic." Dot drank, her grip sending fingers of condensate sliding down the glass, her avid gaze fixed on Drea. "Are you going to try and get his DNA?"

Drea stared at the drops of water splashed on the tabletop. "You weren't kidding about the busybody thing, huh?"

Dot shook her head, expression proud. "Nope. Too many people are scared of reaching out when they should. If there's a way for me to help, I will."

"Well..." Drea popped the last of her sandwich into her mouth and chewed slowly as she contemplated Dot's eager face. "I might just take you up on that, neighbor."

Whatever reply Dot's enthusiastic expression heralded was interrupted by a hard one-two-three knock on the front screen door.

"Ladies, I hate to cut your gossiping short," boomed a hearty voice, "but we've got ourselves a situation at McAllister HQ."

Dot stood up quickly, rolling her eyes for Drea's sake. "Don't mind Jet, he's such a drama queen." She tucked a few stray tendrils of hair behind her ears, then skimmed her hands over her abdomen and straightened the hem of her striped top.

Drea had planned on a lower profile, but it couldn't be helped now. She called out, "Well, come on in, I guess."

The man with the shit-eating grin who stepped inside looked exactly as Drea had imagined—beefy, blond, and brash. Oh this was gonna be good. She put on her best impression of doe-eyed docility. "You must be Jet. Thanks for sparing Dot to bring me lunch. She's an amazing cook."

Jet's eyes pinched at the corners as he smirked. "Wouldn'ta married her otherwise." He took his time surveying Drea from the messy topknot of black curls to the ankle suspended on the chair. "You're just a bitty little thing, aren't ya? Tell you what, if your ankle's giving you trouble, you just holler for Bella, our oldest. She can give you a piggyback ride. She does it all the time for Bumper and Jack."

Dot flapped her hands at him. "You leave Shanti alone. Not everyone comes from Viking stock, you know."

Drea had to bite the inside of her cheek. There was just something so delicious about playing it straight with these people. "Thanks, I'll let you know."

Jet's grin lingered on her for another moment before he addressed his wife. "Bella can't find her flip-flops or something."

"I swear," Dot harrumphed exaggeratedly, "you all would lose your own heads if it weren't for me." She took her half-finished sweet tea to the sink, dumping it out before rinsing the glass and placing it upside down on a folded tea towel atop the counter. "You stay off that ankle, Shanti, for at least another hour or two. You're gonna want to let that swelling come down. I'll check on you at dinner time." She gave Drea an open smile. "If you're good, we'll take you with us to Bremerton tonight. They have the cutest ice cream shop, real old-fashioned and everything."

"Can't wait," replied Drea obligingly. "Who doesn't love ice cream?"

Jet came closer, just far enough to snag Dot by the waist and reel her in. "Come on, woman, your children await." He smirked at Drea again as Dot let out a peal of girlish laughter. "You better listen to Nurse Dot, so you can come with, Shanti." *Shanty*, he said, like a shack. "Why is it something you can have every day, like ice cream, tastes so good when you're on vacation?"

Drea only shrugged, biting her lower lip to keep from laughing. She almost felt sorry for Dot. Almost.

Technically, it was against the rules to take in-between jobs like this. It made for mistakes—like stumbling into a gopher hole, spraining your ankle, then being exposed to well-meaning busybodies. But when emotions were in play, it was impossible to argue rationally. Ephemeral or not, once Drea read that email, there was no going back. Ambivalence was nothing but luxury. It would fuck you up if you didn't commit.

Not that Drea would ever admit to anything but an appropriately professional commitment. She certainly wouldn't waste time observing the man and his loud, boisterous family. A family of people always holding hands, or slinging arms around shoulders, or landing quick kisses on cheeks and lips and the tops of heads. Drea was definitely not fascinated with their public shows of easy affection, and absolutely not comparing it with her own mother's tight-lipped, dark-eyed ways.

Drea had lied to Dot, her wannabe white savior. Drea had known all her life that Randall Simcoe was her father. Among the many secrets she had pried from her mother over the years, sometimes brutally, her parentage hadn't been one of them.

So now, here she was, chosen specifically over other available associates, and sent to her father by her mother's decree. On the weekend of his forty-fifth wedding anniversary. Drea had always known her mother had a mean sense of humor, but this seemed next level even for her.

The heart, though, right? Such an unruly bitch.

Drea knocked briskly on the back door to Cabin One, the largest in the resort. She knew no one was inside. She'd made sure of it, counting fifteen heads as she'd watched the Simcoe clan through her binoculars while they piled onto Randall's pretty boat. The sun was bright, the breeze was fresh, and he'd taken them all on a late afternoon cruise around the lake.

The cocktail of oral painkillers and the steroids she'd injected into her ankle worked their miracles. Drea felt nothing but a distant throb underneath the tight athletic tape. She had almost-full range of motion. Which she needed in order to break into her father's rented cabin.

If she finished up tonight, she'd have a couple of days to heal up all the way before her next job. Not quite the maximum pain her mother wanted to inflict on the Simcoes, but what did she expect when she guilted Drea out here on short notice? What Drea had planned would ensure plenty of suffering to go around. Her mother would just have to deal.

Inside, the cabin smelled like lavender and sweet cream. Drea wrinkled her nose. She hated lavender. A good reminder to hurry up and do what she came to do.

In the bedroom, though, she stilled, staring at her father's shoes lined up neatly beside a tall dresser. Without conscious thought, she found herself opening the dresser drawers, touching his soft T-shirts, inhaling the scent of some kind of woodsy cologne.

Drea wondered if her mother knew this smell.

Simcoe had brought her mother into the business, then abandoned her to fend for herself in the middle of Nebraska. He'd done it right after she'd told him she was pregnant, loving her to sleep, then leaving her to wake to silence—and bricks of crisp hundreds on the kitchen table. Her mother never failed to mention that he hadn't bothered with a note.

Drea thought it more important that he'd left behind some-thing useful. She'd never bothered to find him. To what purpose? He'd made it clear he wanted nothing to do with *this* particular baby. Why would she beg?

She understood her mother's bitterness, of course she did. She'd indulged her own version. For a time. But surely her mother had known what she was getting into. Even then, he worked for criminals. Surely, she'd been smart enough to know it couldn't last. To interpret the gaping silences, the places promises were supposed to fill.

Surely, she'd known what the baby would mean to a man married to another woman.

She'd survived, though, hadn't she, and Drea too? In the decades since, her mother had scrapped her way into a lucrative, respected position of authority. Drea had grown up in the business, excelling at what suited her. They might not have the easiest life, but they'd carved it out, sometimes inch by bloody inch, on their own terms.

Sighing, Drea pushed aside the same tired arguments as she closed the drawer softly. She'd agreed to do this. She'd *committed* to it.

Tight-lipped, she tucked the carefully composed note inside her father's Dopp kit. Whether he read it tonight or tomorrow, they would meet. One way or another.

It struck Drea as incredible that everyone at the resort readily complied with an arbitrary eleven o'clock noise curfew—all because of a dozen signs scattered around the cabins, nailed up to tree trunks. Was this the social contract at work?

Even Jet was nowhere to be seen and Drea had been half expecting him. She'd convinced Dot easily enough to take a rain check on ice cream, but she'd understood the predatory glint in Jet's eyes. Drea laughed to herself. The less Jet McAllister fucked her with his greedy gaze, the better for him. He wouldn't like how Drea could calculate him into her plans.

The curfew came and went as she prowled in and around the edges of the resort, her ankle freshly tended and bound, her black eyes wary and alert, her skin caressed by a soft breeze. Voices and laugh tracks drifted to her through windows left open on a pleasant night, while she slid beneath the trees shimmying in the gentle wind.

At eleven thirty, confident she and her handiwork remained off the resort radar, she re-entered her cabin. As thirty minutes passed in deepening silence, Drea sat, quiet and composed at the little kitchen table.

When her father finally came through the back door, as instructed, she took a steadying breath and turned her face to the light.

He stopped short, blanching beneath his tan. "Rika?" The door, on a pneumatic hinge, closed behind him with a low thump. He flinched.

"Have a seat." Drea gestured to the chair facing her.

He staggered forward, his incredulous stare pinned to her face. He fell onto the seat, the scrape of chair legs across the worn linoleum harsh, discordant. "My God..." he whispered hoarsely, "you look just like her." To Drea's bemusement, tears filled his pale gray eyes.

She pointed to the glass of water she'd prepped for him, and this moment. "Please, take a moment to compose yourself."

His gaze roamed her face, disbelieving. "How...how did you find me?" His silver hair glowed underneath the cheap fluorescent bulb above them.

"Mom's specialty," answered Drea readily. "Research of all kinds. It's an integral part of the business."

"And you?" His Adam's apple bobbed.

"I'm in a different department." Drea half smiled. "I hate desk work."

He swiped at his eyes with his knuckles, falling against the chair back. After another moment, he shakily grabbed the water glass and drank half of it down. "Why are you here? The note—"

"I thought I'd give you a chance to save yourself." Drea blinked. That was *not* what she'd planned to say. She continued briskly anyway. "Give me the login credentials for the Cayman account and I'll help you get square with the Chengs."

His face blanked. "What?" He gulped at the water, his gaze

sliding sideways.

"You don't have a lot of time," she said, careful to speak clearly. "Mom left you alone all these years, but this time..." Drea sighed. "Now, it's *company* business. She traced the money to the Caymans, easy, but they've got excellent encryption and this is time sensitive. Plus I have another job," Drea muttered under her breath.

Her father set the empty glass down, sputtering. "I don't...I can't..."

Drea assessed her father with a clinical eye. Still objectively handsome, his face carved lovingly by laugh lines, by years of living happily. Years spent firmly forgetting about six passionate months, thirty years ago. Years spent raising a family he'd chosen over Amrika and Andrea Agrawal.

"I'm sorry," Drea said softly as something within her settled. She hated when she was dishonest with herself. "I thought I had to try because you're my father. Seeing you in person, watching you with your family...I thought maybe I owed you something. Maybe Mom's narrative wasn't the only one. Maybe you had a side to tell me, too.

"But you had thirty years to find me, if you'd wanted. And clearly, some part of me knew all along—Mom was right." Drea huffed. "I set this plan in motion long before I lied to you about getting square with the Chengs. We both know forgiveness isn't their style. It doesn't matter what you might say. You made your choices. The past...is done."

Drea met his panicked gaze squarely. "I'm sorry your future is over." She flicked a fingernail against the water glass, making it ring faintly. "You're about to have a heart attack, Dad."

A thud sounded to her left, from the cabin's lone bedroom. Drea jumped up, ignoring the crash as her father toppled from his chair. As she hurried down the hall, another thud, then a scrabbling sounded through the flimsy particle-board door, opened a crack. She threw it wide, crouching down in the doorway, ready to draw the pistol from the holster at her back.

In the filtered light from the kitchen, Drea watched Jet McAllister throw the bedroom window screen at her. It sliced to her right, disappearing from her periphery. Jet panted, face shadowed, chest heaving as he swiveled to and fro, clearly searching for another weapon.

Drea stood slowly, leaving her gun alone. She glanced at the rumpled covers of the bed, noted Jet's bare feet and chest, his hair every which way. "If you're gonna sneak into a woman's bedroom, you probably shouldn't fall asleep while you lay in wait to rape her." Drea cocked her head. "'Cuz now I have to deal with you."

Without a word, he rushed her, hands stretched toward her neck.

Just before he reached her, Drea swatted his arms upward and pivoted until her back hit the outside hall. As Jet's momentum carried him through the doorway, she shoved him in the back, smashing his forehead against the opposite wall. His head rebounded backward.

Drea grabbed his wrist and elbow, angling his arm, putting pressure on his shoulder to immobilize him. Clumsy, dazed, he tried to yank away. She jerked his arm just shy of pulling it out of the socket. He cried out, low and guttural. She maneuvered him onto the bed, facedown, twisting his arm until his wrist was along his spine. Digging her knee into his back to hold him, she took the hand from his elbow and set her fingers along his carotid artery. Ignoring the clamminess of his skin, she clamped her hand hard, cutting off blood and oxygen.

"Oh Jet, you poor fuck." Did he hear the disappointment in her voice as he lost consciousness?

As she turned onto the state highway, Drea breathed fully for the first time in five days. It hadn't been to plan, but she'd pulled out a win anyway. Only Dot was left to say some woman named Shanti had rented that little cabin—though resort paperwork would show only Sadie Thompson's info and credit card.

Jet would be found half naked in the cabin's bed, dead from carbon monoxide poisoning. Randall Simcoe's autopsy would suggest he'd died of a heart attack, not long before the CO got Jet. Assumptions would be made, and questions unanswered. The Simcoes would be left to wonder, bewildered and betrayed, just what the fuck had been going on between the two men. Dot would be shell shocked, maybe even shattered.

Drea's mother got what she wished for, after all. Maximum damage.

As a professional, Drea avoided collateral damage as a matter of form. But short notice jobs required a certain...flexibility. Her mother would understand.

Still—it was really too bad about the Thompsons.

THE GIFT
Barb Goffman

June 1992

I've known parents who've tried my patience. Made me want to lose my cool. Loosen my tongue. Maybe even throw a punch or two, abandoning my grandmotherly image. But I've always refrained, arranging my face in a calm manner and speaking to them in a reasonable tone, because I am a high school principal and that is how we roll.

But as I stared across my desk at Mr. Telman, gritting my teeth hard enough to anger my dentist, I realized that today I might be willing to make an exception.

"I pay a lot of taxes to this school," Telman said, pushing his rimless glasses up to the bridge of his nose again. Considering how he kept his nose in the air all the time, you'd think they'd stay put. "My son *will* be returning to classes."

He had such an entitled tone, sitting there in his fancy silk suit. I bet it worked with a lot of people. But not with me.

"Jason was arrested right here two days ago with enough drugs to stock a pharmacy," I said. "It wasn't the first time, as you well know. After he got out of juvie last year, I'm the one who told the school board they should readmit him because I believe in second chances, and I thought he'd learned his lesson." I paused, saddened by Jason's choices. "But your son has blown

51

it. So, he's suspended for the rest of the school year, and I will pursue his expulsion. There's nothing more to say. Good day, sir. This meeting is over."

"Like hell it is. I'm a taxpayer." He tapped his index finger on my desk repeatedly. "You work for me—"

"I work for the school board and for all the families with enrolled children, not for you specifically, Mr. Telman. Now get out of my office. You can consider yourself expelled too."

He sprang up like the Incredible Hulk, rage pouring from him as he leaned over my desk and glared down at me, his bloodshot eyes peeking over his glasses. "Mark my words, Mrs. Clemens. You're going to hear from my lawyer."

As if that would scare me. I slowly rose up to meet him, my resolve as strong as my spine. "That's Principal Clemens. And instead of wasting your time calling your attorney, why don't you spend it teaching your son right from wrong. It seems he missed that lesson somewhere along the way."

Telman's lip curled. He probably didn't like anyone standing up to him, especially a woman. I held my ground, and he stormed out of my office.

His poor kid. Jason probably never had a chance with that cretin for a father. I wished Jason had understood the gift he'd been given when we let him return last year. But not every child could be saved, at least not by me.

I glanced at my watch. Ten minutes until school would let out like an erupting geyser—the joy only a Friday afternoon could bring. Sometimes I stuck around after school to do paperwork, but the Mr. Telmans of the world always made me itchy to get out of here, especially on beautiful June days like this one. I packed my briefcase. I'd do the paperwork at home.

A half hour later I was in my car with the windows rolled down, letting my stress ease away, breathing in the peace of the abundant cornfields that lined the road. Absorbing the bliss of the wildflower meadows on the rolling hills. The air was lush and sweet, the sky an unusually deep azure blue—just like the day we buried my husband three years ago. It was so beautiful it made me marvel how life could be wonderful and sad all at once. It was one of those days that made me happy I lived in Iowa. On the radio Sting was urging listeners to set their loved ones free. I laughed, recalling how disturbed some of my students were several years ago when they heard me quietly singing this song. Principals were never supposed to enjoy the same music teens do.

I pulled into my driveway as the school bus was unloading at the corner. My grandson, Brian, stood talking to some boys. I was blessed he lived three doors down, enabling me to see him all the time. We only had fourteen months before he'd leave for college. I'd miss him terribly, but I couldn't wait to see the man he'd become. Not to be biased, but the sky was the limit with him. Actually, the sky couldn't hold him back. He was brilliant.

Brian spotted me as he headed home. "Hey, Grandma."

"Want a snack?" I often fed him after school since his mom wouldn't be home from work for a couple of hours.

"Okay."

He plodded my way. Looked like the kid had every textbook he owned in his arms—and the world on his shoulders.

A few minutes later Brian sat at my kitchen table. His wavy ginger hair gleamed in the sun spilling through my back window. Amazing how much he resembled his father, my late son, Ron. Their hair was the exact same shade of red, the same one mine used to be before I let it turn gray.

"How was school?" I asked as I slathered spicy mustard on a turkey sandwich. His favorite.

"Fine."

"How'd your math test go?" I brought the sandwich, a plate of chocolate-chip cookies, and a glass of milk over. Most sixteen-year-olds didn't like milk. Brian probably didn't either, but he was a good boy and wouldn't balk, so I took advantage of it.

"All right." He took a large bite out of the sandwich.

"School was 'fine.' The test was 'all right.' You're usually chattier."

He shrugged.

Something was up. I worked in a neighboring school district, so I didn't have any inside information. The principal in me wanted to shine a light on him and make him talk. The grandma in me pushed the plate of cookies closer.

"I spoke to Professor Margolin yesterday," I said. "He's looking forward to working with you."

Brian would be interning this summer in my friend Ken's physics lab at the university here in town—a coup for a kid still in high school. Ken made an exception because Brian got a perfect score on his ACTs, as well as on his mathematics and chemistry achievement tests. Then Brian wowed Ken with his zeal for astronomy. Getting my daughter-in-law, Sarah, to agree had actually been a harder sell.

Brian frowned. Now I *knew* something was wrong. He'd been over the moon about the job.

"Talk to me," I said.

"I'm going to have to start the internship a week later than planned."

"Why?"

"Mom's taking me to look at colleges. The same week I'm supposed to start work."

"Oh. That's okay. Ken will understand."

He stared at his plate and chewed his bottom lip. Ron used to do that too when he was troubled.

"Is something else wrong?"

Brian sighed. "It's the schools we're going to see. A five-day trip across Iowa, touring ten colleges. None of them have a top-rated physics program. I can get into all of 'em with my eyes closed."

"Iowa State has a good physics program." So did EIU, our college here in town. He could definitely get into both. Not that he'd likely matriculate at either one. Brian had a solid shot at Cal Tech—his top choice—as well as MIT, Stanford, and the Ivy League universities.

"I can't apply there."

"What do you mean, you can't apply there?"

"Mom said I can only apply to schools within a two-hour drive."

"What?"

"Places she could drive to quickly in case of emergency. And they have to be small. Two thousand students max. That rules State out. But I could go to EIU if I live at home."

At home. I held back what I wanted to say and went to get a glass of water. I promised myself when Ron died six years ago that I'd give Sarah whatever support she needed. It couldn't have been easy for her to learn that Ron might have been cured if he'd gone to the doctor sooner, if she hadn't insisted her homemade medicines would work if he gave them enough time. So I'd forced myself to put my anger aside. But learning she intended to stifle Brian's dreams riled me up all over again.

"Why the small schools?" I asked as I rejoined him at the table, trying hard to keep my cool. "Did she say?"

"She's afraid I won't make friends at a big school. That I'll 'get lost in the crowd.' Spend too much time in a lab or library."

"Well, balance is important in life."

I said it, but it was a load of horse hockey, to quote Colonel Sherman T. Potter. (I enjoyed a good *M*A*S*H* rerun now and then.) Parents with children need balance. But teenagers— especially gifted ones like Brian—should be shooting for the stars. And if Sarah was so worried about Brian making friends, she should want him to live in a dorm.

"Mom keeps asking me about girls." He blushed. "Whether I 'like' anyone. She makes me feel guilty when I stay home and study on the weekends. I guess that's the balance you're talking about too."

I growled under my breath. Sarah's priorities were screwed up. Kids might put romance before achievement because their hormones run amok. Parents should know better.

It seemed Sarah was still the same girl she'd been in high

school, thinking young love trumps all. She'd told my son she loved him, and before I knew it, Ron's plan to attend Princeton faded away. He followed Sarah to an in-state college. He still could have pursued his dream to work at NASA, though it would have been harder without the Princeton pedigree and pipeline. But then Sarah got pregnant in their junior year and wanted to move back home after college. And once again, Ron's plans faded away. He ultimately became an engineer and lived a happy—though far too short—life. But he gave up a lot of dreams for love. I'd hate to see that happen to Brian too.

"There's nothing wrong with dating," I said, deciding to say my piece. "But there's also nothing wrong with concentrating on your studies if it'll help you achieve your goals. There'll be lots of time for girls later—girls you'll have more in common with."

He sighed, sounding relieved.

"You know, you don't need your mom's permission to apply to college. You simply need to send a check with each application, and I happen to know someone with a checkbook." I smiled. "Cal Tech and MIT will be happy to take my money."

"Go behind Mom's back?"

What kind of principal—or grandmother—advocated that? But these were unusual circumstances. "It doesn't hurt to apply. I'm sure once you get in, she'll see the light." And if she didn't, I'd smack her on the head until she saw reason. Or at least I'd fantasize about doing that.

Brian looked hopeful for the first time since he got off the bus, warming my heart. Then he shook his head.

"I couldn't do that, Grandma. Lie to her. Disobey her. Thanks anyway."

How kids like Brian and Jason Telman could exist in the same world, I didn't know.

"How 'bout if I talk to her?" I asked.

"You think that'll help?"

"I can be very persuasive. I'll come over tonight." I leaned forward and mussed his hair. "Now, go on home and study. If you're going to get into Cal Tech, you'll need to ace your finals."

"Yes, ma'am." With the excitement of a kindergartner on Christmas Eve, he grabbed his books and a cookie, bounced out my kitchen door, and started down a shortcut that ran through the neighbors' backyards to his house.

The tall linden tree behind Brian and Sarah's house had bloomed just this week. That evening I stood by their back door, breathing in the sweet smell of its honey-scented yellow blossoms. The tree's large heart-shaped leaves cast a helpful shadow over half of Sarah's large garden, enabling the flowers that needed part-time shade to flourish. I took a moment to let their beauty relax me. I needed to approach Sarah with an affable smile. Parents and kids often saw me as their adversary. I didn't want that tonight. Sarah and I were on the same side. We both wanted what was best for Brian.

I knocked once and went inside.

"Mule fritters!" Colonel Potter bellowed from the other room. Brian enjoyed *M*A*S*H* reruns as much as I did.

I chuckled, walking through the kitchen, passing the dated but hardy harvest-gold appliances. In the living room, Brian was lying on the couch. A half-eaten bowl of popcorn sat on his chest. Sarah was reading in her favorite club chair, her legs curled beneath her thin, petite frame. I felt more kindly to her than I had that afternoon, having had time to consider her perspective about Brian's college plans.

These last few years hadn't been easy for Sarah. She'd never gotten over losing Ron. Never dated. Hardly had any friends. Her mother died a decade ago. Soon after that, Sarah's sister moved six hours away. Her father still lived in town, but he was a cold fish. Brian was her whole world. It made sense she'd want to keep him close. I'd like that too, but Brian deserved better.

"Hey, Grandma." Brian shut off the TV. "Well, I have homework to do."

He ran to his room with the speed of a dog chasing a treat. It didn't go unnoticed. Sarah's gaze flitted from his disappearing backside to me as she closed her book. "Evening, Debbie." Her voice had a questioning tone.

"Hi, Sarah." I kept my voice warm, friendly. "I hope you don't mind me dropping by."

She knitted her brows. "You know you're always welcome. But why do I have a feeling this isn't a spur-of-the-moment visit?"

"Guilty as charged. I want to talk with you about something."

She waved me over to the couch. She and Ron bought it shortly after they married seventeen years ago. Beige with orange-and-brown flowers. Comfortable but butt ugly, to use an evocative phrase I'd recently heard at school.

"Brian stopped by this afternoon. He mentioned your upcoming trip."

"Ohhhh. I know, he's upset he'll have to start his internship a week late. But that's when I can get off work."

"It's not that. He's concerned—and I'm concerned—about the colleges you're going to visit."

She rolled her eyes. "I know they aren't his first choice, not yet anyway. But that's because he hasn't seen them yet. You know how good the schools here in Iowa are."

"Of course I do, but as you said, they're not his first choice."

"He's resilient. He'll adjust."

"But why should he have to? There's no doubt he'll be valedictorian next year. He has an excellent chance of getting into the best schools in the country, and later, to making a real contribution to this world. So, why are you limiting him to colleges within a hundred miles of here? Small ones, to boot, with small endowments and small budgets."

"What do I care about budgets? He can get a fine education at any of them."

"Fine, yes. But not outstanding. None of them have a first-class physics program. They don't have the money for it."

"He doesn't need first class. It's not like he's going to go work for NASA."

Was that a dig at Ron's old dream? "Why couldn't Brian work for NASA? He's certainly smart enough."

Her mouth dropped open, as if I'd said something ridiculous. "Of course he is. But NASA doesn't have any offices around here. And why would you want him to spend his life doing research in some lab? He spends too much time by himself as it is."

You should talk. I counted to three before I spoke. I often did that with difficult parents so I wouldn't say something I'd regret. "If working at NASA or in a lab—no matter the location—is what he wants, we should support him." *You should support him.*

"He's sixteen. He doesn't know what he wants."

"He's old enough to know what he's good at and what he enjoys. He might get to study under some of the finest minds in the world, people who share the same passions he does. He should take advantage of that. But he won't if you don't let him."

She scowled. "I need some tea." She went into the kitchen.

I blew out a deep breath as I glanced around the picture-filled living room—the center of a life Sarah yearned to preserve, while Brian, like most kids, was marching eagerly toward the future. Funny how life worked that way. You spend so much time helping your kids progress from one milestone to the next, until they're ready to leave, and then you wish you could take it all back.

When I was Brian's age, I loved botany as much as he loves astronomy. But I was a girl. My father said my next steps after high school should be marriage and children. Dad was certain that would make me happy. Not that I was against those things, but I'd wanted more. He finally agreed to pay for college but only if I'd study to be a nurse or a teacher—the only "proper" jobs for a girl with the Second World War finally over. So, I became a science teacher right here in my hometown, and later, an administrator. Now Brian was nearly ready to spring into the world, and like my father with me, Sarah wanted to hold him back, limit his dreams. She wasn't unusual. I saw it all the time. Parents with the best of intentions foisted their own dreams onto their children instead of letting their kids follow their own paths. In some ways, the world had changed so much in the past fifty years. But in other fundamental ones, people were still the same.

"You okay?" I asked as I entered the kitchen.

Sarah was sitting at the square table, drinking her favorite tea, which gave off a woodsy smell. She made it herself with vitamin-rich rose hips and other leaves and seeds she foraged from her garden each fall and then dried for year-round use in jams and this tea. Whenever she got sick, she drank it by the gallon. After taking another sip, she set her cup down. "Can I get you some water?" she said.

"No thanks."

She didn't bother to offer me tea. She knew she was the only one who drank it. Brian hadn't touched it in years. "Sickeningly sour," he once called it. I didn't find it that bad, but I preferred coffee, which Sarah never had.

I sat at the table and squeezed her hand. It was velvety, like snapdragon petals. I wished Sarah were as soft inside, where it counted. "I know what it's like to be lonely. But you won't be alone after Brian leaves for college, honey. You have me."

She was quiet for a moment, then sighed. "All right. If he really wants to apply to those schools he keeps talking about, he can. But I'm still taking him on the tour I planned. They're good schools, and I bet once he sees them, he's going to realize a small college close to home will be the perfect fit for him."

Thank goodness. "I can't ask for more than that. I'm going to say good night to Brian and head on home. Get some reading done before I turn in."

I went upstairs. Brian was hard at work at his desk, a nice breeze coming through the window. When I knocked on his open door, he turned toward me, his eyes wide with hope. I gave him a thumbs-up.

He jumped from his chair and hugged me, his body vibrating in happiness. "Thank you, Grandma."

"Anything for you, dear boy. Sleep well tonight."

"You too. See you Sunday."

"Can't wait."

Most Sundays he and Sarah ate lunch at my house. I'd never been the greatest cook—I'd always been better in a lab than a kitchen—but feeding them comforted me. My husband might be gone, and soon Brian would be off into the world, but Sarah and I would still be able to rely on each other, on our tradition.

I passed her on my way out. She'd already returned to her favorite chair in the living room, her book in hand.

"Good night," I said.

She looked up. "Night, Debbie."

I let myself out the back door. The sun had set, and there was no moon. But the stars were bright, and the air was awash with the fragrance of nighttime-blooming flowers. I neared the edge of Sarah's patio and decided to sit a bit and enjoy nature.

"Brian Vincent Clemens, how could you do that to me?"

I started at Sarah's angry voice coming from above. Brian's room, with his open window, was a few feet beyond the edge of the patio.

"Do what?" he asked.

"You know very well what you did," Sarah said. "Went behind my back."

"What?" He sounded mystified.

"I made myself very clear that you are only allowed to attend college close to home. Yet tonight you blindsided me, sending your grandmother to do your dirty work."

Excuse me?

"No, it wasn't like that," he said.

"Don't you know what those places are like?" Sarah said. "California. Massachusetts. They're dangerous."

"I'm...I'm sorry. I didn't go to Grandma for help. She just got it out of me. But Cal Tech and MIT, they're safe places, Mom."

"How would you know?"

"I've talked with my teachers about them. And I've read their catalogs."

"Catalogs? Where did you get catalogs?"

"At the library."

"So, you want to leave me, like everyone else." Her voice had taken on an anguished tone. "You want to go off to one of those hedonistic cities and leave me all alone. You don't love me."

"That's not true." He paused. "Mom, please don't cry. I'm sorry. I won't go. I won't apply anywhere far away. You and Dad got a great education here in Iowa. I'm sure I can too."

"You swear?"

"I swear." His voice was gentle and sad.

Sarah must have walked away, because the only thing I heard after that were chirping crickets while I nearly ground my teeth to dust.

Lies. Manipulation. Emotional blackmail. I'd always thought Sarah was caring but misguided. Now I saw her for who she really was, selfish and controlling, motivated not by what she thought was best for Brian but by what she wanted for herself. If she had her way, she'd hold him back the same way she held Ron back—the way my father held me back, but at least his intentions had been good.

How had I never realized that Sarah was just like Mr. Telman? He bullied to get his way. Sarah manipulated. If I didn't stop her, she'd ruin Brian's future. Sometimes in life you only got one chance to reach for the stars and achieve your dreams. You couldn't count on another one.

Brian couldn't count on another one.

I needed to figure out a way to help him, and I needed to be calm to do it. I leaned back, taking deep breaths. The sweet scent of Sarah's lilacs and moonflowers usually soothed me. Not now. I sniffed again. I detected something citrusy. Jimsonweed. It was definitely jimsonweed, a beautiful—but toxic—wildflower. Some local kids nearly died fifteen years ago after they smoked its seeds for their hallucinogenic properties. They hadn't known that in the right amount, those seeds could kill you.

In seconds, a plan came together in my mind. It would be easy to gather the seeds. I could make stew for Sunday and mix the seeds into Sarah's bowl. Dizziness, flushing, and fever would set in quickly. We'd walk her home to rest. While Brian got books and clothes—he often stayed with me when Sarah was sick—I'd bring her a large glass of her homemade tea and a jug with more of it for her nightstand. She always included herbs from her garden when she made the tea, so she wouldn't notice the jimsonweed seeds I'd mix in. The sicker she'd feel, the more she'd drink—that was her way. And then she'd die, probably within twenty-four hours. I'd make sure I'd be the one to check on her, to find her. Yes, it could work. I could set Brian free.

But it'd be wrong. We always tell kids the ends don't justify the means.

Yet I knew all too well that life was full of gray corners, and this was one of them. I looked up at Brian's window. While I couldn't see him, I knew he was still at his desk, studying, learning, preparing for the future he dreamed of. The future he deserved. Sting's message floated through my mind. *Set him free.* Sarah wanted to chain Brian to her, but I could free him to chase his dreams. I could. And I should.

My son sacrificed his dreams for a woman who only cared about herself. I'd be damned if I'd let my grandson do the same thing.

This would be my gift to him. I couldn't save every child, but I could save this one.

I stood and headed for home. Time to find a good stew recipe.

CUTS

Tessa Wegert

The cut is small. Just a scrape, really, straight across the top of my wrist. The wrist I awoke to find hanging over the edge of my bed, exposed. The cut is fresh, though, that's the thing, and a drop of blood has dried on my skin like a tiny glass bead. Harmless. My fingernail hovers, itching to pick, but I leave it be. Instead, I reach for my cell phone, charging by the bed, and snap a photo.

Zoom in until the red slash fills the screen.

It's the fourth unexplained cut this week. They arrive in the night, in different quadrants of my body. I thought there was a message in that, at first, but if there is I can't make sense of it.

The first was on my breastbone, hair-thin and straight as a blade of grass, appearing last Tuesday when I woke up much the same way. Tuxedo's young still, only five months old with teeth like needles heated over a flame, and the girls are starting to look like Edward Scissorhands, so I brushed that wound off. Attributed it to a cuddle gone wrong. The next day there was another, this time on my foot. It wasn't there at bedtime, and Tuxedo sleeps in a crate. Locked in all night.

"It's not the dog," I told Josh yesterday, the fourth day. Thursday. His eyes rolled back in his head, and he sighed in that full-body way that means he's all out of patience.

"Who is it, then, Holly?" Lids heavy, mouth set. "Huh?"

Before, when we were still married and Josh still made an effort to humor me, he would have sat me down on the couch and put his hand on my knee. *Let's think this through*, he would have said, tender. He might have encouraged me to examine my negative thoughts and the evidence—or lack thereof—that rationalized them. It's all about evidence with my therapist, too. *What proof do you have that someone took your mail? Where's the evidence?* So now, I take photos.

"If I knew who was doing it," I'd said when Josh picked up the kids, making sure to toss a disparaging glance at the scorched and yellowed front lawn, "I would have led with that."

"Jesus, Holls, don't be so—" He cast a glance behind him at the car, where Cleo and Selena were already buckled in. One month since Josh moved out, and they knew the drill. This was Mom and Dad's time to talk grown-up stuff, which yesterday involved yet another intervention relating to my mental health. Josh was dying to say it, the word our couples counselor, back when we still had one, told him never to use.

Paranoid.

"Fine," I replied, because I'd been down that road before and arguing with my ex-husband wasn't healthy or productive. "Forget I mentioned it. Don't keep them too late tomorrow morning, Selena has dance. Don't let them stay up late, either. It throws them off when you do those late movie nights."

"It throws *you* off, you mean."

He wasn't wrong. Unpredictability is a trigger for me. As he stood there lobbing barbed comments, so smug is his sweat-soaked designer shirt printed with a thousand tiny skulls, the shirt he knows I hate, he was already convinced it was all in my head.

But the girls weren't home last night. Tuxedo was in his crate.

And yet, today, another cut.

The weather guy on 680 CJOB says it's raining. He's been focused on the weather more than usual this week, though in truth it's all about the weather here, where the climate is a study in extremes. Where there can be snow on the ground ten months of the year, but you may still get an F5 tornado. Just yesterday, someone from Environment Canada declared the drought and blistering heat we've seen these past sixty days the worst in more than a century. Weather Guy was right, though; it's pouring now, and I'm thrilled. I waste no time struggling into my sports bra and tugging on my crappiest shoes. I'll be soaked through with a pulpy new blister on my heel by the time I reach the end of the street, but that's the way I like it. It's a trick I learned when I was a teen. A truth, really: discomfort equals distraction. If my muscles burn and my feet are bloodless and pruny and I can't see for all the rain in my eyes, I don't worry. I won't be thinking about the incisions notched into my flesh without my knowing. How they got there. What they mean.

Where they'll turn up next.

Even in the rain, I'm hot and panting. I pause at the corner to adjust my headphones and shuffle the playlist on my phone, already tasting metal as Elton John and Kiki Dee's "Don't Go Breaking My Heart" jangles in my ear. Someone once told me intense exercise can cause fluid to accumulate in our lungs, which causes red blood cells to leak, which leads us to taste iron. I don't how much of that is true, but I can't run anymore without picturing my lungs exploding and my mouth filling with blood. As I tuck my phone back into the holder affixed to my bare arm, I see the cut on my wrist again. It's dry now, a deeper shade of red.

I shake out my hands, take a breath, and run on.

The drought has turned the soil into an impenetrable shell, so the street is a river in no time, rainwater lapping at the curb and gushing down rusted drains. My shoes squelch and spatter my calves with every step, but I don't feel cold. The air is steamy. Stifling. When I was in university, still living with my parents in their overvalued house in Tuxedo, I used to run in Assiniboine Park. The path wound its way past the zoo, the outdoor theater, and the conservatory, a biodome with lush foliage and tropical temps where you could walk year-round without getting frostbite. Every couple of days, after school, I'd run until I was numb before wandering the brick pathways of the Palm House, listening to birdsong and pretending I was in Costa Rica, Aruba, anywhere but Winnipeg in winter.

That was where I first noticed him, sitting on a bench across from a fountain topped with a spider plant. He was there again two days later, and again the following week. He always had a book with him, some mass market paperback thriller with a city on the cover in black and white. I remember thinking he must be a slow reader. The book was always the same.

On the third day, when I walked by, he asked me if I liked to read. Only years afterward did he confess the book was a prop, left behind by some other visitor who'd used the bench, too. The first time, he'd come to the conservatory to meet a blind date who didn't show. The others, he'd come for me. I wish I'd realized sooner how creepy that was. That I hadn't been so easily charmed.

It takes an hour for me to finish my circuit and it's a slog, the humidity a wet blanket on my back. When I finally round the corner onto my street, there's a car parked in front of the house. It's a decades-old blue sedan, a beater with the familiar beach and bison on its license plate, *Friendly Manitoba* in sky blue. Is the car here for me? There's no movement at the neighbors', nobody else on the street. The car is running, wipers frenzied, and it's occupied, but I can't make out the driver's face through the deluge. I've slowed to a walk, body pulsing with exhilaration and exhaustion, skin rumpled by rain. When I'm two houses from home, wondering if I should approach, the driver peels off, leaving a wake in the road behind him.

We got the dog for Cleo. Compulsive behaviors can run in the family, as my ex has reminded me, the note of accusation in his voice sharp as a blade. And though my youngest is only seven years old, the writing's on the wall. Cleo counts things. "How many?" I asked the other day, nodding at the grommets on her high-top Chuck Taylors. A test. Holding my gaze, her round face unyielding, she said, "Fourteen. Seven on each side." I've caught her hoarding things: broken-off pencil erasers, her sister's bobby pins. She lines them up like balusters, and then she counts them.

As of this morning, the cuts total four.

Cleo wasn't home last night. But we watched a show together after school, her Friday treat, and for a minute or two on the couch beside her, I had closed my eyes. Was it possible I was wrong? That this cut came sooner? It was hectic when I startled awake, between packing for the kids' overnight with Josh and shuttling Selena to dance. *I need extra time to put on my pointe shoes. We can't be late, Mom.* Now, standing naked, my shucked running clothes a soggy puddle on the tile, I examine myself in the unforgiving bathroom light. The one on my breast is the longest, a full two inches across. The deepest, though, that was on my outer thigh. Our house—my house now—is too old for central air, and the window units clang and leak onto the carpet, so I sleep in a T-shirt and suffer through. There was blood on the bed when I awoke the next morning, a crimson smear where I'd kicked off the sheet. Breastbone. Foot. Thigh. Wrist.

Four.

Almost ten p.m. The rain has passed. I take Tuxedo for one last pee and find the sky is bright, the street steaming. It's like *Northern Exposure* here in high summer, not quite the constant daylight you get in Alaska, but close to midnight you can still find people gardening, grateful for the heat—and the chemical stench of the DEET on their skin and the milky Revello bars that fill their freezers—because it's temporary. The enduring daylight's why I know there's someone in my neighbor's front yard. A figure, unmoving on the other side of the hedge, and a smell to go with them. In River Heights, the houses are set close together, pale brick bungalows from the '50s separated by skinny paths. Squares of gum in a foil packet, lined up in a row. Still, the smell throws me off, and it takes a second for me to recognize her. Humming to herself and pushing a honey-colored, humidity-induced curl behind her ear.

"Belinda," I say, the puppy straining on his leash as we round the hedge. I've been taking him to pee out front since we got him. The yellow patches piss off Josh. "You scared me."

"Hey. Don't tell my husband, 'kay?"

Something lights up in her hand. There's a flash of teal and a sound like someone sucking an empty straw. She's vaping, and for a moment she's faceless, her head swallowed up by a puff of smoke. She vapes, and she hides it from Jerry. I didn't know this about Belinda.

"Don't you love it out here after the rain?" She sips from the tube. The clouds shift, and it's a glow stick in her hand. She's a one-person rave. "It smells so...green."

I part my lips, and snap my jaw shut. I want to tell her that while green is lush and life it can also be poison. That what she has in her hand is poison, too. Instead, I say, "How's Jerry doing? Up and about yet?" Jerry had a hip replacement two weeks ago, and Belinda has done nothing but complain since.

"I used to like that he ran, you know? Kept him fit. Had I known it would blow out his joints, I'd have told him to skip the jog and have another pierogi. He can't even tie his own shoes right now. Insists on sleeping in the basement on account of the heat, even though he can't get up the stairs on his own. I swear, it's like all of a sudden I have three kids instead of two."

She has one of those smiles that isn't a smile so much as a gnashing of teeth. Belinda's kids are probably in front of the TV right now, licking the neon suckers she brings home from the Magicuts where she works. "I didn't know the two were related," I say. Tuxedo turns in place and relieves himself on Belinda's crispy hydrangeas. "Running and hip surgery."

"You should be careful." Another drag. Belinda's wearing lipstick, I notice, her mouth a salmon O. "You run, don't you? It's not that safe for women. All the break-ins lately, you never know who might be out there prowling."

A mosquito whines in my ear. I use my free hand to do some hopeless swatting, thank her for her concern, and guide Tuxedo back inside. All the while I'm thinking, *you're the one out here alone. Like you're waiting for someone to steal you away.*

The lock on the door is well-oiled, and it slips into place with a comforting click. I don't like being apart from the kids, but there's something about having the house to myself on a Friday. I pull down a box of Old Dutch chips from the pantry shelf, draw the blinds in the TV room, and turn on Netflix. I can't do horrors or even thrillers, with their stories that cling to me like a foul fog, so I settle on a show about a perky lady renovating a Toronto patio.

Then I remember the break-ins. Picking up my phone, I Google *burglary River Heights Winnipeg.*

Break-ins soar in River Heights.

Spike in property crime.

MB crime rates: Burglary spree.

The results are endless, but none of the dates on the stories are recent. Whatever Belinda heard, she must have gotten the news from a neighbor.

The growling starts low, a rumble deep in Tuxedo's throat. A sound I didn't know he could make. Unnatural, and a little demonic. A minute ago, he was on his bed in the corner, but now he's at the window, his face jammed up behind the blind. He's looking outside. At the street.

I remember the idling car. "Tux." I snap my fingers. Make some kissing noises. Tuxedo keeps on growling. "There's nothing out there," I say, trying to sound plucky, but I don't know that, do I? It's the dog who's looking out the window, not me.

I had a friend growing up named Staceyann. She lived in a '70s split-level with huge plate glass windows and a diagonal roof, on a lane in the suburbs with more swimming pools than streetlights. At night, she and I would stand in our sleepover PJs and stare out at solid black until our skin was pebbled and the backs of our necks crawled. I felt like a doll in a big box store, frozen under the fluorescents, but Staceyann loved a good scare. That was then. A few years later, grade ten, Staceyann's mom was attacked in the parking lot outside the convalescent home where she worked. She was mugged and so badly beaten she lost vision in one of her eyes. Staceyann didn't invite me for any more sleepovers after that.

I pick up my cell phone and call Josh.

"We're in the middle of something, Holls."

Josh doesn't like me to call the kids when it's his time. He says I worry too much about every little thing. But am I not justified? Do I not have the right, as a mother, to care? It isn't just about him. Selena's got a soybean allergy, and Josh doesn't always think to check labels. Despite all our visits to the allergist, and the time her throat closed up when she ate tofu, his side of the family doesn't take our daughter's allergy seriously. They think I'm overreacting. *You worry too much, Holly.* If I'm grateful to my ex-husband for anything, it's that he waited to leave me until Selena was old enough to take care of herself.

"This'll just take a second," I tell him. "What do you know about the break-ins around here? I was talking to Belinda, and she said there have been prowlers in the neighborhood."

There's pot-clatter in the background, which means Josh hasn't yet fed the girls their supper. He barely feeds himself half the time, preferring a bottle of Crown Royal to a proper meal. He hums as he cooks, a song that's familiar but that I can't place.

"I might have heard something about that," he says, distracted. More humming.

"Like what? If it's not safe for the kids here, I need to know." Despite what Americans think of Canada, despite it being one of the safest countries in the world, there's crime here too. Winnipeg's one of the most dangerous cities of them all.

"You worry too much," says Josh.

And then I know. What he's humming, and why.

It's all so innocent. Josh and I still share a Spotify account. He must have seen "Don't Go Breaking My Heart" on my playlist and decided he was up for some '70s pop, too. It's nothing.

Except it doesn't feel that way. It feels like I've been followed. Like Josh's been spying on me, the way he did at the conservatory in those early days, before we met.

Josh still has a key. *For emergencies*, ostensibly, but he knows my house—*our house*—as well as I do, including that the door's well-oiled and the threshold to the living room creaks.

It's the idea of it that tortures me most. The knowledge that someone could creep into my room with a razor blade, a scalpel, I don't know what, and carefully drag it across my skin while I'm at my most vulnerable. Do they want to hurt me? No. If they wanted that, they'd press harder. Go deeper. Split me like an overripe fruit and spill me everywhere. I think this is something else, about my brain more than my body.

Someone knows who I am. What I am.

The thought makes me want to scream.

If someone's found a way to sneak into my home and hurt me without my knowing, who's to say they'll stop at these quiet little cuts?

Who's to say what else they might do?

"Mom! Did you sew my pointe shoes?"

The girls are back. I blink into the sunlight forcing its way between the blinds and run my tongue across teeth. My lips feel numb, the teeth furry. Somehow, I spent all night on the sofa, listening for Belinda's robbers. Wondering about Josh. I remember Tuxedo, curled up in his crate. The girls must have set him free. He's at the door now, wagging his hips, no doubt peeing all over the foyer as his nose bumps Cleo's legs, knees smudgy with dirt. No reminder to shower last night, I guess.

I want to know how they spent every minute of their time with their dad, but the girls are busy now, in their own heads. Later, when they've have had their fill of social media and video games and their sleep-deprived bodies go boneless—Josh always lets them stay up way too late—I'll give them a nudge. They might tell me about their night then. For now, I'm just grateful they came back to me.

Selena's pointe shoes. She did tell me she needed them done today, having declared her old pair dead after a single month of classes. I meant to sew the ribbons and elastic last night. Class starts in less than an hour. "On it!" I call cheerfully, hurrying to the drawer in the dining room hutch where I keep my sewing stuff. It's only then that I notice I feel groggy. My mouth is still dry too, like it was stuffed with hospital gauze. Two weeks ago, I switched to a new medication. Fatigue's a common side effect for these types of pills. Maybe dehydration is, too.

No time for that now. I brush the thought aside, and reach for the sewing kit.

My mother's kit was tidy and complete, packed with pin cushions shaped like baby strawberries and every size needle you could imagine. Mine's an old pickle jar of miscellaneous junk, but I find a needle and the pink thread, and I place a satiny shoe across my lap.

"What happened to your face?"

The day before she turned fourteen, Selena insisted that she dye her hair. She settled for candy blue bangs, but now, three months later, the blue is turning green, and standing over me with that probing expression, she looks like some inquisitive tropical bird. "Right there," she says, pointing at me. "What happened to you?"

My hand flies to my chin. There's a seam there. A fine crimp in the skin.

"Give me your phone."

Selena hands it over and I open the camera. Flip it to make a mirror. There are purple bruises under my eyes, and my complexion is sallow. I look no different than I have for the past week, only now there's a cut. A drip of dried blood like a scarlet beauty mark in the center of my chin.

Thumb hovering over the button on the screen, I snap the photo.

It's the first cut to ever appear on my face, and that concerns me. It speaks of boldness. Or is it impatience? Whoever's doing this to me, whatever it means, I think they're almost finished.

We're nearing the end.

"It's nothing." I hand back the phone. Return to my sewing. "Tux, probably. Just a scratch."

I look down. *The needle.* It's sharp enough to puncture skin, but a needle cut would scratch rather than slice.

Catching it between my fingers, I pry open the scissors and snip the thread.

Selena isn't happy about the divorce. I know she blames me for it, my condition and how much it frustrated Josh. Recently, she confessed he talked to her about it. Josh said he was always sick with worry. It wasn't that he didn't love me, just that this was no way to live. He promised Selena he'd get me help.

It was Josh's idea for me to take the new medication.

There isn't time. I need to finish sewing and get Selena off to class. Instead, I take her arm and pull her into the chair beside me. "Your dad," I begin before deciding on a different path. "What did you three do last night?"

"Watched a movie. It was awful, some lame rom-com. Dad was totally into it. It was weird."

"Huh."

Selena studies the run in her ballet tights, and slowly drags her finger over the tear. "We told him we'd rather watch *Survivor*, like, *three times*, but he made me keep it on even after he left."

I swallow. "He left?"

"Just to the beer store. Geeze, Mom, I babysit Belinda's kids all the time, I can definitely watch Cleo for half an hour. Oh my God, you're not done? We have to leave!"

Selena's standing again, bouncing on the balls of her feet. I'm nowhere near finished with her shoes.

"Give me five minutes," I tell her, still thinking of Josh. *What time did I drift off last night?*

"And Mom," Selena says, her tone brisk, "I need a new house key. Mine's lost."

My head snaps up. My cheeks are hot. "You lost your key? When?"

"I don't know, last weekend? I for sure had it when I went to Belinda's, but she hasn't found it. I asked."

She means last Sunday. She babysat for Belinda's kids last Sunday. And then she lost her key.

"Just forget it," she tells me, yanking the shoes from my lap. "I'll wear the old ones today. We have to *go*."

I stumble when she pulls me up and thrusts the car keys into my hand.

I've decided I won't take my pill today.

Five cuts.
Breastbone.
Foot.
Thigh.
Wrist.
Chin.

It was so much better when I didn't know where they were coming from.

It's been going on for longer than two weeks, of course, probably since well before the divorce, but Jerry's immobility has made things easier for her. There's no chance he'll catch her, sneaking across my lawn. Twisting Selena's key in my lock while her husband, whom she hates, snores in the house next door. Josh knows where I am, where the girls are, when I go to

CUTS

sleep, and that the dog won't hear a prowler from his crate. And that means she knows, too. He was furious when I got sole physical custody, but with two DUIs on his record, the judge felt better placing the girls with me.

Josh never did give up easily.

Selena and Cleo are in bed. The puppy, too. Everyone's tucked away for the night, and now, so am I.

Five cuts. I wonder what it felt like, to pull out her scissors and stand over me. Watch them glint in the moonlight as she decided where to cut me next. I wonder, too, what they have planned. Another day, and I would have gone back to my doctor with a story about injuries inflicted by a ghost.

It's possible they want something more than that. If they want to be sure this works out in their favor, Belinda could drive those scissors straight into my heart. My paranoia is well documented, after all. How could anyone look at the photos I took and not wonder whether I made those cuts myself?

It's late, still light out. Soon it will be dark.

But this time, I'm ready.

No matter what happens, I already know.

Tonight's cut will be the last.

STAY HERE, HONEY
Mark Bergin

There were no passing drivers to see Art cross the line as he took his first steps toward his second life. At two a.m., his car crashed, straddling the median and grinding along the raised concrete divider till it banged hard against the sand barrier. Rain had fallen all night and suppressed sparks that might have flashed from the scraping steel undercarriage or the stubby aluminum sign bracket torn apart by the bumper. Ten miles from downtown Minneapolis and the city glow reflected down off the clouds like a full moon.

Braced for impact and ready to jump, Art relaxed as it stopped, one hand on the wheel near the door handle, the other on the seat belt release and said, "Stay here, honey." With luck, the last thing he'd ever say to this wife.

With a glance in the rearview past his awakening kids to see no approaching headlights yet, he stepped out and looked under the car. Amy unbuckled to turn and watch him, concerned but not scared. Art handled problems, fixed things, paid bills. Except for all the bank errands he had her do this week she never handled money. He'd seemed especially confident tonight at dinner with the Johnsons, the girls playing themselves to sleep with friends, and he'd carried them to the car like they were inert lumps. Which made it easier for him.

He opened the trunk, removed two vodka bottles, a filled

and bulky gym bag, and a smaller bag containing the ashes of one thousand dollars in ones, burnt and bashed to a thin powder of gray and black. He knelt at his door and had to bend away from the pungent smell of leaking gasoline as he placed his items at the ready.

Art got back inside the car and, as she smiled, reached to cradle his wife's worried head and slammed her forward, temple-first into the hard steel shroud around the dashboard radio. Once was enough, twice would have ruined the effect. She slumped away against the passenger window, eyeglasses broken on her lap, her flowing blood black in the dark car, the interior light bulb out for some reason. His kids' eyes were wide and the one in the booster seat began a long, ascending moan, maybe "Mommy," maybe just a whine like she did.

He reached out and retrieved the vodka bottles. Turning back in he grasped each by the neck and smashed them together. They shattered in a spray of clear alcohol and glass, and the kids shrieked at the deluge. Still no headlights behind or in front as he stepped back out, crouched to shield his hands from the rain, and struck a match. He tossed it under the trunk.

Art stepped forward as the spilled gas ignited with a rush, low orange flames spreading out from both sides of the open trunk and in a line back toward the sharply mangled sign bracket that had torn open the gas tank. Just like Nora had said it would. He lit another match in the doorway, dropping it on the car's center console, and the vodka lit with a gentle blue glow, flames flowing down to the floorboards where other whiskey bottles lay below the kids' kicking feet. The older one's fingers scrabbled at the door handle like she'd been told never to do, but the child-proof locks were engaged, of course. She screamed more as he stepped back and dumped the money ashes in the open trunk for investigators to find. Nora, a trained crash reconstructionist, had told him he'd have a few moments before the tank blew, enough time to lean over and catch his blazer sleeve on fire to scald his arm. For authenticity.

And Nora drove up now, her cruiser first dark behind her headlights, then flashing red and blue as she activated her rooftop strobes. She turned the nose away from him at an odd angle, toward the passenger side of his smoking car. He knew her dash camera would be recording now, activated along with her police emergency lights, and hoped she'd remembered to advance the time readout by two minutes. Of course she would. She had skills, like he'd never known, like he wasn't ready for. They'd need two minutes to finish the scene.

Nora, it turned out, needed only one.

The first crash she'd worked here at this concrete divider resulted in an explosion that crisped the occupant family, she'd told him in bed. Ten years ago, and few in their small town would remember. That it happened a second time again tonight would be seen as an unfortunate circumstance, at least for Art, his wife, and daughters. But they were of no concern to Nora. With a five-cell steel flashlight on her shoulder like a rifle, she strode up to Art, who stood with his left arm straight out, his tweed sleeve aflame and his face beginning to register the pain of self-inflicted, convincing burns. In his right, he held the gym bag full of all the cash from the family bank accounts, the cashed-out life insurance policies, the second mortgage his wife never applied for but bore her forged signature. Why she did it, Art would tell the investigators, why she took out the money then made him crash, he would never be able to understand. Boo hoo. He squinted through the thick smoke. The red cylinder in Nora's hand would be a fire extinguisher as planned, and he spoke to hurry her.

"Here, honey," he said, and proffered the bag.

She tossed the bucket of gasoline straight at Art's face and upper chest, where it ignited with a whoosh of rolling fire, roiling up over his face and taking his hair. Like she'd practiced it, she plucked the gym bag of money from Art's hand and, with the butt of her flashlight, pushed his flaming body back into the open door of the engulfed car.

"Stay," she said.

He kicked and flailed a moment, till his heart learned his lungs were toasted.

Nora glanced into the back seat where the screams had stopped and walked back to her cruiser. She waved smoke away and smiled. She didn't need to double check that her dashcam image cut off at the edge of the driver's side of Art's car, leaving their dance unrecorded, but confirmed that the altered time stamp would match her radio transmission.

She hid the money in her trunk. Their Mexico money, he'd called it, "for when you go away with me." *Nah, I won't, idiot,* she'd thought. *I can't be with a man who cheats. What kind of woman do you think I am?* In her mind she spoke in black-and-white, like Veronica Lake, or the other girl in *The Big Sleep*, the troubled one. What was the movie word? Noir? Nora swung a wet bang off her eye and keyed the mic, far too late.

"Unit 132, request Rescue for a collision at Duke and Walker Streets, one car fully involved, occupants unknown." She coughed in the smoke. It sounded like a laugh.

THE MINNESOTA TWINS MEET BIGFOOT

Richie Narvaez

We showed our IDs to the beefy security guard, hoping to get past him and quickly through the crowds we saw flowing into the convention center. The frisking I expected. But one staticky two-way radio call later, and suddenly four other cheesehead goons were escorting us past seven Spider-Persons, fourteen Stormtroopers (some purple, some orange), a Batman in breezers, eleven elves or dwarves or trolls, I wasn't sure, and a giant samurai/robot/can opener before we got to an upper level.

"We're just here to meet our client," I said. "What's this about?"

Cece gave me the *cool it* look and I rolled my eyes.

Ignoring us, the goons escorted us to an office between the concierge and a Caribou Coffee. The door had a small sign that read "Lost & Found."

Inside was a small desk, and behind it was a stout, extremely bald man in a sweater, tie, and jacket. Behind him were stacks and stacks of stuff in bins: scarves, umbrellas, toys, laptops, briefcases, suitcases, phones, many looking brand new.

The stout man looked up from his own phone when we came in. Barely. "Bert Ebersol, head of Security & Safety Solutions for the Minneapolis Convention Center. I hope you don't mind my bringing you up. This is the biggest convention center in the state, and this here QuasarCon is the biggest convention we have all year. We can't be too careful."

"If you say so," I said. I gave Ebersol our card.

"The Reyes Agency?" he said. "You two related?"

"He's my brother," "She's my sister," Cece and I said simultaneously, each nodding at the other.

"Bless your hearts. I've never heard of your agency. Are you new?"

"New to the city. We usually work in St. Cloud," my sister blurted before I could answer. She was probably worried about my being too honest—our agency was only three weeks old. "We have plenty of—"

Ebersol cut her off. "So what's your business here?"

I'd had enough of this. We were going to be late and I hated being late. "Look, our client asked to meet us here. He's working his booth all day and can't leave. He's expecting us. Thirty seconds ago."

Ebersol smiled. He actually picked up to his phone and started scrolling, completely ignoring us. My sister gave me the *good grief* look.

There was an awkward pause.

Ebersol guffawed at something on his phone, then he looked up and said, "Well. Anything security-wise going on here goes through me. I understand I don't need to know exactly what you're being hired for, client privilege, yadda yadda. But if it affects this convention center, then it affects me, and then I do need to know."

Again, Cece spoke before I could. "We understand that, Mr. Ebersol. From what the client told us, the case involves something that did not take place on convention grounds. That's all we can say."

Ebersol shrugged. "Just want to make sure we're on the same page. And if you need help, my men and I are always available. Nothing happens here I don't know about."

On the escalator down to meet our client, I bet my sister Ebersol was looking for a bribe.

As usual, she disagreed. "For crying out loud, he just wanted to show us he was the king of the castle."

"Whatever," I said. "But next time we use my fake ID kit. We could have said we were Hollywood VIPs." She ignored me, but it would totally have worked.

Instead, she said, "Let me take the lead with the client, all right?"

The convention center was noisy and hot and smelled like a locker room at the end of the sad and sweaty sophomore year. My brother Casper and I stood in a booth piled high with toys, collectibles, memorabilia, all too spendy.

"You guys could totally dress as Zan and Jayna!"

"Uff-da! I'd do it," I said honestly. "Not Casper, though."

"Or the creepy twins from *The Shining*," our new client, a Mr. Hoxsey, continued. "If you don't mind the dresses. Wait, so you're both in the same line of work? I guess it's like what they say: you're basically the same person, am I right?"

It was clear to me that Hoxsey had had too many lattes for breakfast. He was red-faced, had a clammy handshake. He wore a black T-shirt he must have owned since he was thirteen, a couple-few decades ago. But a trusted friend of ours had given him a good reference, and our agency was brand new. So we had to indulge him. Or at least try to.

"Casper and I are actually quite different," I said. "For example, he crochets and I like paint-by-numbers."

"Sweet!" Hoxsey said. "I guess."

"So you wanted help in retrieving some valuables, Mr. Hoxsey?"

"You guys can just call me 'Conan.' It's actually my real name. My father loved R.E.H. Yeah, anyway, my story is this: as you can see, I got valuable stuff for sale here, and every night

85

I lock most of it in my van. But the primo items I take back with me to my hotel room."

"Primo items?" Casper asked.

"You betcha. I got a complete set of Mission Venus FunGo action figures, including the metallic bookworm and the clown-faced Van Johnson."

I pointed at a series of squat plastic figures in plastic packaging, each about fifteen centimeters high. "Those dolls. They're that valuable?"

"No, not those. But that primo set of mine is. Each figure is worth ten thousand. I like to show them off here in this case behind me, which you can see is now empty. They're not really for sale, but it brings customers over."

"Were these figures insured?" I asked.

"Yeah, sure. All insured. My wife hassled me about that and good thing. But that's not the point. It took me years to assemble that set. That set is priceless to me. And I can tell you right now who took them. It was Yadhira Tsuki, Spaceborne Princess, don'tcha know."

"Spell that for me." My brother started to take down the name.

"That's an anime character," I said, stopping him. "You mean someone dressed as her, of course. How did she get into your room?"

"Weh-hell, there was a little after-party after the first day of the con yesterday, and she was at the bar all the dealers go to. This woman was in full, super-accurate costume."

"Which doesn't cover much," I said.

"Gosh, no, it does not. It's basically a bikini with wings. But hers were beautifully done, 3D-printed feathers, little claws at the end, fully articulated wings. She even had the lightning bolt antennae. Lit up every time she spoke. She practically flew over to me at the bar and came on pretty strong. Wait, here's a picture I snapped with her. As soon as she started putting out the vibes, I knew I had to get a picture. No one would believe me if I didn't."

The photo showed an even more red-faced Hoxsey with a

woman in a multicolored bird-alien-warrior-swimsuit model get-up. A hell of lot of her upper body was showing but most of her face was hidden behind a mask.

I pointed at the ring on Hoxsey's left hand and said, "Didn't you say you had a wife?"

"What happens at the con stays at the con, am I right?"

I did the professional thing and resisted rolling my eyes. "So you brought the princess to your room?"

"Yep. *Things* happened."

"And you showed her your primo collection?" my brother asked, and I dreaded the response.

"In more ways than one!" Hoxsey said. There it was. He snickered to himself, but then stopped when he saw we weren't laughing with him. "But, um, yeah, when I woke up, she was gone and so was the set."

"Did you get a look at her without the mask?"

"She insisted on keeping the room dark."

"Uh huh," I said.

My brother chimed in. "Isn't it likely this Tsuki has fled the state by now?"

"Gosh, no, that's the thing," Hoxsey said, "and why I'm hiring you two. With that gear she was wearing, she is obvi an A-level cosplayer, and this being the biggest convention of the year in Minnesota, and only the second day out of four—dudes, there's no way she's going to miss a chance to show off. She's still here. I know it."

A lot of people think that because we were twins, my sister Cece and I were somehow psychic, two brains linked as one. This was nonsense. Not that Cece I weren't on the same page a lot. Just not always.

Walking through the crowd, I said, "Are you thinking what I'm thinking?"

And she said, "His lightsabers are way too spendy."

"What? No, I was thinking that this Yadhira Tsuki could have borrowed or bought the costume just to get to this guy's toy set."

"Possible," she said. "But if she was as tricked out as he said, that takes time and skill, even a little obsession. Cosplayers don't just put on a costume. This is a serious hobby, even a career for some people."

Cece suggested we stroll around the convention. "You never know, we might trip over a six-and-a-half-foot-tall woman with wings."

We waded through the crowd and into another long aisle of booths. The third one we came to was similar to our client's—collectibles, comics, etc. Standing in the middle of the booth was a chubby man in a black T-shirt and brown leather cowboy hat. He was having a heated conversation with a tall woman made taller by thick-soled boots and a three-foot-high faux-fire headdress. Over the consistent din of the convention, I could only make out: "Keep calm already and it'll work out."

Cece and I looked at each other. We couldn't be that lucky...

As we walked over, the man in the hat smiled. He also clasped his hand around the wrist of the tall woman. Before we could introduce ourselves, he said, "Anything I can help you with today?"

I took the lead this time. "Yes. How much would a complete set of Mission Venus FunGo action figures go for?"

"Hah! Those are super valuable, ten grand for each figure, at least," the man said. "Now, if you're interested in super-valuable items, I've got a Diamond Encrusted Barbie, the Mountie G.I. Joe, and a 1954 Superman lunchbox, all in mint condition and right here."

"So you don't have that set?"

"Dang. No. Wish I did. But no."

"Would you be able to procure that set of FunGo figures somewhere?"

The man shook his head. "Sorry. They say they only made

three clown-faced Van Johnsons. You want that set you can try to pry it away from Hoxsey over in the next aisle, but I doubt he'll ever sell it. Now if it's rare collectibles you want, I have Sylvester Stallone's compression socks from *The Expendables 3*. Never washed."

The man handed me a card that said:

Brent McCoy
Darn it, Jim, I'm a Fan, Not a Businessman

I looked over to see my sister smiling at the spiky-headed woman. "Hi," Cece said. "Nice Faerie Assassin Witch costume."

The tiniest smile crept into the corners of the woman's lips, but her face remained impassive in glittery white face paint

McCoy said, "This is my girlfriend, Luna Rinehart. She's one of the top cosplayers in the country. If she moves her face too much, she'll ruin her makeup. No offense."

We thanked him and went on our way.

Casper and I made the rounds of the con and found four Yadhira Tsukis. Two were children, one was a male with a hairy belly and a churlish attitude, and the last had just arrived that morning and produced an airplane ticket to prove it. We eliminated them as suspects.

Armed with an image of the set as well as the picture of Hoxsey with Tsuki, we visited the Ray J's American Grill on Central, the bar where Hoxsey said he'd met his outer space assignation.

We found a bartender in white shirt and black pants, smoking on the sidewalk outside. "For cute!" she said when we showed her the picture. "But, no, I don't recognize the face, not that that's where my eyes go, if you know what I mean. But she's no regular. There's someone inside you may want to ask though."

"Another bartender?" I said.

"You could. But I'd say try the couple by the jukebox. You'll see what I mean."

Over by the neon-lit jukebox against the wall were two patrons dressed head to toe as lizards.

"Oh that'sssss lovely," the first one said. "It could be Ssssandi Piñero. Or Luna Rinehart."

My brother and I resisted giving each other a look.

"Could be Luna, yeah," the other lizard said. "Thissss could also be Ssssssuzie Sssseeley."

"It'sssss not a great picture isssss the real issssue. But honessssstly there are about only ssseven or eight coplayers at this level at the con who kinda ssssssorta look like this."

The second lizard person said, "Cossssssplayers live for attention, especially thessssse. They won't be hard to find at the con. Besssssidesss there'ssss the massssssquerade."

"Massssssquerade?" my brother said.

I nudged him. "Big cosplay contest at the end of the con."

"Big cash prize, I bet."

"For Pete's sake, not just. It's for glory, for bragging rights."

The lizards were warm-blooded enough to give us names to follow up on. Luna Rinehart topped the list. But she did not return our phone calls and emails. But the other cosplayers were eager to talk and agreed to meet. My brother and I split up—I took ones at the con, and he met some at their hotels.

It was easy to spot Anna Caprica. She was dressed as Taco Belle, the character from *Beauty and the Beast* but with a dress made of lettuce and taco shells. "I prefer doing costume puns," she said. "Yesterday I was Jon Snow White."

No, she had never met Conan Hoxsey. Yes, she knew what FunGo figures were but didn't know they could be so valuable. She'd spent the previous night in her hotel room, sewing the tomatoes, onions, and cheese onto her dress. I believed her. I moved on.

Alana Craig made it clear she would only speak in Klingon, so I didn't get very far with her. One of the warriors standing nearby said to try again the next day, when Alana would be a rhyming demon.

I hoped my brother was doing better.

Later that afternoon, I met my sister in the lobby of the Holiday Inn Express. Another cosplayer, a something purple and gold, had told me that Luna Rinehart was staying there. Cece said her day had been a bust and would give me a full report later. I asked her to type it up instead of just sending a voice file the way she usually does.

"I'm not going to type it up," she said.

"We need to have everything in writing."

"Fine, I'll get an app to transcribe it."

"I just want our agency to get off on the right foot."

Before the elevator doors opened on the fifth floor, we heard a super-shrill scream. We ran toward it and, through the open door of Luna Rinehart's room, saw what looked like, well, Bigfoot. Well, someone in a ghillie suit with a Bigfoot mask.

"That's different," I said.

It—he?—was trying to wrestle a duffel bag out of Luna's hand. Cece jumped in, karate-chopped the cryptid's forearms, and he squealed and turned toward the door. But I was in the way.

He barreled toward us like a truckload of fur and knocked me upside down. I went, "Ope!" and on the way down—while hitting my skull against the doorjamb *hard*—I reached out and grabbed for Bigfoot's foot and yanked. I heard the cryptid yowl and I ended up with a tennis shoe in my hand. I turned to see him limping down the hall.

"Go after him," my sister yelled.

"Gosh darnit," I muttered, feeling pain radiate all over. I stumbled after him but couldn't find him in either stairwell. He was gone. I went back to the room and announced, "So, I got his tennis shoe."

I heard my sister sigh. She was trying to calm Ms. Rinehart down. Eventually, we got me an ice pack and the whole story.

There'd been a knock on the door and through the peephole

Luna had seen this person in a Bigfoot outfit. "No biggie," she'd thought, thinking it must be a fellow cosplayer, so she opened the door. But he'd pushed in and demanded the FunGo set. She denied having it. Then he started to shake her but she yelled like a "B-movie Scream Queen" (her words) and he turned and that's when we showed.

My sister asked her if she had been cosplaying at Princess Tsuki the night before, but Ms. Rinehart didn't want to talk about that. Neither did she want to go to the hospital, but she still had the shakes. So Cece said she'd stay with her for a little while.

On my way back to our office in St. Cloud, I called Hoxsey to give him an update. He was happy to hear we had the set. We agreed that I'd store it in our office safe, and that we'd meet in the morning and I'd hand it over.

"You guys are great," he said. "I'm going to give you the best darn Yelp review anyone's ever gotten, you betcha!"

I decided to hang back with Luna Rinehart. My instinct told me she knew more than she realized, and that getting my brother to skedaddle would help her open up. I called the hotel desk and told the concierge I'd give him fifty bucks if he'd run across the road and get a bottle of rum and a liter of pop.

Her room was filled with cosplay paraphernalia and smelled of glue, burned latex, and makeup. I handed her a filled plastic cup.

"This is all very impressive," I said. "How did you get into this?"

"It's a long story," she said. Then she took a sip of the drink. "Oh wow!"

"You're not from around here. Minnesota, I mean. I hear the accent." In Spanish, I asked her what town she was from.

"Ha! San Juan!"

"Ha! Our family's from Arecibo."

"That's amazing. My real name is Luisa Ruiz."

"Nice to meet you, Luisa. When did your family come over?"

"After Hurricane Maria. We really had no choice. We ended in Roseau because they *said* there would be jobs."

"Roseau?"

"It's about six hours north of St. Paul. My parents, they were looking for work. It was a weird change, you know. And the kids in town, they called me 'Pocahontas' or 'Wetback.' I hated it. I hated them. I had been messing with cosplay back in San Juan. Over here it became everything I was about. With cosplay I get to make my own identity. I don't gotta be this or that, you know. I can be whoever I want one day to the next."

After another round of drinks, I got her to talk about the Bigfoot in the room.

"He was definitely really tall. That wasn't lifts or stilts. But that was a cheap suit—it smelled. No self-respecting cosplayer would wear that."

"Noted. And now we have his shoe. Which could be useful, I guess. You want to tell me about taking the figures," I said. "Was that your boyfriend Brent's idea?"

"He's always wanted that stupid set. But, it wasn't his idea."

"Where is he right now?"

"At the convention, of course. He's always stays really late. It's his whole life. The toys and the collectibles. They fill up everything in his house. There's barely room for me, really."

"If you don't mind my saying, I thought your boyfriend was a little handsy with you the other day."

"He was, but not for the reason you probably think. He knew I was freaking about what I'd done the night before, and I would have freaked out more if he hadn't anchored me for that moment when you and your brother came over. Seriously, I know Brent comes off like a jerk. He likes people to think that. But he's not."

"Still, he had you seduce someone to steal their stuff?" I said.

"No! I don't know what you think happened, but that Hoxsey guy was snoring like a chainsaw two minutes after we got in the room from the stuff I put in his drink."

"What stuff?"

"The guy who hired us sent it to us. He said, 'Whatever you do, don't actually have sex with him.'"

"He said that specifically?"

"Yeah."

"Tell me everything he said."

"Yeah, so, some guy called up Brent about a week ago. Said that if we stole the action figures, we'd get a cut of the sale. Brent was so turned on about the idea of messing with Hoxsey—they've been, like, frenemy rivals for years—he barely asked questions. I went along with it because I love Brent, and because I was kind of turned on by the idea of doing it, too, you know, like being a spy."

"Another identity," I said. "Let me guess: You and Brent decided to double-cross this person?"

Luisa/Lucy hung her head. "Yeah. We were supposed to contact her, but Brent and I were talking and we said, 'Screw that' because we realized we had the figures and could sell them and keep all the money for ourselves. What were this person on the phone going to do, you know?"

"But then along comes Bigfoot, so you know these people are serious."

My sister was never going to let me live this down.

I was opening my car door when Bigfoot came up behind me. I could smell him. He slammed my face into the car. My skull was not having a good day.

I woke up when my sister kicked me. Gently, but it was still a kick.

"Bigfoot returned?"

"Holy buckets, he sure did."

"Got the dolls."

"Suckin' A."

"But you made him work for it, gave him a run for his money, a few good licks?"

"Sure did."

"That's my big brother—by fifteen minutes!"

"Fifteen more minutes of experience therefore wisdom therefore strength and agility."

"Let's go to my dojo one day and spar, so you could show me this strength and agility," Cece said.

"We don't have to."

We decided to grab dinner to talk the case over. I got a Juicy Lucy, and Cece said she wasn't going to eat but she ended up wolfing down all of my tots.

She told me what Ms. Rinehart had told her.

I said, "So the guy who hired them didn't want Hoxsey to get the satisfaction of getting satisfied. A jealous lover then? You think Hoxsey's gay?"

"I asked Luna that. We both agreed definitely not. But it gives me an idea."

She said we should call the client again. I said I didn't want to. She said to put him on speaker.

Mr. Hoxsey was understandably surly and disappointed.

Cece, out of nowhere, assured him we'd get the figures.

"Gosh darn, the con ends in two days," he said. "After that, everyone scatters. I'll never get my set back, and I'm going to give you the worst Yelp review anyone's ever gotten, you betcha!"

"Mr. Hoxsey, I know you're upset," Cece said. "But we have some ideas."

I looked at her with my *what gives?* face.

"Tell me, Mr. Hoxsey, who knew you were coming to the con with the FunGos?"

"Everyone! For the past two years, they've been my thing."

"So, literally hundreds of thousands of people know you had them. How many of those people might want be about six and a half feet tall and possibly violent?"

"Most of them."

"That's not helpful, Mr. Hoxsey. How about this: what does

your wife do for a living?"

"Sonja? She works at a Thrifty White Pharmacy in Milaca."

I saw where she was going. I said, "Can we ask: where is your wife at the moment? And, just for elimination purposes, how tall is she?"

Saturday was the loudest, most crowded day of the convention. Our client suggested that my brother and I dress up as Men in Black, in order to blend in. I was into it, Casper not so much. But there we were, in black suits and shades, taking turns wading through the three floors and dozen halls and rooms.

It had turned out that Hoxsey's wife was only five-four. But she hadn't been home at eleven p.m. My gut told me she was somehow involved with our sasquatch.

We reasoned that whoever nabbed the dolls would have to come back to the con. We hoped that he was planning to sell the dolls, and there was no better, more immediate place to offload them.

But in the sea of bodies, it was impossible to spot anything besides the odd full-size Transformer.

To top it all off, the masquerade contest was starting in Hall C. Thousands of people flowed into the room. Inside, it was like George Lucas or Stan Lee or one of those guys had exploded. It was a parade of IPs. There were more than a few Chewbaccas. But no Bigfoot.

"This is hopeless," I said.

My brother shrugged, ready to give up. "There's just too many people."

"I seriously don't know how we're going to find them."

At that moment, Casper and I turned to each other. We were searching in the wrong place.

Simultaneously, we said, "Lost & Found."

* * *

96

Where was the easiest place to buy and sell in stolen goods in a giant place like this?

That was the real reason Ebersol had pulled us into his office the first day we arrived. It wasn't so much to show us he was king of the castle. He wanted to make sure we weren't investigating him.

We were looking around for a spot to stake out the office when we got a lucky break: along came Bigfoot, heading straight for the "Lost & Found."

It was a distinctive enough costume. But we knew it was him because he was carrying Luna's duffel bag. And when he started to run as soon as he saw us, he limped.

"See," I said to Cece. "I did do some damage."

"Well done!"

We caught him making his way for the stairs. But with his limp and the compact crowds, he saw he had lost.

He collapsed against a wall and sank slowly to the floor. It takes a long time for a giant to sink to the floor.

"I've had enough," he said. He pulled off his mask. Steam heat came out of it.

Cece took a picture of his face. "I'm texting our client."

A moment later he texted back: *That's Ted! My neighbor and BFF.*

"Best friend, huh?" I said to Ted. "Have you been having carnal relations with Sonja Hoxsey?"

Ted nodded, his face slick with sweat.

"Hold on," Cece said. She had opened the duffel. "There's nothing here. Only newspaper."

"Aw, cripes!" Ted looked genuinely surprised.

"She set you up," I said.

"He's a distraction," Cece said.

In the car, my brother kept nagging me about Ebersol, that we had to turn him in, let the authorities know about the racket he was running.

"We're not cops," I reminded him for the hundredth time since we started this profession. "Besides, we have no proof."

Casper shook his head. "Ted admitted that he was going there to sell them."

"But Hoxsey's wife tricked him."

"But why? What does she want with the figures?"

"Something Luna said made me think of why. That this con and these fantasy things were her boyfriend's whole life. I just hope we get there in time."

Casper turned into the lot of the Metro Inn, where Ted had told us Sonja had been staying. Night had fallen, but we could see light coming from the back of the lot. It was a fire.

When we got out of the car we saw Sonja Hoxsey. We could tell by the bright red hair Ted had described. She sat in a foldout chair in front of a barbecue egg that was burning up something good. At her feet were the boxes the FunGo figures had been in.

When we approached, it was obvious she knew who we were by the way she rolled her eyes.

"So it wasn't about the insurance?" I said.

"Maybe. At first. See, Conan kept these things on our mantle. Took up more space than our kids' pictures. At night he'd move them into the bedroom, up to a shelf above our TV. I fell asleep every night looking at these gosh darn things. I ain't sad to see 'em go."

In the cool night, the fire was warming, but my brother and I had to move away from the toxic smoke.

Casper turned to me and said, "We better call Mr. Hoxsey."

"Yeah, we better," I said. "Oh hey, I was going to ask, how is the website coming along?"

"Well, I thought we could put a picture of Bigfoot's shoe on the front page. That'll bring in lots of traffic."

"Good idea, yeah, sure. You betcha."

NIGHTMARE WITH A TWIST
L.A. Chandlar

He became my nightmare. Everything he said or did came with a twist, like a knife dug deep into flesh with a little extra spin of cruelty to top it off like hot sauce. Of course, not when he thought anyone was watching, then he was always a charming beacon of friendliness.

Tonight was the night. Eddie was going to force me far out onto the Lake Michigan Triangle in his new boat. The thought of it made itchy tingles of sweat break out all over my body. Of course, he fed off that fear which he'd been using against me all week. I could see it in his mean, pink-rimmed eyes. The eyes that now carried the look of someone used to whipping dogs and children. Eddie was still a handsome man and his suitcoat and tie fit like he actually had the job to afford it. He was one of the administrators for our public school system and well-respected in the community. Well. Most of the community.

As we walked across the street in town, he put his hand on my shoulder. His grip had the power of a vise and was just as yielding, reminding me he was in control as he simultaneously smiled to passersby, leading them to believe my husband was lovingly possessive. *Isn't that sweet.*

I nodded a greeting with a smile that was merely a grimace of resignation. They'd never understand. And to think, he'd brought us to this place not because he loved the lake, but because he knew

I feared it. This little Wisconsin town that was right at the corner of where the Michigan Triangle touched the shore. Every Scooby-Doo and Hardy Boys / Nancy Drew fan knew about the Bermuda Triangle, but we had our very own. A triangle of deep water in the middle of Lake Michigan full of ghosts and mysterious disappearances of people and entire ships over hundreds of years. Everyone just accepted it as part of our colorful culture, but to me it was a looming shadow over my life. The lake near to shore was my friend. Once land was out of sight, it was menacingly deep and held unknowable secrets. I had a paralyzing fear of going far from shore. So much of my life was uncontrollable and the thought of being in the middle of ghostly, dangerous waters with no land in sight was enough to make my heart race and my mouth go dry even as I was simply walking across the street.

Lake Michigan was breathtaking but it was not a regular lake. The Great Lakes are each the size of a small ocean that hold ancient spirits and fickle winds that one moment are as soft and rolling as a lazy summer day spent upon a hammock, then suddenly as wicked as an icy, bone-crushing nor'easter. The waves, though fresh, could be as high as the sea's and would turn from a deep royal blue to a murky yellow green at a moment's notice, as volatile as a wild animal.

"So you're sure you want to go out on the lake tonight?" I asked my husband, Eddie. He'd been wavering a bit, so I wondered if I could sway him. My voice shook just the tiniest bit.

"Well, honey," he said as the vise gripped my shoulder a fraction harder, "I think it's turning out to be a great night." *Sure. If I could just survive.*

Just then a buddy of his passed us on the sidewalk and we stopped.

"Hey Eddie, Cass. How are you?" I had to be careful around this one, he was an officer from the local precinct who was a buddy of Eddie's and known to cover for any indiscretion of his friends. Male friends, that is. I looked distractedly into the shop window next to us.

"Doing great, doing great, John. Say, how's it going with Pete's case? I'm real sorry about that, sorry to lose such a great guy."

John hung his head as he replied, "Yeah, actually it was definitely a DUI. His blood alcohol was way over. Just can't believe he's gone. Feel real sorry for his wife and their new son, too."

I kept my eyes focused on the shiny new purses in the shop window. This was exactly what I was talking about; that idiot Pete had been drunk more nights of his life than he'd been sober. And a cruel drunk to boot. His wife—Jen is her name, which Eddie would never remember—and baby were lucky and in my opinion she looked as if she knew it. I hadn't known her for long, but I knew the signs. The occasional flinch in her husband's vicinity, the flair of pain if someone bumped into her near her ribs where bruises were concealed by clothing. And as usual, he'd gotten worse when she was pregnant. The highest rate of maternal mortality is not from genetics or illness of any kind, it's from domestic abuse. No one seems to know that fact. My girlfriend Olivia, also an officer at the precinct, told me that statistic. A sense of dread had filled me with such fear, I started secretly using the pill again, taking great pains to conceal it from Eddie who wanted me to get pregnant.

Then one day Jen came to visit with me and talk about my business in essential oils, some healing potions that helped with bruising and finicky infants, among other things. Olivia had been my only friend at the time, but slowly I started making a few new ones here and there. Mostly from my business, like Jen. The business I loved inherently turned into a way for me to help others, especially women, which made it even more satisfying. Women *need* to help each other.

I interrupted the men's chummy conversation, "Wasn't Pete's accident right by the bluffs at the edge of the lake?"

"Uh...yeah it was," stuttered Officer John.

Eddie rolled his eyes. "Isn't she just the cutest, most superstitious little thing? Cass here thinks the Michigan Triangle is real." He laughed a low chuckle that held a promise of pain. He pretended to kiss my temple but whispered in my ear, "Shut. Up. You're embarrassing me."

Officer John looked a bit awkward, but they finally ended the bro chat and we got to leave. Every second that passed inched me closer to facing my biggest fears that night. *God help me.*

At home, Eddie sat down in his recliner with his beloved newspaper while watching a football game, yelling out tidbits of the news about the weather and sports interspersed with demands for beer.

"Get me a Bud, Cass. Make sure it's from the back, real cold." I had to stop working on an article for a health magazine to retrieve it. "Say, did you hear about that hiker who got lost on the trail near the Sheboygan Falls?" he asked.

I handed him the cold beer and said, "No, I didn't."

"They found his body. Been missing three weeks. Finally got some dogs on the trails and they sniffed it out—fell off a cliff, looks like. He'd hit an outcropping of rocks, so his body wasn't near any popular area. It's what kept them from finding him sooner, I guess."

"Huh," I said distractedly. At least that one was a little farther from the Triangle, but superstitious or not, we definitely had more than our share of strange disappearances. I felt another surge of alarm about the night ahead.

I forced myself to return to my article and knocked out a few more paragraphs. During the day, I usually worked on my recipes for herbal remedies and positive energy practices, and lately I'd also attained a still and had been learning how to make my own essential oils. I even dabbled in making my own whiskey. But Eddie hated my business, called me a hippie incessantly, though he certainly enjoyed my paycheck and gave me a very *gracious* allowance. When he was around I kept to the bookkeeping and writing tasks to stay as invisible as possible.

In the beginning I'd thought his teasing was endearing, that the allowance thing was part of both of us investing in the family, that he liked our differences. I hadn't realized I was the metaphorical frog in the pot. Couched in loving, charming ways at first, Eddie slowly turned up the heat taking more control over the finances, forging my signature on a second mortgage and secreting away the money, making me feel like his dark moods were my fault, and he even eased me away from my former friends and family. Not to mention the bruises and occasional broken ribs that began to "happen" to me.

"Well honey? Tonight's the night! I will make a boater out of you if it kills me."

I had to get out of the house. Knowing Eddie would be enjoying his football game for another forty-five minutes, I softly eased out and ambled around our neighborhood to enjoy the ancient trees and small streams. The beauty was refreshing and never ceased to remind me of who I was.

I recalled a sweet memory that happened on one of my walks. A few months ago, I had sat on a small bench enjoying the thriving summer leaves and bright green grass dotted with plump honeybees in the wild bergamot and purple clover. Out of a close group of trees, a doe emerged and gently came up to me so close I could almost touch her perfect nose. I was stunned that she seemed unafraid. But like her, I had learned a hard-won patience. I knew the best way to steer clear of danger was stillness, invisibility. Perhaps she felt a kind of kindred spirit with me.

The doe's muscled body was strong yet delicate. I loved her all-seeing black eyes, the very kissable nose. I felt a love and a strength radiating from her. I once read of a Native American spirit called the Deer Lady who appeared either as a beautiful woman or a deer and as that memory had flitted into my consciousness, the doe tossed her head in a quick salute and bounded off, leaving waves of peacefulness in her wake.

The memory boosted my confidence and I turned to go back. I was walking up to our house just as I saw Olivia's patrol car pull up in the street. My heart started to pound; Eddie couldn't see her here. We only ever visited in town and only when he'd be at work. *Shit.*

"Hey there, Cass!" Olivia called out with a friendly wave. I waved back but tried to give her a look that said she needed get the heck out of Dodge. She started to get back into her car and I gave a sigh of relief. Just then, Eddie came striding out of the house.

"Well look who's here. Officer, is there a problem?" he asked. But before he could master himself, I saw a look of desire run across Eddie's face as he got closer. He was attracted to power and it reminded me of how powerful I used to feel. He put that possessive hand on my shoulder as I fought a twinge of disgust.

"Not at all," Olivia replied in that low, mesmerizing voice of hers. "Just got a call about a deer that might've been hit by a car, but there's nothing about. I'll keep an eye out in the area just in case."

With a sincere yet revolting jolliness, he reached out in a gesture to shake hands with her, and said, "Well then, that's great to hear and you're looking quite fine today. Is that a new uniform? You do fill it out nicely, you know." He gave a wink as she made an obvious move of getting out her notebook so she didn't have to shake his hand. It was difficult restraining an annoyed roll of my eyes.

"Just move it along, Eddie, I have to get going," said Olivia, putting her notebook away and fingering her duty belt, right near her holster. I dreamed of her writing him up a ticket for anything at all, even something stupid like the flagpole being too tall, if only he wouldn't take it out on me. But she knew he would. *They always do.*

"Take it easy, don't get hysterical, Officer. Just joshing. Hey, you know? You should come and see me some time on my new boat. Just got her last month and have been fixing her up."

Thinking of going out on the lake again made me queasy and I tensed. Eddie felt it and looked at me grinning with malice. "Oh honey, you're just going to love it. I know you hate those old ghost stories about the Triangle, but I'm telling you, you'll enjoy every second." He gave my side what was supposed to be a playful tickle, but he pinched harder than necessary and I flinched like he'd elbowed me.

Olivia said, "You know, Eddie, if your wife isn't up for it, maybe you should bring someone else along."

His one eye squinted and he shot a look to her, clearly loathing being contradicted and unused to it. "Are you applying for the job?" he asked with a smarmy tone.

"Nope, just saying that you'd have a lot more fun if you were with people who wanted to go out on the water."

"Are you saying my wife doesn't want to spend time with me? Is that what you're saying, *Officer*?" With the last word, a little spit flew out of his mouth as he became brittle with anger.

"All right, all right, Eddie. Like I said, let's just move it along. *Now*." With everything in me, I wanted her to add *don't get hysterical* but she knew it was not in my best interest. She turned to me and instead of saying anything else, she gave a little up-tilt of her head that reminded me of the deer's salute.

"Bye, now," I said as I nodded.

A few hours later, we were ready to take the boat out. It wasn't a sailboat, thank God, but a used cabin cruiser. If I stayed within sight of the shore, I thought it'd actually be fun to tool around. I shot a look to Eddie, wearing dark jeans and a white button down. I no longer felt an ounce of attraction, but his slightly longish black hair and strong jaw were the epitome of male handsomeness. I'd watched many women ogle him over the years. He touched a few controls on the boat as he steered and then smiled to himself at some inner joke. Which could only mean bad news for me.

We slowly made our way out far from the sight of the lighthouse and the creamy sands to the point where the lake didn't feel like my friend any longer. We were smack dab in the Triangle now. There was just nothing around us. I knew my directions well and I made sure I knew how that boat worked from studying it online as I went over it in my mind again and again, fighting the nausea that came with the fear.

"Eddie? I think we should turn back now."

He cackled. I threw up overboard and he laughed louder as a rumble of thunder hit and the waves rose up suddenly as if some kind of cosmic mechanism had just been flicked on by a god. His face didn't show an ounce of fear. He *knew* it was going to storm. Every damn nightmare came with a twist.

He was drinking. A lot. And not just beer but Jim Beam. Then he decided on yet another twist. He threw the empty bottle into the lake and prowled toward me unbuttoning the top of his jeans. I gripped the side of the boat harder, wildly looking around as if I could find help nearby.

A large wave suddenly crashed right into our starboard side; we rocked perilously close to overturning because he hadn't been careful to remain perpendicular to the waves. In his delight of tormenting me, we'd drifted parallel. A flash of lightning hit and as an enormous green wave was eerily lit up by the lightning, I saw the staggering image of a beautiful woman with flowing hair, tipped with fire like a goddess, just off the bow. Then everything went black.

I awoke wrapped tightly in a blanket, on another boat streaking toward the shore. The storm had let up, though I was soaked through. The side of my head had a lump on it and I was shaking all over. A small trickle of blood dripped from my eyebrow and I tenderly wiped it away. Someone handed me a flask that contained whiskey. I took a gulp and the fire going down warmed me quickly. The Lake Michigan Coast Guard had come to the rescue and I turned my head to see Eddie's boat being driven by someone else right behind us.

I tugged on the coat of the nearest person and rasped as loudly as I could over the wind, "What happened? Is Eddie in the other boat?"

"Who's Eddie?" he yelled.

"My husband!" I yelled back.

"Lady, there was no one with you in the boat. We were informed someone went out when a storm was arriving quicker than expected. Your boat took on a lot of water, but it was upright when we got there. The engine was cut and you were drifting. We found you knocked out and bleeding, your arm over the side so we saw you right away. No one else was there. We have a crew out sweeping the area. I'll notify them that there was a confirmed second person on board, now missing."

I wanted nothing more than to set my head against a pillow and go to sleep, but the rescuers wouldn't let me, figuring I had a concussion. So I just soaked in the friendly sight of the lights of the coast coming nearer and nearer. I felt nothing.

But I survived.

Four weeks later, I stood at the shore of Lake Michigan as the wind swept in with the power and danger of an ancient spirit. But as I breathed in the rushing air, the force of it cut through my soul with a crisp, sparkling slice of unexpected hope. My head had healed nicely though I had quite a concussion and several stitches were needed. I told the police everything about the abuse and the foolish boat ride to torment me; x-rays of healed broken bones and hospital records confirmed that. The authorities eventually found Eddie's body after about three days, which was surprising that they'd found him at all. Cause of death was clearly drowning and though they couldn't discover blood alcohol levels after forty-eight hours of death, reports of Eddie drinking straight from the bottle came in from people at the marina also confirming my story.

As I walked back toward my house, I smiled as I glimpsed several does frisking around together in an open patch of a commons area. I got to my home and it had never looked so good. I'd changed everything and did all the things Eddie would never let me do. I placed lights in the windows; I painted every single room in the house and even the siding of the outside in all the colors that I loved and not one of them Green Bay green, which was Eddie's favorite color. Inside, I peeked into the den that was now my office and a burst of electric joy ran through me. I'd finally be able to make my life what I wanted it to be. I went to my room and changed for an evening with a few friends coming over.

At the kitchen bar, I clasped my dirty martini and rolled the stem of the glass between my fingers like an unholy prayer bead. After two hearty sips, my shoulders unclenched and I realized a strange, unrecognizable feeling had stolen over me the past few weeks. A lightness of spirit, and a noticeable lack of *something* that used to clutch me around the chest, tightening and grasping at my lungs with every breath. I ate an olive in total peace. Eddie hated olives.

The back door opened and closed. "Well, don't you look relaxed and happy. You do know you're smirking?" said a teasing, low feminine voice coming into the kitchen. That voice. Something within me never ceased to be drawn to Olivia's lilting tone full of steamy summer evenings drinking Kinnickinnic Whiskey with fireflies and bonfires in the silky night. I took a contented breath and allowed the last fractured bits of the past nightmare to softly fall away.

Olivia sat down next to me as I made her a martini neat with a twist of lemon. "How's your head? You really did a number on it, didn't you?"

"Yeah, I definitely know how to get the job done," I joked. "It's healed well, though."

We clinked glasses as she said, "Cheers, Cass. To your new business, your new life, and to helping women."

A knock on the front door sounded. I bounded up and greeted my two other friends, Jen and Barbara. We cozied up to the bar and I made drinks for us all. I brought out more olives and a charcuterie board.

Olivia looked at me with pride and said, "Well, we are so happy for you, Cass. The business is booming and you've made your home a welcoming place. We've not only helped women, we've changed lives."

I put my head on her shoulder and said a heartfelt, "Thank you. I couldn't have survived without you three." I perked up and declared, "That calls for a special toast." We all raised our glasses. "Cheers to the Deer Ladies. We are going to do great things, girls." We clinked glasses with smiles all around as they echoed *to the Deer Ladies*.

"All right," said Barbara, putting her glass down and rubbing her hands together in anticipation. "Now that we solved my predicament, Jen's, and now Cass's situation, what's next on the list?"

I brought out a bottle of my experimental new whiskey for us to try in a 1.75 liter of Jim Beam and poured scant amounts in four shot glasses. "Well here's my new batch. Now, remember, don't drink it, just touch your tongue to it. Eddie gulped it down fast and a lot of it. It absolutely did the trick."

"Worked with Pete, too," said Barbara. "Aiming the car toward the cliff was easier than I thought. He was agreeable to anything I suggested but didn't pass out. He could still walk, talk, and drive a car. Even floored it right into the darkness."

"Yeah, when they drink this, they'll do anything you suggest," I said.

Oliva chimed in, "Just next time don't go so crazy with the concussion bit, Cass."

I rubbed my head that was still slightly sore. "Good idea."

They tried the concoction and gave rave reviews—only the whiskey flavor came through. Given the okay, I quickly poured out the rest from their test glasses and made notes about my recipe.

"Excellent," Olivia declared. "Now, let's brainstorm some new ideas. We need to make sure there are no connections and under completely understandable circumstances. Ladies, we are just getting started."

L.A. Chandlar

* * *

I already had three new names on my list and was going to make a trip to the neighboring town just south of us the next morning to a woman who came forward about a rape that no one believed was a crime worth formal charges—despite abundant evidence—because you know, *his career was at stake*.

I took a deep breath and looked each of them in the eye, feeling a fire within me. "We've lived a nightmare. But there is hope." The powerful vision of the woman in the stormy lake came vividly to mind and I grasped Olivia's hand. I leaned in close to the center of the group and whispered, "Every woman deserves to give her own twist."

Deer Lady, or Deer Woman, is a Native American spirit who is associated with love, fruitfulness and protection. However, for men who have harmed women, she is known to lure men to their deaths. She appears as a beautiful young woman or a deer.

110

BIRCHWATER

Jessica Laine

Snowflakes christened my arrival in Birchwater, an exclusive bedroom community nestled along Lake Minnetonka. It was a few days after Christmas and professionally installed holiday lights sparkled from the eaves of older cottages and newer homes built to look like gigantic barns. Rooftops were covered in a tasteful dusting of snow, and everything was white: the barn-like homes, the expensive SUVs parked in the driveways, even the doodles owned by a pair of men who stood gabbing in the middle of the road, blocking the entrance to the Birchwater Police Department. When I beeped my horn, the men turned and glared at me as if I'd run over their designer, shed-free dogs. Bundled in goose-down parkas that cost more than my monthly mortgage, they ambled toward the slushy sidewalk at a snail's pace.

The police station was attached to a tiny village hall, the kind you'd see in a Hallmark movie where a woman takes a leave from her job in the city and returns home only to throw away her high-paying career so she can live in poverty with the hot carpenter down the road. This wasn't my hometown, and I wasn't getting paid the big bucks as a private investigator, but there was a hot cop named Chad Patterson waiting for me inside the station.

It was late morning and the receptionist eyed me curiously as she ushered me into Chad's office. Chad stood up from his desk and greeted me with a big smile—as if he hadn't sent me a pissed-off text last Friday reminding me that I owed him, big-time, for his help on a missing persons case.

"Officer Patterson, nice to see you again."

He hadn't changed much since the police academy other than he looked a little tired and there were some new worry lines weaving their way across his forehead. His blonde hair was still cropped in a buzz cut which showed off his nicely shaped skull.

Ignoring my outstretched hand, he swept me into a hug. "Margarita O'Neill, my favorite P.I." Releasing me, he looked me up and down. "How is it you get prettier with every passing year?"

"Prosecco and good genes." It wasn't always fun being the only Peruvian Irish person I knew but little to no wrinkles was a definite plus.

He looked at his smart watch. "Are you up for lunch? I can clock out early."

My stomach grumbled loudly.

Laughing, he said, "I'll take that as a yes."

Chad liked to post photos on social media that showed him cross-country skiing, snowmobiling, and ice fishing on the lake. With his broad shoulders, flat stomach, and muscular legs, he was a walking advertisement for outdoor living. Driving to The Anchor, an old-fashioned sports bar on the lakefront, Chad pointed out landmarks along the way. The views of Lake Minnetonka in its frozen state were so eye-catching that even a city girl like me could see the appeal of lake life.

The Anchor's specialty was a Juicy Lucy, a burger with melted cheese in its center, served with tater tots and a dip made of sour cream on the side. I took a bite of my burger and exhaled happily.

"Tasty, right?"

"It's not good unless the cheese is burning your tongue."

Chad smiled as he took a sip of his Summit Pale Ale.

"What's it like to be working in your hometown?"

"I like it." He shrugged. "We get our share of car accidents, domestic disturbances, accidental drownings, and home break-ins, especially in the winter when the snowbirds are in Florida, but that's about it. Not as busy as St. Paul."

Birchwater had been a summer resort for the wealthy and even though the trolley from Minneapolis and the enormous wooden hotels were long gone, it was still a rich town with rich people problems. If Chad had wanted more action, he would have stayed in St. Paul.

As if he knew what I was thinking, he changed the subject. "You staying with your cousin tonight?"

I nodded. My cousin Pati and her husband lived in Birchwood and I had wrangled an invitation to stay with them this weekend.

"How's your mom?"

"Busy." Mom ran a popular Peruvian restaurant in St. Paul. "And yours?"

"Good. She sends her regards."

I raised an eyebrow. "I'll bet."

He had the decency to blush. We'd been an item for a hot minute in the police academy, but his mother had hated the idea of her only son ending up with a Catholic and a Latina— something she'd made extremely clear during our first and last family dinner together.

I pushed aside my plate. "Why am I here?"

He gave me a look. "You never were one for pleasantries."

"True." I waved away the waitress. "How can I help?"

"Oh, I could think of a few ways." A small grin touched his lips, and I felt the warmth of his gaze for a moment before his face turned serious again. He was flirting with me because he thought I'd like it, but something was bothering him. He stared down at the scarred table and played with his bottle of beer. "Did you hear about the snowmobiling accident that happened

113

out here last week?"

"The one with the pregnant lady?"

He nodded.

I'd seen the story on the news. A husband and wife had been ice fishing on the lake in a clam shell tent. At sunset, the couple heard the loud buzz of approaching snowmobiles, and the husband went outside to investigate. A pair of snowmobiles thundered past him, one weaving erratically until it plowed into the tent which held his wife who was seven months pregnant. The husband watched as the snowmobilers stopped and spoke to each other briefly before taking off at full speed.

"How's the woman doing?"

"Her husband, Tyler, is my cousin." Chad took a large swig of his beer. "Kelsey's going to make it, but she lost the baby."

Although I didn't have kids, I could imagine how devastating it would be to lose a child you'd carried almost to full-term.

"I'm sorry."

"They've been trying to have children for a long time. The doctor said Kelsey's injuries are such that it might not happen for them now." Chad looked down at his hand and seemed to realize he was clenching the beer bottle in a death grip. He set down the bottle on the table with a thump. "I want you to help me catch the sons-of-bitches who left my cousin and his injured wife on the lake."

On the way back to the police station, Chad told me Tyler used his sled that night to push Kelsey across the lake to where their truck was parked. Chad had always been laid-back at the police academy, blessed with a boundless patience even during the most unpleasant of tasks like rounding up disruptive drunks at closing time. Seeing him like this, I wouldn't want to be the snowmobilers who'd screwed with his family.

"What's happening with the case?"

"Chief wouldn't let me work on it. Said I was too close to

keep it professional."

"Which is true."

"The cop assigned to the case is a Barney."

As in Barney Fife, the fictional small-town cop who was only allowed to have one bullet which he had to keep in his pocket. At least I knew what I was doing here now; Chad was running his own unofficial investigation and he needed help from someone outside of his department. As we pulled into the police station's parking lot, I asked, "Any leads?"

"A few. There's a ten-thousand-dollar reward on any information leading to an arrest. Some tips have come in, but nothing solid. I think it's because this one hits a little too close to home."

My ears perked up. "Why would you say that?"

He pointed at my coat. "That all you got with you?"

My winter jacket was almost as old as my car. Once upon a time it had been fluffy and black, but now it was threadbare with a dark grayish-green tint from too many cycles in my washing machine. "What? I bought it at The Land's End Outlet."

He reached into his back seat and handed me a heavy coat and a set of waterproof mittens. "Put these on. I want to show you something before the sun goes down."

It had stopped snowing but was cold enough that I could see my breath in the air, making me regret my decision to wear thin jeans because they were flattering. No one else was out and several of the homes were dark, giving Birchwater a deserted feeling.

"Are you seeing anyone?"

I shot Chad a sharp look.

He held up his mittened hands in front of his body. "Just making small talk."

"Uh huh," I said. "Not at present."

"For the record, I'm single, too." His eyes zeroed in on mine. Despite the Arctic wind that dipped down into Minnesota making it colder than most of Canada, I felt heat creeping up my neck.

"I'm not interested in being in a relationship right now."

"Who said anything about a relationship?" He waggled his eyebrows, making me laugh.

A charged silence enveloped us as we trudged down the snow-packed streets of Birchwater. The neighborhood was surrounded by water on three sides and glimpses of the frozen lake were possible if you looked between the houses. We walked until the land narrowed to a point where there were a handful of impressive homes. I asked Chad what these people did for a living.

"Mostly inherited wealth mixed in with some holdouts like Old Man Larson." He pointed out a run-down home with old cars and machinery parked on its wooden lot.

He cut through Larson's yard and onto the lake. I followed, not wanting to admit that walking on frozen water gave me the willies. Every time I heard a creak underfoot, I pictured the ice breaking open and sending us to our watery graves at the bottom of Lake Minnetonka.

"Relax." He laid a hand on my shoulder. "We're almost there."

Waving at a bare spot in Larson's side yard where a large willow tree grew, its naked branches rustling in the wind, Chad asked, "Do you know what this is?"

I shook my head, moving my feet from side to side to stay warm.

"It's an old fire lane. These were public access areas created along the shoreline so the fire department could draw water from the lake when houses and other buildings were on fire. Unfortunately, they didn't prevent the old wooden hotels in Birchwater from burning down." He pointed at the mature willow tree. "A previous homeowner planted a tree in the middle of the fire lane to make it less appealing, but it hasn't worked. See the snowmobile tracks?" I followed his line of vision and saw the parallel tracks that crisscrossed the fire lane.

"What makes you think the snowmobiles we're looking for used this particular fire lane?"

"Kids like to party in Old Man Larson's yard because they can evade the police by hiding behind his broken-down cars and whatnot. Nick Larson got sick of finding crumpled cans of White Claw and used vape filters on his lawn, so he installed a Ring doorbell."

Back at the police station, Chad pulled up the grainy home surveillance video from the day of the hit-and-run on his computer. The resolution wasn't great, but I could make out two snowmobiles going through the fire lane and then returning a few hours later. It was hard to say much about the snowmobilers other than they had slim builds and their vehicles looked expensive.

"What are you thinking? Two teenage boys? Maybe a teenage boy and a girl?"

Chad ran his fingers through his buzz cut. "I'm not sure. Tyler never got a good look at their faces, either, but there were a few things we were able to keep out of the papers."

He reached into his cabinet and rifled through a folder before plucking out some photos. The first was of a damaged yellow tent.

"Tyler's clam shell tent is relatively unique. I doubt anyone else on the lake would have a tent like it. He purchased it as an exchange student in Sweden."

The next photo was a close-up of the tent's bright yellow metal poles that had been twisted out of shape during impact. Chad pointed out a black gouge. "This is glossy black paint, like the kind you'd find on a snowmobile. I think the snowmobile we're looking for hit this pole. It should have streaks of bright yellow paint along its front bumper."

"Do you have a list of registered snowmobiles for Birchwater?"

He dug through a pile on his desk and tossed me a huge three-ring binder. "This includes everyone around here who has actually registered their vehicles. It wouldn't include anyone who has purchased a used snowmobile or one from out of state and not registered yet. It's almost easier to find the people in

Birchwater who *don't* have a snowmobile."

He pulled out an aerial photo of Birchwater. "This is where we were." He circled the fire lane out on the point. "Theoretically, people could drive in from the lake, but this fire access is hidden from view thanks to the tree and Larson's junk. Not many people know or use this particular fire lane."

"Unless they live in the Birchwater."

He smiled at me. "Bingo."

It was getting late, and the burger and beer were making me sleepy. "I should head over to my cousin Pati's house." I grabbed my phone. "I just need to look up her address."

He picked up the aerial photo and circled a home close to the fire lane that had been used by the snowmobilers on the video. He tossed the photo at me.

"Here you go."

I raised an eyebrow. "Thanks."

"Don't mention it." Chad didn't look at me as he rifled through the paperwork on his desk. "Give my regards to Patricia, Wesley, and Brayden."

After we made plans to catch up on Sunday, I left the police department, walking the short distance to the parking lot. It was a moonless night, and unseen animals rustled and chittered in the nearby woods. There was only one other car in the lot, a large pickup. I quickened my pace. As I opened my trunk to get my overnight bag, the pickup's engine roared to life. Whoever was in the pickup turned on their high beams and drove straight at me.

I threw myself onto a nearby bush and felt a rush of air as the pickup zoomed by. It sped out of the parking lot before I could get a good look at the driver or write down a license plate. Heart racing, I stood up and dusted off the snow, dirt, and dead leaves from my winter coat. Taking a quick inventory, I was thankful that both my body and car had avoided major damage.

Hands shaking on the wheel, I drove the short distance to my cousin Pati's house. We'd grown up together in the same blue-collar neighborhood in St. Paul but had drifted out of each other's orbits as adults. I saw her at family reunions a few times a year and that was about it. She was smart and industrious, but she'd always been what I called a "need to know" Latina; if you needed to know Pati was Latina, she'd tell you. Otherwise, she was happy to let you think she was white.

I'd never been invited to her house in Birchwater and might have gone to my grave never seeing it if I hadn't received the request for assistance from Chad. I hadn't planned to spend more than a few days investigating this case since my fee was gratis, so I'd asked Pati if I could stay with her through the weekend.

Pati lived with her husband, Wesley, and their son, Brayden, in a gigantic Tudor which included a three-car garage, a large shed, and nice views of the lake. Pati and Wesley had good jobs, but not good enough to pay for this house. I'd always assumed Wesley had family money.

A figure peered down at me from a bedroom window on the second floor. When I looked again, they were gone. Nervously, I walked up the front steps and onto the porch. There was an impressive winter topiary near the door and a doormat that said BLESSED. I pressed the Ring doorbell.

Pati opened the door wearing expensive stretch pants and a slouchy sweatshirt, her dyed blonde hair twisted into a top knot. She smiled at me with teeth which were whiter and straighter than I remembered.

"Hello, stranger. Come on in."

The foyer was even nicer than I thought it would be, with original hardwood floors and oak paneling. She hugged me and tried to take my overnight bag from me, but I shook her off.

"No need."

"Follow me. I'll show you to your room."

We walked down the hallway and ended up in a guest room with an attached bathroom. The room was painted forest green, and the walls were lined with bookshelves.

"We converted Wesley's study into a guest bedroom last year. He's working late but should be home soon. He keeps all of his books in here." She made a face. "I hope you'll be comfortable."

"I love it," I said, trying to reassure her. "This is perfect. Thanks."

She smiled. "Why don't you freshen up and meet me in the living room for a drink?"

I unpacked my bag, showered, and changed into some sweats. I'm a nosy person and took advantage of this short break to peruse Wesley's books. I didn't know too much about Wesley other than he taught English at a nearby college and wrote a mystery series in his spare time. Although I'd never read any of his novels, I'd heard from my aunt that he'd won a bunch of awards. I found the first book in his mystery series and pulled it out of its spot on the shelf. *HER NAME WAS B*TCH* by Wesley Connor. I read the blurb on the back cover:

HER NAME WAS B*TCH *is the raw and powerful debut by Wesley Connor, one of best new storytellers in the mystery genre. Voluptuous twenty-three-year-old Candy Griffin has been victimized by men her whole life. Armed only with her brains, an AK-47, and a heart as big as her double-D cup bra, Candy hits the road as a stripper-for-hire and exacts vengeance upon the men who have wronged her, beginning with dear old Dad.*

¿Qué carajo?

I placed the book back on the shelf where I'd found it and scurried out to the living room, ready for that drink.

The living room was decked out with plush sofas and a fireplace made of boulders. Pati had lit a fire and the room was toasty warm. She sat on a couch typing on her smart phone. She hit send and then looked up at me.

"I asked Wesley to stop at the store on his way home. What would you like to drink?"

I pointed at her glass. "I'll have what you're having."

"Easy customer." She got up and poured me a glass of red wine from an open bottle. She placed it in front of me, then sat down on the sofa next to me and raised her glass.

"Salud."

"Salud."

We clinked glasses and sipped our wine in silence as the fire crackled and hissed. Pati set her glass down gingerly on the coffee table, making me wonder how much wine she'd had while I was in my room.

"How's work going?" I asked.

"The market is hot. People are buying and selling houses como loco. How about you?"

"My services will always be in demand as long as people lie, cheat, and steal."

Pati laughed politely. "What are you working on with Chad?" she asked casually, but I could tell she was dying to know.

"I'm sorry, I don't think I'm at liberty to say. You understand."

Pati looked disappointed. "Of course."

"She's working on the snowmobile hit-and-run, Mom," a voice said. "Obvi."

A look of annoyance crossed Pati's face. "Brayden, why don't you come out here and sayhello to your *tía*?"

A teenager wearing a hockey jersey appeared from out of the shadows. "Isn't she actually my cousin?"

"Whatever," Pati said.

"Hi, Brayden," I said. "It's nice to see you again."

"Likewise."

Brayden had olive skin like his mother and was tall and thin like his father. It seemed like only yesterday he was in diapers. Soon, he'd be out of the house and on his own.

"How's hockey going?" I asked.

"We'll probably make it to finals this year."

I smiled. "Impressive."

"Totally." He turned to his mother. "Can I go over to Jaxon's house?"

Pati looked at her phone. "Be home in an hour."

"Okay, bye."

We watched as he slouched out of the room.

"Cute kid," I said.

"You want him?"

We both laughed at that.

We had a couple of drinks, waiting up for Wesley but he never arrived home. When wesaid good night, I told Pati I'd be out and about on Saturday.

"Will you be home in time for dinner?"

I nodded.

"Oh good, then you can teach me how to make aji de gallina."

"It's a deal."

Once Pati was upstairs, I took advantage of being alone to look through the rooms on the first floor. Most of the rooms were as expected, stuffy and littered with expensive furniture, but one room caught my eye: the library. It had even more books in it than the guest room, many of them literary works. It made sense since Wesley was a professor. I pictured one of his female students stumbling across HER NAME WAS B*TCH and grimaced with distaste.

One of the walls held a gun locker. Curious, I tried opening it.

"It's locked."

Pati's husband stood behind me dressed in typical professor gear: horn-rimmed glasses, a sweater vest, and corduroy pants.

"Wesley, nice to see you again."

"Likewise."

Now I knew where Brayden had gotten the "likewise' from. Wesley didn't try to hug me or even shake my hand. He just stared at me.

"Well, I should go."

Wesley nodded primly and gave me a look as if he'd caught me cheating on an exam. "Sweet dreams, Margarita."

The creepy way he said it, I knew I would have nightmares instead.

The next morning when I walked into the kitchen. Pati was making a pot of coffee. Brayden was leaning against the island, looking at his phone and Wesley was reading *The New York Times* while seated at the table.

"Do you guys have snowmobiles?"

The family froze for a moment before Pati answered me.

"No, why do you ask, chica?"

"I'd like to go out on the lake. Take a look around."

Pati's shoulders relaxed. "We have an old Norwegian kick sled that belonged to Wesley's father in the shed. Would you like to borrow it?"

I nodded. "Is the shed unlocked?"

"The shed is older than the house and in very poor condition," Wesley said. "I'll have Brayden fetch the kick sled for you."

"There's no need—"

"It's about to fall down," Wesley said. "I'd hate for something to happen to you in there."

I had no idea what I was doing out on the lake, but at least using the kick sled was fun. As I was cutting through the fire lane, the front door to Nick Larson's home opened. An older man stepped out and asked me, "Want some hot cocoa?"

I didn't learn much from Nick Larson other than he, too, thought Wesley was a pendejo. However, when he said he'd seen me through the video monitor on his Ring doorbell, a light bulb went off. I headed back to Pati's.

Pati was standing over a rice steamer. She smiled when she saw me.

"You're home."

We worked together preparing the aji de gallina for dinner. She was good at following directions and soon we had a pot of the creamy chicken dish bubbling on the stovetop. Like risotto, it needed to be continuously stirred to create the perfect texture. I watched as Pati rubbed her temple.

"You look tired. Why don't you take a rest? I can finish up here."

"Are you sure?"

I nodded.

Pati, looking relieved, said, "Call me if you need my help."

I listened as her feet padded up the wooden staircase which led to the bedrooms upstairs. Once I was sure she was gone and not coming back, I opened her phone and scrolled to her Ring app. The Ring doorbell faced the fire lane, and I wondered if the app had captured any additional video of the snowmobilers. I looked up the video taken a week ago, on the day of the hit-and-run, and found footage of two snowmobilers driving away from Pati's driveway that afternoon and returning later that night.

Carefully, I opened the door to the garage and looked around. There was a pickup truck, about the size of the one that had tried to run me over at the police station, but that wasn't saying much as trucks were a dime a dozen out in the suburbs. No snowmobiles. Relief swept through me until I remembered the shed on the back of the property, the one I wasn't allowed to visit.

The door to the shed was unlocked but jammed with rust and age and it creaked as I forced it open. It was close to midnight. Turning on my flashlight, I crept past clutter until I reached two objects covered by tarps. I reached for the tarps and pulled. One of the snowmobiles was dented and had a streak of yellow paint on its front bumper. The overhead lights clicked on. Wesley stood at the door, a gun in his hand.

"Brava, Margarita. You're not as stupid as I thought you were."

I pocketed the flashlight, wishing I'd brought my gun with me, and looked around the shed for something to use as a weapon. "I'm sure there's a good explanation for everything."

Wesley snorted.

Pati ran into the shed, holding a damp kitchen towel in her hands. She looked at Wesley as he continued to point the gun at me.

"What's going on?"

"Call 911," I yelled.

Wesley shot her a look. "Lock the door, Pati."

Pati did as she was told. Glancing at the snowmobiles, I noticed a detail that had escaped me before: the word "HIS" had been stenciled onto the seat of the undamaged snowmobile, and the word "HERS" had been stenciled onto the seat of the damaged snowmobile.

"You hit her, Pati?"

She twisted the kitchen towel into knots. "I didn't mean to. We'd been drinking. I don't want to hurt you," she said, not looking at me.

"You don't want Wesley to take the blame for your actions, do you?" I scooped up a tool lying on the workbench.

"She won't have to if I shoot you," Wesley said. "You're a real pain in the ass, you know that? Now drop that lug wrench."

I dropped it but kept my hand in my pocket, edging closer to him.

"I'm going to enjoy shooting you. In fact, I think I can use this visceral reaction to power the emotional arc of my next mystery—"

"Shut up!" I screamed, startling him. I used the momentary distraction to throw my flashlight at him. It bounced off his temple and he fell with a loud thump. I picked up his gun and aimed it at my cousin, the one who'd been at both my christening and my quinceañera.

Things happened quickly after that. I called the police. An ambulance took Wesley to the hospital. Chad took Pati into custody. Cursing me, my uncle came and picked up Wesley. I was interrogated for several hours at the police station until Chad demanded I be released.

The sun was rising as he drove me to Pati's house. We drank coffee as we sat next to each other on the plush living room couch.

"I can't believe it was Pati." Chad sat next to me, our legs touching. "I'm so sorry. Is there anything I can do for you?"

He gave me a look, the kind that used to signal it was time to shed our clothes and jump into bed. I caressed his handsome face and drew near him so that our lips were almost touching.

"Vete a la mierda," I said.

Chad jerked away from me.

I pinned him with my ex-cop stare. "How long have you known it was someone in Pati's family?"

A wave of emotions rippled across his face. Finally, he said, "For a while now."

"Leave."

Silently, he got up and walked out the door.

Family bonds would always mean more to Chad than anything else, which is why we hadn't made it as a couple. It was also why he'd been willing to sacrifice my family to get vengeance for his. I wouldn't miss Chad and I sure as hell wouldn't miss Birchwood. I planned to drive back to St. Paul in the afternoon, but first—the open bottle of red wine was calling my name.

TROUBLE IN SPADES
BV Lawson

So it's summer, and I'm back at this hell hole they call a "camp," even though there isn't a sign of a tent anywhere. Guess whoever built this place was crazy, which you'd kinda expect since it's next to Loon Lake. Didn't think they'd let me in again, not after last year and the whole incident with the missing C-note. Good thing I'd thought up that fake tornado drill that solved the case or the moolah would still be AWOL. I didn't ask for any credit, mind you. Not that I got any.

Anyway, I suspect my old man cajoled the camp bigwigs and maybe even passed 'em some extra scratch just to get me out of his hair for a few weeks. He gave *me* some blah-blah song and dance about all that fresh air being good for me, but I knew him and his latest moll just wanted to go "fishing." Heh. Sammy Spade is no fool.

Sure, I tried my usual protest pranks: the shoeblack in the shaving cream, the dead rats in the icebox, the salt in the sugar shaker, but the old man was having none of it. He put his size thirteens down with a thud heard all the way across San Francisco Bay.

Long story short, the old man dumped me and my footlocker halfway across the country at Camp Mooshaka in what's known as the Gopher State of all places, with a "Don't get into no trouble again" line, and that was that. Guess he didn't know about the bottle of Aunt Mathilde's peach schnapps squirreled away next to my baseball cards and skivvies. Hey, it's not like I'd got some kind of tree religion after all that "Kumbaya" bit last year.

They still called the flophouses "cabins," and there are still ten of us schmucks sardined into each one. But the grub is better than last time 'round, so my sentence here in tree-land wouldn't be a total loss. I still hadn't figured out how to jailbreak my way outta here to get a gander at the Gunflint Trail—anything named Gunflint Trail had to be a lot more exciting than this Kumbaya crowd. Might even catch a sighting of a Wendigo, which would be a hell of a lot more interesting than gophers. Not that I believed in all that monster business. Probably a guy in a rubber suit some innkeeper hired for the tourist dollars it'd bring in.

Anyway, we were strong-armed into picking "activities," but I didn't see anything about making fake IDs or disguises and nothing whatsoever about shivs or bean-shooters. Not even throwing tomahawks. Just archery. Okee, then. Shooting pointy things just might come in handy.

The staff were okay, especially the archery instructor, Miss Skye. I kinda took a shine to that dame, a real tomato. She sported a smile that could light up a dingy hash house and didn't treat us campers like the types who'd enjoy that idiotic "Bunny Fru-Fru" crap. Had this necklace she wore every day with these fire-agate stones. Looked expensive.

One day she shows up for our shooting-pointy-sticks class and her eyes were kind of red. I'd seen that look before on one of my old man's molls. Miss Skye had been crying. Found out later her necklace went missing, right from her quarters while she was sleeping.

Who knew summer camp was such a flimflam paradise? Here we go again. But this time, it was personal.

First, I had to sneak into her place. She had a flophouse all to herself, not that I begrudged her that. I got the layout: one door, two small windows, and only one medium-sized table near the door. Had all her combs and potions and all the other mystery goo that dames used—bet she kept her necklace there, too. Okay, so the perp didn't have far to go to snatch the goods. Duly noted.

Then I started asking around. Mostly Sally Snitch 'cause she was always good for a squeal or two. The name wasn't really snitch, but you know that. Her old man had a "consulting" business in Jersey. I was wise to the type. Mob money.

So here's the skinny. Sally says she'd overheard the chief cook, Zelda, chatting up that necklace, as in how much she'd love to have one just like it. Zelda had a steady back home, a down-and-outer who was a horse player. She was suspect numero uno.

Suspect number two was one of my fellow inmates, Sticky Fingers Finton, born with a golden spoon in his mouth. Got whatever he wanted. And whatever he saw, he wanted. Turned out he was a rock collector. Fire-agate gems were rocks, weren't they? As good as.

Then, there was ole Gus Greer, the live-in handyman. Had a secret stash of homemade hootch, a spiked lemonade thing, in a rain barrel behind the tool shed. Liked to "sharpen his tools" a lot. Was stinko half the time. A fire-agate necklace would buy a lot of hootch, the kind that didn't smell like turpentine with a lemon chaser.

Fortified with the usual punch-flavored sugar water and bun-based grub from lunch, I decided to do a little poking around. See if I could stir up a few hornets. We could sure use a bit of excitement around here. Sewing leather wallets? No, thanks. Good thing I'd smuggled some dice along with the peach schnapps. Taught the other guys how to shoot craps.

First thing I found out was Gus pulled a no-show the evening someone lifted the necklace. As in, he was in the local hoosegow cooling off after crashing a wedding party, ranting about some imaginary blue cats that were after him. He showed up at camp the day afterward, though, and didn't get canned. Guess maintenance bums are hard to find.

Next, I offered to help Zelda, the cook, clean up after all of us pigs finished snuffling through the trough at lunch. I sweet-talked her. You know, the ole "Gee, the punch-flavored sugar water and bun-meat-of-the day sure were yummy." Even made her a little daisy-chain. Look, you gotta do what you gotta do. Found out she was a holy roller, the fire-and-brimstone kind. Guess she wouldn't risk eternal damnation for an agate necklace, right?

That left Sticky Fingers Finton. All I needed was a chance to jimmy his footlocker when nobody was watching. I had the bright idea to use the "tummy ache" fake out during the campfire rigmarole, but no joy. Oh, sure, I got excused and got inside that footlocker—did you have any doubts?—but no sign of the necklace. Next time I saw Finton, he smirked at me. He knew. But you didn't think I was just going to leave it there, didya?

Sally Snitch had seen Finton sneaking off into the woods more than once. So during "nap time," I grabbed some stuff and waited 'til I saw him making a break and followed. Found him at an old abandoned outhouse. And then I wiped that smirk right off his face when I aimed my pointy-stick-thrower at him.

"Hand it over," I said. He hesitated, and I launched a stick. Went clean into the wooden door, right between his legs. Lucky shot. More for him than me.

Later that day, I overheard Miss Skye talking to the cook about how her necklace had magically turned up in her cabin. She guessed she'd just overlooked it. Well, whadya know.

Any time I caught Finton looking at me after that, I just started singing "Little Bunny Fru-Fru." He got the picture.

SPURGALING FOR GENIUSES
Meredith Doench

October 2003

I met Jessica Basko at the Red Cow Uptown, a queer bar in the Twin Cities where grad students liked to hang out. I was in my final year of med school, and Basko was a senior lab tech for an elite section of the University of Minnesota's medical school. Both of us were transplants to the city, she from a small town in Indiana and me from an even tinier town in Ohio. We both loved Red Cow Uptown, a safe space that never existed in our own hometowns, where we regularly caught up over beers and darts.

One Friday night, I was on my own and texted Basko. My gal, Marnie, had gone home for the weekend to catch up with her friends from high school. I managed to escape and was relishing in the full weekend ahead of me.

"How's domestication going, Pen?"

I chuckled. Basko liked to refer to Marnie as my soon to be trophy wife. It was true Marnie and I were from different worlds, hers full of family money and success. I wasn't sure I even loved Marnie, but I loved that she knew what to *do*. She had our futures planned out beginning with a marriage only a few months away. Marnie wanted a fancy wedding in the Chisago County countryside. She wanted the four-string quartet and a soul-filled lesbian singer to wail on about love and trust. She wanted a legal Minnesota document to prove our union. And after all that showy-show of devotion and love, Marnie wanted something I could never give her—a baby. Not just any baby, but a genius baby.

"I'm here for you when the Marnie illusion crashes." Basko took a pull from her beer.

"Marnie and I are solid." I tossed a dart and missed the bullseye. I tried not to think about how many times Basko and I had hooked up over the past few years. We connected in a way that Marnie and I could not—Basko and I paid our own way through school. And it was a fortune, even with all the scholarships combined. Unlike Marnie, who had handfuls of relatives with higher ed degrees, Basko and I were first generation college students. I felt the weight of all my living and dead relatives riding on my shoulders, and I know she did, too. It's a horrific thing, to have that kind of generational pressure. You could even feel it in your sleep.

"I'm keeping an eye out for you at the lab, Pen," Basko said. "It's a good job to have before heading out into the medical field."

Basko was known around our department as the failure to launch case. She failed out her last year of med school despite all the second chances the department had given her. Basko was smarter than everyone in her cohort put together, which is why the university wanted to keep her as a research lab tech.

"Don't worry." Basko gave me a wink. She always wore a Minnesota Wild hat with the bill turned to the back. "It's a whole lot more than a glorified security guard position."

Basko worked in the cryobank of Minnesota University's Medical Center, a frozen depository for sperm. The unit conducted research on the intellectual components of reproductive materials and DNA. They were only interested in donations from the top researchers and scholars in their fields as well as artistic geniuses. It was rumored the cryobank had Prince's frozen semen in its deep freezer. Freddie Mercury's, too.

There were many speculations about the studies conducted in this lab. They reminded me of the word problems of my youth, and math—whether with words or numbers—was never my intellectual strength. What do you get when you cross the sperm of a rock star and an older egg of a master flutist with inflammation? This was the kind of daily work Basko was knee-deep in as she monitored and filed reports.

"Any new famous sperm?"

Basko threw me a wink. "It's all about intelligence, my friend."

She explained that all the reproductive material used an intricate numbering system. No one had access to the names of the donors other than the lead scientists who dictated the research.

Basko leaned closer to me. "I can't confirm or deny, but my boss says our current celebrity is Sebastian Simon."

Sebastian Simon had been dubbed a pseudo-scientist by the research community. He loved nothing more than himself and seeing himself in the press. He'd become the scientist pop culture loved, and in the last few years, his name had become synonymous with private sector rocket travel to Mars. Now, almost seventy-three years old, he still invented parts for his rocket. *Time Magazine* had hailed him as one of the most innovative humans of the century.

"Impressive. Marnie would kill for sperm from Sebastian Simon."

"Marnie's not alone. Smart sperm goes for thousands on the black market."

That's when I realized Basko had sold some of the sperm from her lab before. When I pushed for details, I learned she'd paid off a half year of med school with the sale of four sperm vials stolen from the lab.

"If you really want that picture-perfect family, I could get you some genius sperm."

"Are you kidding? I'm so far in debt, my eyeballs are swimming."

"I've been looking for a partner," Basko said as her dart landed just to the right of the bullseye. "The Twin Cities' queer community is an untapped market. Just sayin'."

"Just sayin' what?"

Basko shrugged. "Isn't it our duty to help our fellow queers reproduce?"

"A noble mission. But what's in it for me? Besides a prison sentence?"

"Money. Lots of it, if we do this thing right." Basko reached for another stack of darts. "And sperm for Marnie. All that genetic material to create your smarty-pants baby."

We spent the rest of that weekend in front of a whiteboard in her apartment mapping out the queerest locations in the Twin Cities. We put together a plan, both of us fired up over how easy it had been for her to sell a few vials in the past to desperate couples. Basko had replaced the empty slots in the freezer with vials of a milky concoction from the lab. It had been months, and no one noticed a thing while the couples succeeded in their pregnancies.

"It's called spurglary," Basko said. "Or spermjacking."

When I finally stopped laughing, I asked, "What if someone wants verification the sperm came from a genius? We could have paid drunk undergrads in the dorms fifty bucks to fill some vials, right?"

"Every sperm in the lab came from a genius. It's the required entry ticket."

"Yeah, but how do we verify we got it from the lab?"

Basko paused, blinking at me.

"Don't overthink this, Pen! Who doesn't trust queers other than the government? Besides, I have two beautiful healthy babies to show for my past work."

Hours later, after way too much beer and pizza and spurglary planning, we fell into each other in our usual way—two speed boats crashing and bursting into flames. Later, I lay naked beside her, floating along like wreckage in the water, hoping Marnie would never find out how many times Basko and I had crashed together like this.

"What if we get caught?"

Basko reached for me, pulling me close. "We never get caught. Marnie's clueless."

"I meant the sperm stealing."

Basko chuckled. "Then it's all my idea. You had no knowledge of what I was doing. We keep you out of it so that you can go on to your career, marry the fancy trophy wife, and have kids."

I held her eyes with mine. The skin around them was just beginning to show permanent laugh lines. "Why are you doing this for me, Basko?"

"Isn't it obvious? You're doing what I can't. You're doing everything your family ever dreamed of."

Later, as Basko snored on in the early morning hours, I moved to the couch for some sleep. Instead, I spent those hours staring at the scribbled ideas on the whiteboard. I'd always been a risk-taker, but this seemed more like flinging myself off a cliff. My head spun with possibilities of what this business could open for me, for Marnie, for our to-be picture-perfect family. I felt something unexpected. I hadn't been this excited since I was accepted into medical school and moved to Minneapolis.

Sometime that Sunday morning, Basko stumbled into her kitchen for some coffee. I already had a pot on and some cinnamon rolls in her oven.

"I'm in," I told her.

She rubbed her eyes. "You sure?"

"I'm all in."

We toasted over mugs of steaming coffee.

Stealing someone's frozen sperm from a prominent university medical lab and selling it on the black market turned out to be a lot easier than one would think. Bottom line: women from across the sexuality and gender spectrums wanted smart sperm.

135

They were willing to pay top dollar for donors who graduated from prestigious colleges with high IQs, maxing out their credit lines for two small vials of genius level sperm. These same women were fine with scrimping on the insemination packets from a no-name retailer on Amazon that provided nothing more than a cheap turkey baster for application.

My entire undergrad career was funded in large part through Domino's Pizza delivery. I'd saved the uniform and the stupid little golf hat thinking I'd probably end up back there again before it was all over. I even saved my oven-warming delivery bag. That bag lined with dry ice carried the first ten vials of sperm in mylar bags to five recipients in the Twin Cities area.

Our method was simple, really. I mean, everyone's excited to see the delivery person with a stack of pizzas and cheesy bread by late afternoon. It's the perfect cover. While I unloaded the food I purchased at a local Dominos, Basko slipped the goods into the bag. The cryobank crew dug into the pizza as I walked out the door, careful to avoid the security cameras Basko had staked out.

From the moment the sperm left the deep freeze, we had about two hours before they began to lose potency and eventually die off. Sperm could not be refrozen, so it was a one-shot deal. Good thing I was known to drive with a lead foot.

On one sperm run, I exited the building with a pizza bag full of goods to find a campus cop peering into my car. I parked it where I always did, at the curb on the side of the building, away from the emergency loading areas with my blinkers on.

"Sorry, I was running in a delivery."

The campus cop turned to face me. "You're parked in an illegal zone."

"I deliver here a lot. I usually park here," I rambled on. "It's only for a few minutes, and I could lose my job if I deliver cold pizza."

"Where's your delivery sign?"

My heart jumped into my throat. The blinking roof light. It

was the one piece of Dominos gear I didn't have.

"We don't always use them," I said. "We have a shortage of them at the store, and it's peak delivery time."

"Peak, huh?" He leaned over again and investigated the back seat through the dirty window.

I shifted my weight from one foot to the other. I held the bag of sperm away from my body, trying to keep any form of heat away from it. "I really need to get back to the store for another pick up. I promise not to park here again."

"Too late." He ripped off a parking ticket from his stack.

I watched him go then slammed the ticket inside the glove compartment. I had a delivery to do.

Those first five deliveries paid off the remainder of my undergrad bills and helped cover my portion of Marnie's dream wedding.

"We need to talk about our baby," Marnie announced on our honeymoon. We sat side by side on a South Carolina beach. The low tide waves were full of children in colorful bathing suits and bucket hats. "I want one of those," she said, watching a toddler waddle around the edge of the water.

It's a hopeless feeling knowing that you can't give your partner what they most desire. And I wanted that perfect family, too, even if it was only a shiny shellacked image from the outside.

Marnie would not be deterred. We were now married, and she wanted to take that next step. She'd already been on all the websites and priced out the specific kind of semen she wanted. "I'd prefer a donor with dark hair and blue eyes, but that combination adds an additional five hundred dollars. It's more important the donor is college educated with no known health complications."

"It's like ordering a build your own pizza online. Check the boxes for types of cheese, sauce, and toppings," I joked.

"Well, it's important! We don't want a dumb baby."

A gaggle of small humans squealed over a sinking sandcastle.

"Why is the baby's intelligence so important to you?"

"Why *doesn't* it matter to you?" Marnie asked. "I want our baby to do amazing things. To change the world for the better, to cure cancer, to solve the environmental crisis. Big things, you know?"

"Intelligence does matter to me. So much of what you are talking about has to do with passion, Marnie, not necessarily a ginormous IQ."

She sighed and adjusted her oversized sunglasses. When she turned, I could see myself reflected in them. "Is it too much to ask to give our kid a head start in the intellectual sphere? Please don't talk to me about fate. Fate is as flimsy as luck."

"Maybe."

"Trust me, babe. This is an act of love."

I didn't argue with Marnie, mostly because I understood where this was coming from. Marnie's older sister had mild intellectual disabilities. Marnie spent most of her childhood taking care of her sister, both at home and at school. Her sister would always live with her parents, and Marnie worried what would happen once they passed on.

I understood how precarious DNA could be, how it was a building block full of surprises. There were no guarantees, no matter who the donor. Marnie wanted so much to hold steadfast to the belief that only a genius could produce a genius baby, and I let her have that.

Our sperm runs became regular, and I fell into the familiarity of it. I got to know the security guard, Scott, and brought him his favorite garlic knots with each run. I learned all the building's exits and security cameras. I found a new parking location with an expired university handicapped pass Basko used when she broke her ankle. We doctored the date on the pass, and I had quick and easy access to the building.

One afternoon I came out to find a university parking truck

blocking my car. I ran out to the lot just in time to see them clamping my tire with a large metal contraption.

"You're booting me?"

The same campus cop who'd given me a citation loaded his gear back into the truck. "Yes. You're in violation of parking in a handicapped spot with an expired tag. You also have an outstanding ticket."

"I'll pay the ticket now," I shouted. "I have cash!"

"Take that up with parking services. They close at five."

It was well after six.

I stood in the lot, watching his little campus cop car drive away.

Basko was able to borrow a coworker's vehicle, and she ran the keys out to me. An hour and fifteen minutes after we'd removed the sperm from the deep freeze, we finally found the car in the back of the lot.

"You didn't tell me you had a ticket."

I groaned. "It wasn't a big deal."

"Dammit, Pen! They have a record of you in this lot. Twice!"

I slammed the car door and gunned the engine. I hadn't considered the record or how a ticket might be used as evidence if we were ever caught.

Nine months and almost two hundred fifty thousand dollars later, The Minneapolis *Star Tribune* ran this headline: *Frozen Reproductive Material Stolen from Medical Lab at the University of Minnesota.*

The article detailed how some of the vials were missing and exactly what they were doing with the sperm in the lab. "We collect reproductive material from donors who are exceptional in their intelligence. It's not only about IQ scores—it's also genius in all its forms," a representative from the labs stated. "We even have samples from some of the most notorious criminals and serial killers who have tested with a high IQ."

The article went on to express Sebastian Simon's outrage over his missing sperm, the lab's latest celebrity to donate. "How could this even happen?" Simon complained. "I should have a say where my DNA lands, and it could be just about anywhere."

Officials from the lab claimed that most likely the sperm died before it could be used for reproduction of any kind. "It's remarkable how delicate the life of a sperm actually is," a representative stated. "They lose potency within seconds of exposure to room temperature and die within minutes. The chances of Mr. Simon's sperm reproducing anything are almost impossible."

I went to the only place in my apartment where I could be alone. I let the shower water pound over my head long after it ran cold. We'd taken fifty-eight vials. Basko had replaced them with a milky substance, but it was only a matter of time until those were found. I choked on stomach bile. Every person we'd helped to impregnate had played a version of DNA roulette.

That night, Basko texted me to meet her in a grocery store parking lot. I ran in for eggs, milk, and bread before climbing into her truck.

"The ticket. That fucking boot." I still thought about the way Basko had gone into the university parking services office and charmed them with her smile and cash. The boot had been removed in less than twelve hours. No matter how delightful Basko could be, there would always be a paper trail.

Tears brimmed in my eyes. "The police talked to you, didn't they?"

"We're okay, Pen. I promise we'll be okay."

I stared out the windshield at the dirty snow piled along the edges of the lot. "I just keep thinking about all those people. How many of them received DNA from a serial killer?" I pictured the frozen vials lined up, Prince and Frank Sinatra next to Ted Bundy, Jeffrey Dahmer, and John Wayne Gacy.

"You can't think like that. It's the whole nature vs nurture argument. There's no evidence of homicide in DNA."

Basko reached under her seat and pulled out a worn Star Wars thermos. She unscrewed the lid and dumped two smoking cold vials into her hand. "For you and Marnie. I'm about ninety-five percent sure this is the last of the Sebastian Simon sperm. She's been taking hormones, right?"

I nodded. The timing of Marnie's cycle was nearly perfect.

I pulled Basko into a tight hug, gripping on to her jacket as if she were an anchor. I fought to stay afloat. Her warm hands found their way inside my flannel. I gasped when she slipped the frozen vials inside my sports bra, horizontal between my breasts. "Nesting," she told me and kissed me hard while tears streamed down my face.

Basko had tears in her eyes, too. "Go make your genius baby."

August 2018

It had been fifteen years since Jessica Basko and I spurgaled our way through higher ed debt. Basko had gone on to run a private research lab in D.C. She pulled in more money than I ever could as a pediatrician in Mankato. I still thought about that ticket and boot to my car. No one had come for us, and Basko said this proved her theory correct. The university didn't really care about the missing sperm, they only minded the bad press.

Marnie left me five years into our marriage for a woman who competed in weightlifting shows. Basko liked to point out how blind I'd been to Marnie's shortcomings. It was true; I never saw the weightlifter coming or the tennis player before that. At least I had our son, Tyler. He'd just turned fifteen, and he had Marnie's blue eyes that could melt any heart. He'd been living with me since his mother moved in the weightlifter.

Basko had been the one constant in my life even if we were separated by miles most of the time. We still crashed into one another regularly, and on her latest visit, we talked about the future.

"Tyler will need to start looking at colleges soon," Basko said. "He's so smart, they'll take him anywhere."

"This is exactly why I should have taken you up on that lab job," I joked. She held me close, and I listened to the way the breath moved throughout her body.

"Marnie will help. Tyler will get scholarships, you know." Basko recounted her first college visit, and I thought about Tyler. My Tyler. Our Tyler. *Rocket genius man.* Marnie liked to call him that after Tyler's guidance counselor tested his IQ. His results were off the charts.

"He's certainly not using that brain power in his classes," Basko said, referring to Tyler's failing grades.

Sometimes Basko's bleak outlook on life tainted everything. She didn't always see the good in Tyler the way I did. He held a sensitivity she didn't quite understand. For example, those rabbits in the shed. Sure, Tyler loved to go to the shed to read and be alone. He also liked to organize the many collections he kept out there: rocks, coins, pocketknives. But to say Tyler had something to do with the dead rabbits? Ridiculous. I'm sure the neighbor's dog found the hidden nest.

That stray cat Basko loves to go on and on about? The one she found inside the shed shriveled in death with blood-matted fur? A fox disemboweled that poor thing, slicing its belly wide open. The morning Basko found the violence, she burst into the house screaming for me, then walked with me out to the shed.

"Please." She begged me to see. "A fox doesn't line up organs beside a carcass."

I'd covered my nose with the collar of my shirt and turned away from the collection of freshly polished hunting knives stacked neatly beside the innards. "Neither does my genius son."

THE CROW
Mindy Mejia

I watched my brother's funeral on a laptop at my kitchen table, the front of my T-shirt wet and stuck to my skin, fingers clawing furrows into my sides. No one except Angie and her parents were allowed inside the church, and even they had to be masked and distanced from the minister. They placed roses on my brother's chest, mouths shrouded, eyes dry. The casket bulged ugly and white, an Ectomobile headed for the land of ghosts. I hated it. I hated the roses. Jeff would've wanted a growler of unfiltered wheat beer, a Stephen King book, and a utility knife. If he'd known he was going to die at thirty-eight years old, he would've made me promise to blast Pearl Jam's "Alive" at the funeral, just to fuck with everyone. But no one asked me. They called him Jeffrey, cut his folded hands with their thorns, and closed the lid.

Afterward I curled myself into a corner of the patio in my backyard, where last year's dead leaves decayed into mush, and stared at nothing until a crow landed on the edge of lawn. Not in a tree or on top of the fence, where birds usually chattered. He flew down to my level, strutted to where dead grass met dirty pavers, and cocked his head, as if unsure whether I was breathing. I wasn't sure, either.

It had to be a crow. Not a cardinal or a spring robin, but a plague bird, here to feast on what COVID-19 had to offer. This one had a bad wing, slightly crooked, held gingerly from his side. He paced while the ground leached heat from my body, my vision blurring and clearing. Somewhere they were putting Jeff into the ground, but he had no heat left to take. Were crows watching him, too? Waiting? I pulled a tissue from my pocket and part of a cracker flew out. The crow grabbed it, stretched his bad wing, and flapped away.

He came back the next day, the same tilted-wing bird landing at the edge of the brown, winter-beaten grass, not stopping in the yard for worms or twigs or whatever crows want; he cocked his head at the same angle, strutted over, and cawed. I jumped, startled at how completely one creature could tear apart the neighborhood hush. Quarantine had stretched into a second month, and the only sounds I heard from other yards were muted televisions and the neighbor yelling at her children to pick up their mess. I flapped a hand at the crow, but he didn't move. He'd scented food, dark and rotting in the shadows, and he wasn't going to leave.

The crow came every day and always with the same routine: head tilt, strut, call. He knew me. I wanted to tell someone, but every phone call was about Jeff, the soft how-are-you-doings and abrupt transitions to how some store had toilet paper last night, but no hand sanitizer. The crazy thing was that Jeff would've been the first person I called. He'd told me, years ago, how crows had the brains of primates, that they used tools, held grudges, and mourned their dead. Jeff would've let me recount the crow's entire routine, the number of times I'd seen it, the exact tenor of the bird's stare, and agreed without hesitation that yes, of course the crow knew me; he'd probably been watching me for years before life stopped and I'd been forced to pay attention.

Jeff did that; he normalized the fringes, comforted you with the logic of your own delusions. When I'd first moved into my St. Paul bungalow, I was terrified the guy across the street was a serial killer. He seemed textbook—bland looks, polite avoidance, a locked shed and military-neat garage. Everyone told me I was being ridiculous, everyone except Jeff.

"Obviously he's a serial killer," Jeff said over beers on my front step. "Which means you're in the safest possible place. Serial killers don't shit where they eat. Look at him; he's been doing this awhile. He's disciplined. His killing grounds are way across town, somewhere that would never lead back to him."

Jeff pulled up a story about a hockey coach who disappeared outside an arena in Hugo. Two weeks later they found his hand on the banks of the St. Croix, in the same general area where an unrelated foot had been discovered three years ago.

"See? Secluded location, thirty miles away. Honestly, you couldn't have picked a better spot to live. All you need to worry about is your interview with the press in five to ten years, looking shocked while telling them he was such a nice, quiet guy."

"Does that mean you're safe, too, with Angie right in the same house as you?"

He laughed. "I know how to deal with Angie."

Asphyxia, the medical examiner said. Jeff died in bed, while Angie slept next to him. She claimed she hadn't heard anything, that she'd been taking Ambien since he'd started coughing so much. They tested him for COVID-19, reported his case to the growing death toll, and released his body.

April became May, the first time I flipped a calendar without Jeff in the world—an entire month of blank boxes and more waiting behind them, an endless supply of days without my brother. The calendar was a yearly Christmas present from Angie, because a holiday card wasn't enough Instagrammable superiority, she needed to remind you whose life was better all year long. The thing reeked of bronze pineapple cocktail shakers, staged gingham picnics, and shots of her in random places: sunglasses in sunflower fields, oiled-up legs on tropical beaches, balayage curls whipping at the north shore. The May picture, though, was of Jeff. He walked away from the camera, through a grove of old pines, their bleached trunks aiming for the sky.

I taped it to my fridge and burned the rest of the calendar in the fire pit while the crow watched.

By May, everyone walked. We'd become pallbearers without caskets, moving in huddled groups down sidewalks scrawled with messages from children who didn't know better. *You are awesome. We'll get through this.* I skirted the rainbow drawings, afraid something of me would contaminate them. The Mac-Groveland neighborhood was a peninsula plateauing above the Mississippi, lassoed by the river and freeways on all sides. Most businesses were shuttered, with hasty signs taped up in dark windows. There was nowhere to go and I walked anyway, further every day, as though I could reach that grove of pines, find Jeff among them, and lead him home. Instead, I hit the edge of the city, hundreds of feet above the Mississippi, and stared at the slide of water.

All the benches were taken, so I climbed onto the rocks at the edge of the bluff where a strong wind could have the final say. There were pigeons here, no crows in sight. I opened Facebook, where Angie performed her grief like she was helping the app test drive their new care emoji. Today, there were no sunsets or empty doorways, though—she'd posted a picture ten minutes ago of her feet in front of a pool. It wasn't pool weather in Minnesota.

The call connected on the fifth ring.

"Where are you?"

"I'm bearing up as best as I can. So sweet of you to check." Angie always dipped her hatred in thick coats of pleasantries. She could disembowel you with a weather report.

"I asked you where you are, not how you are."

"I needed time and space to heal. We couldn't get out of the country, so we're in Key West."

"We?"

She named some friends, as someone in the background laughed.

"How could you fly right now?" The skies over St. Paul were empty of everything except birds.

"We were basically the only people on the entire plane. The stewardesses were so understanding. Did you see my stories?"

"Jeff had COVID. You could have it, too."

She danced around it for a while, before finally admitting she hadn't got tested. "You can't find tests anywhere. Besides I waited the two weeks, and I feel fine. Thanks for your concern."

"How are you paying for this?" Angie worked part-time at a store selling forty-dollar candles and distressed signs that said *Bless this Home*. On her own, she wouldn't have the money to go to Wisconsin. Jeff worked seventy-hour weeks to pay their mortgage and bills and provide all the shit Angie acquired. Until the pandemic hit, and he'd been furloughed.

"I'm not destitute. We had savings." Her voice turned brittle. Jeff had mentioned taking out a loan from his 401(k). Would he do that if they had savings?

"And," she continued, "thank god for the life insurance."

She cut the call short and I dropped the phone, swaying forward over the bluff's edge. I felt dizzy, sick. How much life insurance had Jeff had? Enough that two weeks after his funeral, his widow and her friends were sunning themselves poolside in the Caribbean.

On the way home, I passed the serial killer from across the street. He nodded, hulking and awkward in a beige sweater, his eyes sliding past me. The neighbor said he worked in IT, that his ex-wife lived across the river. Right. I wondered if he'd looked her in the eye when he killed her, whether he surprised his victims or if he wanted them to know what was coming. Jeff said he was disciplined, strategic. You'd have to be, to end a life. Or you'd have to want something badly from their death.

The crow waited on my front lawn, twitching his crooked wing. I tossed him a peanut as I let myself in the house, but stopped to stare at the ring of keys. Jeff had given me a key to his place years ago, so I could water Angie's plants while they were away.

They were away now.

I looked up the number for the medical examiner's office and left a message. Asphyxia. Lack of oxygen. If someone had COVID, and their lungs were already drowning, would they be easier to suffocate? Angie said she hadn't heard anything, but they'd been in the same bed. How could she not hear her husband dying a foot away?

I spent the rest of the afternoon researching Ambien. It was a sedative-hypnotic, not to be used by anyone with lung disease or problems breathing. One of the side effects was listed as complex sleep behaviors. Patients had reported walking, driving, talking on the phone, having sex—all while asleep. In the morning, they remembered nothing.

I thought about my brother's deathbed, Jeff struggling for every breath while Angie—what?

What had Angie done?

There were no chalk messages on the sidewalk in front of Jeff and Angie's house. Even children knew it was pointless here. They lived in a planned community in Stillwater with faux gates, shrub art, and porches no one sat on. Their neighbor's houses were dark, the street apocalypse-empty. I eyed the video doorbell and stepped over a pile of Amazon packages. I hoped someone stole them. Inside, there were plants everywhere, not just the ones I used to water, but potted flowers wrapped in cellophane, fresh bouquets decomposing in vases, covering tables and shelves, typed sympathy cards wedged between spiky leaves. Cards and bills sat on the dining room table, unopened. I looked through the stack until I found an envelope from the insurance company and ripped it open.

Jeff's life insurance had paid out one million dollars to Angie as his sole beneficiary.

In the living room, Jeff's favorite recliner was draped with a throw blanket, the fabric he'd worn smooth and dull over the years covered up with West Elm palm tree patterns. He'd moved that chair everywhere with him, from college apartments to downtown lofts, until the cushion had molded to his exact frame. I could still see the impression where his shoulders would fit, the ghost of his silhouette holding a craft beer and flipping through channels to find the game.

He'd probably sat here the last time we talked, a week before he died. He'd sounded fine—tired, but still Jeff, telling me about a woman wearing a full inflatable dinosaur costume at the gas station. Fossils pumping fossils. Jeff always found the joke, always flipped the tedium into our private amusements. The punchlines faded into decades of laughter coating our lungs, ready to contract at the least appropriate time. I had no idea it would be the last story, the last time we would ever laugh.

I'd offered fodder, trying to cheer him up. "Did you hear about people drinking bleach?"

"Who, white supremacists?"

"No." I thought for minute. "Well, maybe."

"We should get that going on Facebook. Want to be whiter?"

"Feels like a solution to a lot of things. I can deal with a bleach shortage."

He sighed, a thin, rattling sound. "Angie would probably end up trying it. Not that she's a white supremacist. But the COVID thing."

"Again: problem, meet solution."

I'd tried being nice to Angie for years while she treated me like we were in some fucked-up competition for Jeff's time and attention. Now, though, I didn't know. Maybe I'd read her all wrong. Maybe it was never about my brother, only about what she could get from him. One million things she could get from him.

I ripped the palm tree blanket off Jeff's chair, knocking over a decorative table and sending a spray of sympathy plant dirt across the wall and carpet.

Upstairs, the master bedroom curtains were shut, leaving

nothing but shadows inside. I paused, scared to turn on the light, not because of the virus or that I would get infected from the room; I didn't want to see where Jeff took his last breath, the place where my brother ended. I stood in the dark, shaking, my body threatening to come apart, until an engine noise outside startled me back into motion. I flipped the switch.

The bed was made, the covers smooth and stiff. I went to Angie's nightstand first. I didn't even know what I was looking for, but I had the crow's eyes now. I wouldn't miss a thing. I picked up a small pineapple statue by her pillow—why the hell did she have pineapples and palm trees all over her house when she lived in Minnesota?—and shoved it in my pocket. Her drawers were stuffed with magazines, candles, an aggressive collection of eye masks, and a half-empty bottle of Ambien. She must not have trouble sleeping in the Florida Keys. I shook out the pills, staring at them until the coating stained orange circles into my palm. Sedative-hypnotic. If Jeff had taken one, while COVID was eating his lungs, would it have caused him to stop breathing?

A clicking noise downstairs made me freeze, the hair on the back of my neck standing up. A floorboard creaked.

"Hello?"

Silence.

I moved toward the door, but a box on Jeff's nightstand made me freeze. I'd completely forgotten about his CPAP machine. Heart pounding, I walked over and pulled the tubing out of the holder. Jeff's last breaths could still be caught in the plastic, pockets of condensed virus couched in the coils. I lifted it anyway and saw white residue coating the inside of the triangular mask. The sheen of it shifted in and out of focus, there and gone, like a breath.

"Hands up."

I screamed, dropping the ventilator. Pills scattered everywhere. Two police officers stood in the bedroom door, faces covered by masks, weapons pointed at my chest.

* * *

They charged me with misdemeanor trespassing and attempted burglary. Angie had seen me through the video doorbell and called them from the Florida Keys. She'd called the police on me, for the crime of walking into my brother's house. The hair on the back of my neck stood up when I thought about the residue coating Jeff's CPAP machine, the life insurance policy, all the things Angie didn't want me to find.

"How do I open an investigation into my brother's death?"

"You don't."

"But, his wife..." I tried to explain about the sleep apnea and the Ambien, but the officer cut me off.

"She's filing a restraining order against you."

They held me overnight, and released me on bail the next morning.

While everyone else compulsively refreshed their news feed, shell shocked by the shutdown of the entire world, I spent every waking minute researching the appallingly simple mechanics of shutting down a single human body.

Breathing is a strange thing. We can't live without a constant intake of oxygen. We need a hit every few seconds, sucking it through the labyrinth of our mother's bodies even before we're born. Then we spend eighty to ninety years inhaling it like greedy, entitled kids, giving nothing back for our entire lives.

In the first two minutes without oxygen, we lose consciousness and our brain cells start to die. After three minutes, our neurons become irreversibly damaged. At the ten-minute mark, our brain dies. In fifteen minutes, we're gone. We're all fifteen minutes away from dying. Sometimes less. I didn't know how long Jeff's body struggled, how much he fought for oxygen against the virus, sleep apnea, drugs, maybe even his own wife.

Angie's phone went straight to voicemail and she refused to answer any of my emails asking for the CPAP machine. I wanted to test the white residue, to see what it was. When I tried the medical examiner's office again, they explained they couldn't disclose anything to me.

"My sister-in-law had a prescription for Ambien. What if she gave him one and disconnected his CPAP machine?"

"You should be having this conversation with law enforcement."

The Stillwater police gave me the runaround every time I tried talking to them. They treated me like I was the infected one.

"Did he have Ambien in his system? Did you run a toxicology panel?" I paced the patio as the crow mirrored me at the edge of the grass, strutting and cawing, demanding his treat.

"I'm sorry for your loss, ma'am." They hung up. Everyone hung up in the end.

The restraining order came in June. I wasn't allowed to come within five hundred feet of Angie. If I tried to make contact, I would be arrested for violation of the order.

I tossed it in the firepit, but before I could light it, the crow swooped down. He grabbed the paper and flew away, struggling under its size and weight.

I chased him down, running through the gate and into the front yard. A bubble of laughter rose in my throat as the conversation played out. *No, I didn't read the order, officer. A crow took it.*

The crow landed in the middle of the street in a whirl of white pages and black feathers. I dug in my pockets for a peanut, a crumb, anything to give him. All I had was Angie's pineapple. It had slipped through a rip in my coat lining and the police hadn't found it when they arrested me. Now it had become a talisman, a symbol of everything I knew and couldn't prove.

"Good bird. Good job. Hang on." I checked my pants pockets, looking for a reward.

The crow paced around the restraining order, his bad wing drooping, until a car came around the corner. He spread his wings to take off, but not fast enough. The bumper clipped him as the car sped down the road and disappeared.

"No!"

I ran to the curb, dropping next to him. His eye was open, unmoving. His wing, bent at an impossible angle, was motionless. I looked for the smallest stir or rustle, any sign that his lungs were still inflating. There was nothing.

I moved his wing back into place, the feathers as silky as they'd always looked, but matted and sticky now. As carefully as I could, I scooped him up, cradling his limp body.

I didn't know how long I sat, rocking back and forth in the gutter. Cars drove by. Pedestrians crossed to the opposite sidewalk, six feet not far enough away. The restraining order caught in the wind, blowing into a parked car and down the block.

I heard the crows before I saw them, first one lone caw, then multiplying into a chorus. Perched high above the street, blotches marring the budding green, they called over and on top of each other, a sentinel of noise. An older couple hurried away, alarmed by the number of birds above them, the volume of their anger and grief.

A shadow fell over me. The serial killer stood on the curb, wreathed in a halo of screaming birds. He stared at the black shape in my hands, then leaned over and took the crow from me.

"What are you doing?" I demanded.

He turned and walked away.

"Give him back." I chased after him, stumbling over his precisely manicured lawn, through a cedar privacy fence, and into his backyard. He handed me the crow in front of his shed, transferring it back so gently that new tears pricked into the corners of my eyes. I didn't know what to say. He turned, unlocked the door, and moved inside. Tools hung from the walls of the shed, shears and picks and an axe with a curved, shining blade. My heart raced, looking from the mounded mulch in his garden to the fence blocking the neighboring houses from view.

I heard Jeff, the confidence of his warm and persuasive tenor, telling me I'd picked the perfect place to live, that this man would never hurt me. You're safe, he'd said. I rocked the dead bird in my arms. The serial killer turned to me, holding two shovels.

We buried him where the patio met the grass in my backyard, working silently as the screaming crows flew away with the sun. The dirt was compact, resistant, but the serial killer cut through it like warm butter. He had a hundred pounds on me. In daylight he seemed bland, but he came to life in twisting shoulders and quick, sure jabs in the dark. When I laid the bird in the grave, he plucked a feather from the bad wing and handed it to me.

I cried then, standing over the dark mouth of the bird's grave. The whole story poured out, from Jeff's death to my suspicions to the restraining order, and how the crow had been the only creature in the world I hadn't alienated or scared off. It wasn't a eulogy, exactly. The longer I talked, the more I felt a hard pit in my stomach, an unquenchable place ripped out by the screaming birds. It was telling me something, but I didn't know what.

Afterward, we put the shovels away. I walked into the shed with him and noticed a hockey puck tucked into the frame above the door.

"Do you play?"

"Sometimes, when the timing is right." He stared at the puck. "That's more of a memento."

His voice wasn't anything like I expected. He sounded conversational, intelligent. The pit in my stomach started to hum, like a call or a warning.

"A memento of what?" I remembered the hockey coach from Hugo, the hand found at the river's edge.

He didn't answer, but turned toward me, filling the doorway. His eyes darkened to the color of the crow's feather clutched in my hand.

My breath seemed to echo in the small space, the pulse of oxygen desperate, heady. I took the brass pineapple out of my pocket—Angie's ornament, the last thing she saw before she closed her eyes—and placed it next to the hockey puck.

A request.

Something in his face shifted, unveiled. The humming in my stomach grew and clenched.

"Let's go inside."

I followed the serial killer into his house, Jeff's voice echoing in every step, leading me on, telling me I was safe. I was safe.

THE JUROR

R. Franklin James

"Prospective Juror Number Five, have you read any articles or followed any news about the defendant, or about this case, in the newspapers or social media?" The attorney for the defense peered under thick bushy eyebrows.

Caught off guard, Joya Sinclair straightened in her seat. She'd almost forgotten she was Juror Number Five.

"What?" She shook her short dreadlocks. "No. I avoid the news—too depressing."

There were a few acknowledging chuckles in the courtroom.

She was a little skeptical when she'd gotten the jury notice. It wasn't her first service. She'd been dismissed twice before from serving.

The attorney nodded to the judge. "The defense accepts this juror to be impaneled."

The prosecution, a friendly-looking young woman, stood and walked leisurely toward the jury box.

"This is a first-degree burglary case," the prosecution said, projecting her voice. "First-degree burglary is the more serious of the two types of burglary. It's when a person enters a private residence, someone's home, with the intent to commit a felony or theft once inside." She crossed her arms. "Do you think you could listen only to the evidence provided to you here and give an appropriate verdict?"

Joya heard herself say in an equally steady voice, "Yes, I think I can."

The prosecution gave Joya a long look. "Have you ever been incarcerated, or have relatives or friends who had run-ins with the police?"

"No," Joya lied. This was the question that had gotten her thrown off the last time.

Again, the prosecution scrutinized her, and then turning to the judge said, "The people accept this prospective juror."

The judge gestured to the jury box. "You will be impaneled as Juror Number Five."

Joya swallowed deeply and nodded. The jury box contained a double row of six chairs. She took her seat in the first row. Glancing at the jury pool, she noticed she was the only African American.

Except for the man on trial.

She gazed at the defendant. He was really just a kid. He had large brown eyes, a groomed short afro, and a scraggly goatee. From where she sat, she could see his left knee bouncing erratically. He stared down at his clasped hands.

For the next half hour, Joya turned her attention to the new jurors being questioned. When the eighth juror was accepted, the judge sat back.

"Let's stop for lunch," he said, motioning to the wall clock. "The court requires four more jurors, and two alternates. In the interest of sticking to an agreed schedule, I hope we can complete jury selection this afternoon and start with opening statements in the morning." He took off his glasses. "Does counsel for either side have an issue with this?"

"No, Your Honor," was the joint reply.

After lunch, and back in the courtroom, Joya listened as Jurors Nine and Ten were quickly selected. Nine seemed self-assured, but she had never served on a jury before. Ten was the other side of middle age and had doused herself in Guerlain. The heady fragrance caused the Prosecution to blink and sniff repeatedly.

Joya's interest was caught by prospective Juror Eleven, a self-affirmed housewife who appeared from the way she dressed to have money. You didn't see many rich people on jury duty.

The Defense asked her, "Do you think you could participate on this jury and give an unbiased judgment?"

"Sure, why not."

Sure, why not.

Juror Eleven was impaneled.

Joya wrinkled her brow. This time it was the questioning of prospective Juror Number Twelve that captured her attention. He appeared familiar, but she couldn't think of where she'd seen him. His graying brown hair was combed over covering a pale pink bald spot. Wearing a deep blue polo shirt and pressed tan Dockers, he resembled a chubby Mr. Rogers. But his dark brown eyes darted about the room, never remaining on a subject more than a few seconds. Then his gaze settled on her and he winked.

Joya knew she wasn't going to like him.

He answered the Defense and the People's attorney's interrogations confidently and succinctly. Counsel must have sensed something about him too, because they asked him more questions than any other juror. But in the end, after the judge glanced pointedly at the clock, both attorneys accepted him.

"Since it is almost five o'clock," the judge said, "I will swear in the jury now, and trial will begin tomorrow promptly at eight thirty a.m." Once again, he peered over his glasses at the defense table. "Any questions? Good." He banged the gavel without waiting for an answer.

The jury was sworn in.

The next morning Joya entered the small, windowless jury assembly room. She chose a chair in the corner hoping to avoid connecting with anyone. She was here to do her civic duty, not make alliances. She could hear the voice of her of her now dead grandmother, insisting "...our ancestors died so you could have the opportunity to have jury duty. Don't turn your back."

Joya was supposed to be here.

Thankfully, the room was relatively quiet. Several had their heads bent over cell phones. A couple of people conversed quietly. Except for Juror Number Twelve who went around the room grasping everyone's hand in a hardy, damp shake. After he released Joya's hand, she wiped his imprint off against her pants leg.

Is he running for office?

She regarded her fellow jurors around the large, oval, walnut conference table. Seven women and five men, half appeared to be over fifty, most wore casual clothing. They smiled at each other tentatively as if it was a violation to be friendly.

Joya noted an energetic conversation underway near the entry door.

Juror Number One, an elderly woman with tightly coiled fog-gray hair, wore two gold crosses, a string of pearls around her neck, and a pair of tiny matching pearl earrings. She seemed to be a little deaf. She was loudly whispering to Juror Number Two that she was retired and that she'd been on seven juries. Two nodded and responded that he was an adult college student.

The door opened.

The bailiff, a tall, solid blonde who wore her uniform as tight as a second skin came into the room. She announced that court was in session and to follow her to the jurors' assigned seats.

"It's about time," Juror Three, the only juror wearing a business suit and spiked heels, murmured to Joya. "If the judge wants things to run on time, he needs to set an example."

Joya flashed a smile in understanding but said nothing.

They all made their way into the courtroom and the jury box.

The judge made up for lost time by quickly running through his court rules. Turning to them, he spoke sharply. "I will insist on your full attention. This is a felony trial. Except during your lunch time, there will be no checking emails, sending texts, monitoring the stock market, or any other diversion currently available on electronic devices—period. Any violation will result in having your device confiscated until the end of the session. A man's future is in question."

He droned on for a few more minutes about jury duty and gave them each a stern look. Squinting, he pointed, "For example, Juror Number Eight, remove that ear pod—now."

Eight was a young man dressed in tan slacks and a black T-shirt. He wore his hair long, but evidently not long enough to cover up his ear.

He pocketed the device in a backpack and muttered, "It was just a little background music."

The Judge raised his eyes, and said, "Bailiff, make sure my rules are followed." Then he nodded toward the prosecution. "Counsel for the eople, please come forward with your opening statement."

The Prosecution stood directly in front of Juror Number One. Clearly ill at ease, the old woman leaned back as far as she could in her seat; her hands gripped the arms of the chair. Her right ear was tilted toward her shoulder as if trying to catch sound with her left. One smiled nervously at the Prosecution's singular attention, and she blinked rapidly under the attorney's glare.

Joya felt sorry for One.

"The People will show that the defendant showed no mercy or sympathy for Mr. Givens, the owner. Instead, he knowingly and with deliberate planning burgled Mr. Givens's home in order to take his hard-earned valuables."

Joya listened intently to the prosecution's detailed case—the reason why this young man was on trial. If what the prosecution said was true, there appeared to be little questioning of the facts. She sneaked a look at the defendant, who slouched in his seat, seemingly captivated with his folded hands rather than the words being said against him. From time to time his attorney would pat his arm, mouthing it will be all right. The boy only hung his head lower.

The prosecution took a long pause, and then continued.

"Due to the terrible nature of this case, the people will be asking for a jury conviction and the maximum sentencing. We will prove to all of you that it is well-deserved." She stared pointedly at One.

Juror One hurriedly nodded.

The prosecution stepped back and said, "Thank you." She returned to her seat.

The people had taken a little more than an hour, after which the judge stated that both attorneys should approach the bench before the defense commenced with his opening statement.

The three huddled.

Meanwhile from her seat, Joya continued to assess her fellow jurors.

Jurors Four and Seven were both middle-aged men sitting dejectedly with chins on chests. Already, at the urging of the Defense, Four had to be warned by the judge to stop playing with his Apple Watch. Four said he was diabetic and watched the time to monitor his medication. The judge encouraged him to use the oversized clock on the wall across from the jury box instead. And Seven, despite his pleas that his dog was at the vet and he was waiting for a call back, had his cell phone taken away until the break. Both frowned at the defendant. He was, after all, the reason for their inconvenience.

Finally, the Defense began his opening statement. He slowly made his way to the jury box with his head bent over a yellow legal pad. He frantically flipped through sheets of paper. He appeared unprepared, as if he'd stumbled into this trial by mistake.

"Good afternoon members of the jury," he said, without looking up from his pad. "I represent the defendant in this case. The defendant stands here today wrongly accused of the crime of first-degree burglary and murder, a very serious matter. At the end of this trial, we are going to ask you to render a verdict of not guilty, the only appropriate verdict."

And, after avoiding making eye contact with any juror, he returned to his seat.

The defense had concluded its opening statement.

The judge barely hid his shock at the short presentation, but recovered quickly to strike his gavel. "The people may call their first witness."

The prosecution supported her case with several forensic testimony witnesses. She was methodical and deliberate. There was no cross-examination by the defense.

Close to the end of the day, out of the side of her eye, Joya noticed movement behind her in the corner of the jury box. She turned slightly to see. Eleven took out a cloth handkerchief and dabbed at flushed cheeks. Twelve leaned forward in his chair with a smirk on his face.

What had happened?

The judge noticed it too. "Is everything all right, Juror Number Eleven?"

Juror Eleven, an attractive brunette, had dressed today casually in tan slacks and a seafoam-green sweater that matched her eyes perfectly.

"Oh, yes, yes, I'm fine." Eleven said. "Please, please go ahead. Don't let me...Don't let me interrupt."

Joya frowned. Where had she seen Twelve before?

Juror Number Ten, also stretched to see what the matter was. She shifted in her seat sending another plume of perfume to scent the air. She shrugged at Joya and patted Eleven's shoulder. But now it was Juror Number Nine who caught Joya's notice. Nine was average-looking with nothing to distinguish her except, when Joya turned to see, she caught such malevolence in Nine's face it caused Joya to catch her breath.

The object of Nine's glance, Juror Twelve, appeared oblivious.

Two more prosecution witnesses took the stand. A young woman, looking to be in her twenties, said, even though it was dark, she was sure it was the defendant who entered the backyard. Then there was a homeless man who said that he was positive it was the defendant he saw running away from the victim's house.

Joya heard Twelve mutter something under his breath. Nearby, Six and Eleven stirred in their seats.

The defendant gripped the edge of the table with both hands as if to jump up, but his attorney laid a restraining grip on his arm. The young man slammed his back against the chair.

Again, Twelve mumbled incoherently.

Joya could feel her own irritation rise. She was more frustrated because the identity of Twelve kept slipping just out of the reach of her memory.

The people's next witness was the owner of a hardware department store who said that the defendant had purchased the knife in question the week previous to the killing. He remembered because he asked if it was "good for gutting."

A gasp came from the courtroom.

At that, the defendant immediately whispered in his attorney's ear, who merely nodded and made a note.

Twelve grunted.

The Prosecution rested. There had been no defense objections.

The judge said they would end for the day and start with the witnesses for the defense in the morning.

The Defense's first witness was the defendant's mother, a trim, professional-looking woman with smooth, dark chocolate-colored skin and dark hair pulled back into a bun. She was sworn in. She spoke about how her son had a good heart and fair grades in school. With tears in her eyes, she went on to tell the story how after his father died, his grief turned to anger, and he fell prey to a gang that used him as a pawn. But that was over, he'd turned his life around. Her son was innocent.

At her words, the young man gazed at his mother with total love.

Joya heard Twelve choke down a guffaw. Neighboring jurors shifted in their seats.

The prosecution did her best to discredit the defendant's mother. For the next ten minutes, she brought up her once job as a "bar maid," and the fact the defendant's mother was raising three other children by different fathers.

At that the judge stiffened. "Ah, is there something the defense might wish to say?" He leaned forward over his bench. "Like, oh, I don't know, maybe 'Objection'?"

The Defense had been taking notes and jerked his head up, startled. "I'm sorry, Your Honor. Yes, yes, objection. The prosecution is...is harassing the witness."

The judge shook his head.

"That's not a problem, Your Honor." The Prosecution smirked. "I'm finished cross-examining this witness."

The mother rose up in her seat. "But they aren't my bio—"

"Your Honor, please excuse the witness." The prosecution cut her off, and hurried back to her seat.

"The witness may step down," the judge ordered, then frowned. "Unless, of course, defense would like to clarify any confusion that could be left in the mind of the jurors with a redirect question?"

The Defense smiled. "No, Your Honor, we are sticking to our agreement with this court to keep things moving."

The judge stared at him for a long moment then leaned back. "The Defense should call its next witness."

After calling four more character witnesses, who over the next hour were asked nearly the exact same questions, Joya couldn't help notice that Six had started to nod off. Four stared as if in a trance at the clock on the wall.

The Prosecution had no questions for cross-examination.

Joya wondered if the defense had any intention of calling witnesses to dispute the incriminating facts against his client. It was clear from the judge's expression that he wondered the same thing.

He slammed his gavel. "The court will break for ten minutes. Bailiff, remove the jurors."

The bailiff led the jurors back to the assembly room. "Take advantage of the break," she said. "Remember there's to be no discussion of the trial. I'll be back to get you." She closed the door behind her.

They all took the same seats they held from the morning.

"What a numb-nut," Twelve called out. "If that guy was my attorney, I'd go after him for malpractice. He's a total incompe—"

Nine extended her hand in protest. "Didn't you hear the bailiff? We're not supposed to be talking about the trial," she said with slow deliberateness. "We shouldn't talk about the case until after the judge turns the matter over to us."

Twelve leaned forward with a squint. "Who in the hell are you to—"

"Hey, hey let's just give it a rest," Four said. "She's right."

A thick silence followed. Moments later the door opened and the bailiff poked her head in. "Okay ladies and gentlemen, you're up."

They all stood and shuffled back to court.

"Wait, wait just a minute," Twelve said shaking his forefinger at Nine as she approached the door. "I remember you. You're—"

"Juror Number Twelve," the bailiff interrupted. "This is a trial, not a reunion. Get together with your friends on your own time." She pointed to the hallway. "Let's go everybody, the judge is waiting."

Joya joined the others in the corridor. Twelve tapped his forehead in final recognition. Nine sent Twelve a knowing sneer.

Back in the courtroom, the defense continued to elicit character references from the defendant's former classmates and neighbors. Joya almost cheered when the prosecution called out: "May we approach the bench, Your Honor?"

"I thought you'd never ask," the judge responded. "If the defense has no more questions, this witness is excused."

The three once more huddled in muffled tones. Moments later

the attorneys returned to their posts and the judge turned to the jurors and spoke.

"The prosecution accepts for the people that the defendant has affected the lives of many persons in a positive manner, and the defense accepts that while the exemplary background of the defendant leads credence to the argument that the defendant may not have the temperament of a stereotypical burglar, that is in fact the crime he is charged with today." He motioned to the defense. "Proceed, counselor."

The Defense moistened his lips and turned to the jury.

"I call the defendant to the stand."

"This ought to be good," Twelve said under his breath.

The young man was clearly nervous as he entered the witness box. He began to cough repeatedly, and his attorney brought him water.

"It's my...my...my asthma," the defendant stammered, after gulping down half the glass. He set it down and hugged himself with his hands gripping his upper arms.

And that's when Joya remembered where she'd seen Twelve before.

Four years before, St. Paul's North End Marydale Festival was a regional favorite. Diverse, loud, and fun-seeking, families milled around leisurely. This was why the altercation that broke out midday garnered an almost universal groan from onlookers. Joya looked up from a table of pottery when a woman yelled out, pointing to a man holding his head as blood oozed between his fingers—Joya's cousin. Nearby, another man was taunting him. Then she saw her cousin grip his upper arms not wanting any fight. But there was a third man egging them on, clearly an ally of the instigator. She gasped when the troublemaker pushed her cousin. He pushed back. A tussle ensued. A few men tried to pull them apart. Another ran for security. It wasn't until her cousin fell to the ground at the feet of the third man that the crowd was able to hold his tormentor back.

Later, in the hospital, Joya told police that the incident was not an accident as the sideline bully claimed. It was not an accidental stumble when the third man stomped his heavy boot to her cousin's eye. Her cousin had screamed out in pain, but it was nothing compared to the anguish he suffered when he was told he would never have sight in that eye again. That loss, and the accompanying brain damage, were listed as reasons for his depression and subsequent suicide a year later.

That third man was Number Twelve.

He had aged and changed his look. His thick brown hair was gone, replaced with a skimpy mustache and a hefty paunch of a stomach. But he couldn't change his eyes, flat and cold like a shark's.

Joya seethed and clenched her jaw.

"Want to catch a bite to eat after court?" Nine asked Joya, as she soaped her hands in the restroom basin.

"Sure," Joya said. "Someplace close, all right?"

"Perfect. There's a deli across the street on the corner." Nine smiled. "I'd like some company."

The afternoon dragged on much as the morning had. Finally the Defense called his last witness who swore that the defendant was with her at the time of the burglary. Joya, and the rest of the jurors, straightened in their seats.

An alibi?

Why were they just hearing this now? She could tell from the scowl on the judge's face that once more he was wondering the same thing.

From behind her she could hear Twelve mutter what sounded like "liar."

Listening to the defense witness, the Prosecution turned with a look of annoyance and glowered at the police detectives behind her, who frowned.

The witness explained that the defendant had been helping her with a term paper in a café, three blocks from the university campus and about eighteen miles from the burglary scene.

"Is there anyone from the café who can verify your story?" the Defense asked smugly.

The young woman nodded. "Sure, we're regulars. A lot of people saw us. We were there almost four hours. We've been studying there at least once a week for months."

Murmurs rose in unison from the courtroom.

At this the Prosecution leaned back in her chair and once more glared over her other shoulder at two uniformed policemen. Their faces had frozen into grim masks.

The judge just stared at the defense, then said, "I'd like both counsel to approach the bench."

From the agitated tone of the muffled discussion, all was not well. Finally, the lawyers returned to their tables, and the judge observed the jury box.

"As you've heard there has been very revealing testimony this afternoon. Both sides must consider and be prepared to respond to this court, with what had better be a very good explanation about the timing for what has been said here. Therefore, I am excusing you for the rest of today. However, you should report back to your assembly room at eight a.m. tomorrow morning. Again, you are cautioned not to speak about this case or anything you have heard today."

Down went his gavel.

"Wow, want to go for coffee instead?" Nine held the front door open for Joya to pass through.

She smiled. "Sure."

Starbucks was half full, and the welcoming aroma of coffee and baked goods filled the room. The two women took chairs at a small round table at the rear of the store.

"I can't stand that he's behind me. Juror Twelve, I mean. He destroyed my family," Joya said, draping her coat over the back of the chair. "I saw the way you looked at him. You know him too, don't you?"

"Yes, I know him," Nine said. She peered into Joya's eyes. "Twelve killed my fiancé."

"What?" Joya gasped. "How awful, I'm sorry...that's terrible. I...I—" Joya sputtered.

Nine gave her a half smile and went to pick up their order.

Back at the table, Joya just stared as Nine nonchalantly opened a sugar packet and the crystals slowly slid into the cup.

Nine spoke as she stirred. "It was a result of the pain pills he needed. He...he was on his way to a bad addiction. He got into a rehab program," Nine said and paused and sipped her coffee. "He'd been to others before, but this place was working. I work as a pharmacy nurse—I know. He was ready to get healthy."

Joya sipped and nodded for her to keep talking.

"He was ready to get clean of pills, and clean of the so-called friend that got him started." Nine shook head, and tears glistened along the rims of her eyes. "I loved him. It was a second marriage for both of us. He was a beautiful person." She swiped at a tear making its way down her cheek. "I did everything I could to get him away from his crowd. We lived together so he couldn't get more. He was...He was..."

Joya reached across the table and squeezed Nine's hand.

Nine flashed a small smile. She withdrew her hand and reached for a tissue in her bag. She remained silent as she dabbed at her eyes.

"Was Juror Twelve your fiancé's friend?" Joya asked.

"No, Twelve didn't know my fiancé. He was the hospital worker who supplied drugs for my fiancé's so-called 'friend.' Twelve helped my fiancé's friend to track him down to the rehab program. When my fiancé was back in his clutches, he got back on pills and...and he overdosed. Twelve made it all possible. I told the police, but I couldn't prove anything and he got away with it. My fiancé's friend got five years, but Twelve, Twelve got nothing."

Nine suddenly halted speaking. She paled and stiffened. Joya looked over her shoulder to see Twelve enter the Starbucks. She quickly sought Nine's eyes, but they were already fixed on the approaching figure.

"I thought I saw you two come in here." He grinned without sincerity. "Mind if I join you? I'm not going back to work. I still get paid on jury duty."

"I mind," Nine said.

Joya interjected. "We're having a private conversation."

"Not a problem." Ignoring her, he shook his head and brought over another chair. "I can only stay a minute. I drink the other guy's stuff." He motioned his head toward Nine. "I finally remembered where I know you from."

Nine did not respond.

"Yeah, it was you who got me fired from my job," he said. "Sorry about your boyfriend, but nobody made him take those drugs. He was weak. Your pals at the hospital and the jury agreed with me."

Twelve hadn't yet sat down. He stood with his hands on the back of the chair waiting for Nine to speak, but she remained silent, her eyes glued to his. Joya caught a small movement of Nine's fingers slowly and deliberately slipping into the purse resting on her lap.

Joya's heart beat a rapid staccato. She eased her hand onto Nine's arm, halting her effort. Nine's eyes widened but stayed on Twelve. She didn't face Joya but she stopped.

"What?" Twelve teased. "Cat got your tongue?"

Nine slowly pulled back her hand.

"Please go," Joya demanded, her adrenaline pumping like water through a fire hose. "Just leave. Like I said, we're having a private conversation."

Twelve sniffed. "A private conversation, huh? Sure, I'll give you your privacy." His eyes narrowed and headed toward the door only to turn around again. "By the way," he whispered loudly to Nine, "you may have shut me down for a little while, but people like your wimpy boyfriend are out there for the taking."

"You are a monster," Nine yelled, standing with balled fists. Her chair fell backwards and her purse hit the floor with a thud.

Joya quickly snatched it up and placed it on the seat of an adjacent chair. She frowned; it held something very heavy.

Twelve smirked and sauntered to the door, pausing once more with a backward glance, shaking his head and chuckling.

Finally, he was gone.

Joya spoke quickly, "I know you're upset, but don't give him the satisfaction of knowing he got to you."

Nine didn't look at her. Instead, she picked up her purse, eyes focused on the door. "I'm not in a social mood right now, sorry." She finally turned to Joya. "Let's talk later. Here's my number." She scribbled on a piece of paper.

"Are you okay?"

Nine gave her a tight smile. "No."

Later, Joya heard it was One who had gone for help. The older woman half-ran down the hallway pushing past the jurors and barreling through clusters of people making their way into to the various courtrooms. Puzzled, but continuing to the assembly room, the remaining jurors entered, straining to look around each other. Joya stood to the rear of the line.

The scream, within the room, came from Eleven.

"I think he's had a heart attack," someone else called out.

Twelve's body was positioned at the table in the assembly room, his cup of coffee nearby, in the chair he'd claimed from the first day the jurors had convened. His arms draped over the sides, face in a grimace, right hand gripping his chest, and eyes staring at nothing.

Joya felt the presence of a juror behind her and without turning around, she moved her fist behind her back for the mutual bump.

SPINOUT
Michael Wiley

On the second morning, the cargo van left the highway and bounced along rural state routes and small-town streets until it reached a road that wound in and out of a chain of ravines. At the end of the road, the van stopped and backed a quarter mile up a gravel driveway. When it stopped again, for a long time no one came.

Inside the cargo area, Missy Denners sat on a crate. A rush and hush of breaking waves sounded in the distance.

Then footsteps and voices approached. A lock rattled against metal. The doors opened.

Victoria Beauvien looked in at Missy. "I hope you had a pleasant trip," she said.

The cargo van had driven from Nogales, Arizona, on a hot dry night. But here, the air was cold and wet, which meant Missy was...she didn't know where.

Pitch pines and birches lined the gravel driveway. Northern trees. The air smelled of woods and lake water. A large house, built of split logs, stood next to an industrial shed.

"Where am I?" Missy asked.

"Come inside," Victoria said.

Two weeks earlier, Missy had tried to kill Victoria's brother,

Marcel. An attempt at revenge—Marcel murdered Missy's husband for failing to pay the Beauviens the money he owed. So Missy had pumped two bullets into Marcel, but he was like a starfish, surviving after it loses a limb.

Then, for the past two weeks, the Beauviens had kept her in a locked room and fed her from their table. As they handed Missy a bowl of *pozole* or a plate of chicken, they treated her as a marvelous joke. One morning when Victoria brought her a plate of fried eggs and tortillas, Missy asked, "What am I now, your pet?"

Victoria laughed. "Yes, you're my wild cat," she said.

"You know that's a cliché," Missy said.

The woman smiled. "Then you are my cliché."

So the Beauviens fed Missy from their table, and when Victoria went north, leaving her brother behind to clean up Missy and her husband's mess, she took her with her. She shoved her into the back of a cargo van full of guns and ammunition. She said, "The kennels won't board a wild cat." Then she slammed the van door.

The inside of the log house was paneled with knotted pine. Wooden carvings of ships and taxidermied fish lined the shelves. An antique farming scythe hung over the mantel. A pair of red-collared Weimaraners trotted from the kitchen and greeted Victoria and her company. A bay window looked out over a sand dune toward gray, rolling waves on a vast lake.

A man took Missy to an upstairs bedroom. There were padlocks on the outside of the door. But the door itself was made of thin pine planking. A window, without bars, faced the driveway.

"Where are we?" Missy asked the man.

"You know when you're so lost you don't know up from down or inside from out? That's where you are." The man closed the door.

Missy washed in the sink in an attached bathroom. Then she

watched through the window as a half-dozen men carried crates from the cargo van into the industrial shed. When they finished the job, she lay on the bed. Sleep tugged at her after the long ride, but she got up and went to the bedroom door. The man had left it unlocked. Missy walked downstairs. Victoria sat on a brown leather couch, drinking a mug of coffee. The Weimaraners lay at her feet.

"Refreshed?" she asked.

Missy said nothing. She went to the bay window and stared at the rolling waves. She wanted to plunge into them. She grew up playing in the warm water along Florida's Atlantic coast. She swam and she dived. Most of all she water skied—rising through local and regional competitions until she won the national junior championship at age sixteen. Now, at twenty-three, her life had gone to hell.

She asked Victoria, "Where are we?"

The woman gave her a curious smile. "A few house rules. If you follow them, you can relax while you're here. First, you may go anywhere you like when you're inside. Except my bedroom. Second, if you're hungry, you may use the kitchen. Don't touch the knives. If I find you with one, I'll break your fingers. Do you understand?"

Missy understood that the lake water would be colder and less buoyant than the Florida salt water, but she still wanted to immerse herself in it.

"Third, stay away from the shed," Victoria said. "Fourth, you may walk to the beach, but you'll stay in front of the house. If you try to escape, I'll send my men after you. They *will* catch you. And when they do, I'll reduce your freedom. Severely."

Missy said, "Why didn't you just kill me in Nogales?"

The woman smiled. "I want you to see what I'm capable of."

"Why does my opinion matter?"

"I see something of myself in you. I wonder if you can be saved."

"For what? You want me to be like you?"

"I need someone who's smart—and fearless. I need someone I can trust."

"If you think you can trust me, you're insane," Missy said.

For the next two days, Missy lived by the house rules. As she watched from her window, more cargo vans arrived with weapons and ammunition. Sometimes, late at night or in the early morning, cars came and men carried packages out of the big shed. But most of the movement remained inward, with Victoria supervising the unloading. When no vans came, Victoria drank coffee in the living room or walked the dogs on the beach.

She kept an eye on Missy. Missy overheard her asking the man who did the cooking whether she was eating. When Missy went to the beach, she felt Victoria's eyes staring at her from the window as she sat on a sand dune and watched the waves break.

On the third morning, as Missy stood at her bedroom window, a van driver argued with a man unloading cargo. The driver threw a punch. Soon the two were rolling on the gravel. The driver bloodied the other man's face. Victoria came from the house. Without shouting or pulling a gun, she stopped them. The men tried to fade back to their work, but she kept them there and chastened them with words Missy couldn't hear from her window, though she saw the fear in the men's faces.

Missy left her room. The stairs went down to a hallway outside the living room. Missy turned toward Victoria's bedroom door. Rule one: *Stay out of the bedroom*. Missy tried the handle. The door was unlocked.

Victoria had a white king-sized bed with a white bedcover. Next to the bed there were matching white night tables. Across from it there was a long white bureau. Missy opened the drawers in the bureau. There were sweaters, shirts, underwear, bras, a vial of Xanax.

Missy went to a night table and opened the top drawer. There was a Glock 26, wrapped in a green bandana.

A voice spoke from the doorway. "I would've thought by now you would live by my rules." Victoria's voice was calm, cold.

Missy lifted the pistol from the drawer, unwrapped the bandana, and aimed at her.

"The only question now," the other woman said, "is what to do with you."

Missy pulled the trigger, and metal slapped against metal. The chamber was empty.

The woman said, "I keep the ammunition in the bottom drawer."

Missy dropped the pistol on the bed and headed for the bedroom door. Victoria stepped aside and let Missy go, saying, "What *will* we do with you?"

Throughout the day, Missy expected the men to come for her. She carried lunch to her room and ate alone.

Later, she sat silently at the dining room table and ate dinner.

Then, that night, as she lay in bed, men whispered outside her door. She'd thought about bringing a fork from dinner but that would only anger an attacker. She would fight empty handed, and she would lose. A man laughed outside the door. She would kill *him* first with her bare hands if she could. Another man whispered. She would kill *him* second.

But the men stayed outside. They played with the locks on the door, snapping them shut, metal against metal, as loud as the hammer on the Glock closing on an empty chamber.

Missy stayed awake through the night. As the sun rose the next morning, she cleaned herself, dressed, and checked the bedroom door. Locked. She kicked the door. Kicked it again. The pine planking split from the cross supports. After five kicks, she climbed through a gap onto the upstairs landing. As she came to the first floor, two of Victoria's men stepped out of bedrooms.

"*Hola*," said one of them.

She crossed the living room to the door leading to the path to the beach. Then Victoria came from her bedroom and asked what she was doing.

"Leaving," Missy said, and opened the door.

The woman shook her head. "Don't be foolish."

But Missy stepped outside. If the men shot her, she would die running, not cowering in bed.

No one shot her.

She reached the beach and ran. Waves lapped at the shore. Missy followed a hard-packed lane of sand and pebbles at the water's edge. She went past a long stretch of wooded land. She went past a dark cottage, its windows covered with storm shutters. She went past more woods. Then light footsteps approached from behind—the footsteps of Victoria's two Weimaraners. The dogs shot past her, as if they too were escaping. Then they circled back. When she dodged around them, they closed on her and barked. She stopped and held a hand toward them. They growled and forced her back.

She stepped into the cold lake water. The dogs followed.

She moved into the sand dunes. The dogs followed.

She threw handfuls of sand at them. They lunged at her legs.

Only when she turned toward Victoria's house did the dogs stop barking. As she walked, they strolled beside her.

When Missy stepped into the living room, Victoria was sitting on the couch, drinking coffee and reading a newspaper. The dogs trotted to her and she petted one on the head.

Missy went upstairs. She climbed through the broken door. She got into bed. When a man brought a breakfast plate of eggs and bread, she left the food on the floor. When a new argument broke out on the driveway, she stayed in bed.

At noon, a cargo van arrived, and Victoria went to the driveway to supervise the unloading. Missy got up and watched from the window. The Weimaraners ran around the men, barking happily.

"Stupid," Missy said to the window.

She climbed through the door and went downstairs. Two men were talking in the living room. She passed them as if she had every right.

She went out the door to the beach. The waves had built through the morning. A steady wind was blowing wispy clouds across the sky. Seagulls hung in the air. Missy walked. She passed the stretch of wooded land. She passed the dark cottage. She passed the second stretch of woods. She passed rolling sand dunes and crossed a narrow creek, its icy water stained brown by pine tannin. She knew better than to look back. Only losers checked over their shoulders. She walked for more than an hour before she saw the next cottages—three gray wooden houses in a row, built at the edge of woods that backed the sand dunes. Plywood covered the windows of two of the three. In front of the third, a small sailboat rested on a hand dolly between the dunes, the sail reefed to a little aluminum boom.

Missy ran to the house and pounded on the door. She yelled for help. When a soft-looking gray-haired man, dressed in khakis, wearing wire-rimmed glasses, came and unlatched the screen door, Missy burst inside. She said she needed him to call for help. She'd been kidnapped. The house she'd escaped from was a few miles away. She needed the police *now*.

The man got her to sit and calm down. He asked her to explain again. When she finished, the man, who said his name was George Fellows, got the phone and dialed it. He identified himself. He said he had a woman at his house who'd been assaulted by a neighbor. Assaulted was his word, not hers, but it was close enough to the truth. When he hung up, he offered to make tea. Tea seemed a ridiculously insufficient remedy for all Missy had experienced. She said tea would be nice.

They sat together for a half hour. The man told Missy she was in a town north of Milwaukee. He said he moved to this house thirteen years earlier, after his wife died. Now he spent spring, summer, and fall days sailing or fishing on the lake. Not much to do in the winter other than watch the deer and drink. The conversation was so normal it hurt her ears to hear it.

When the knock came, she smiled at the man and pulled

herself out of her chair. "Thank you, George," she said, as he
went the door.

But the men he let in weren't police officers. Missy recognized
them from Victoria Beauvien's house. They seemed relaxed, letting
their guns hang toward the floor. "Let's go," one of them said
to her.

George Fellows sucked his lips.

"You bastard," she said to him.

He raised his eyes to hers and stared hard. "I need to live
here. You're just passing through."

When Victoria came to the bedroom, Missy was lying on the
floor with an ankle shackled to a bedpost. Victoria sat by her
on a folding chair. Missy studied the wave patterns in the grain
of the pinewood floor.

The woman said, "I hate stories that victimize women and
kids. Or animals. I won't read them or watch them on TV. But
some of the guys who work for me like those stories. The things
they'll do to you should never be done to a person, living or
dead. You understand?"

Missy thought life itself seemed to come in waves—mostly
harmless—mostly offering the little ups and downs that keep us
from killing ourselves out of boredom. Then the big one comes.
An earth shock levels a mountainside village. A rogue wave
sinks a fishing boat.

"What I'm saying," Victoria said, "is I've been indulging
you."

"You have a funny way of doing it," Missy said.

"You'll know when I stop."

Either the big wave kills you, or you float up and ride it.
Those are the only two possibilities. Missy said, "Can I have a
cigarette?"

Victoria looked surprised. "You smoke?"

"Only when I'm nervous," Missy said.

"Bad for you."

"As opposed to the rest of the life I'm leading?"

A smile flickered on the woman's face. "Yes, I see in you the girl I used to be. You once were a champion athlete, is that right?"

"Sure."

"Child's play," Victoria said. "Welcome to the big-girl world. You have guts, but you doubt yourself. Once you are sure of yourself, you'll be brutal. I can use you then."

A half hour later, a man brought Missy a pack of Marlboros and a Bic lighter. Later, Victoria brought dinner and sat on the folding chair until Missy ate. She eyed the unopened pack of cigarettes. "No?"

"I'm not feeling nervous right now," Missy said.

The woman said, "You're a funny one."

"If I promise to stay in the room, will you unlock me from the bed?" Missy asked.

"Every chance you get, you try to escape."

"Where would I go? You have the dogs. The neighbors."

"I don't underestimate you," the woman said.

"I don't underestimate you either," Missy said. "I'll stay."

"I'll tell you what—in a couple days, we'll try again. Fresh start. Can you live with that?"

"Could *you* live with it?" Missy asked.

"I've lived with worse."

Nonetheless, two hours later, as Missy lay on the floor, a man came with a key. When he unlocked the chain from her ankle, he told her, "Victoria says if you run again, you die. Don't mistake her unchaining you for softness. She'll shoot you herself."

"Nope," Missy said. "No more mistakes."

* * *

At two in the morning, she unclipped the window screen in her bedroom and set it against the wall. Men talked downstairs, but the driveway outside was dark.

Missy eased herself through the window feet first. She lowered her body until she hung against the outside wall of the house. She looked down at the dark driveway. It appeared a long way away.

She pulled herself back up to the window but only high enough to peer inside. She held herself like that. Then, as her muscles tired, she relaxed her arms until she hung between the window and the ground.

She loosened her fingers and fell.

The impact knocked the breath from her lungs. She lay on the driveway without moving. Waves rushed and hushed out on the beach. A breeze blew through the pine trees. Men talked inside the house, their voices muted by the sounds of the night. Missy gazed at the sky. The stars shined bright. The glow of the Milky Way looked like a path to somewhere better.

Missy moved her hands. She touched her fingers to her ribs. She moved her head, raising it off the gravel. She moved her legs.

Slowly, she got to her feet.

She breathed deep—in, out.

Then she crept along the edge of the driveway.

She hid between a Jeep and a pickup truck. She watched until a man guarding the shed left his post and went to the house. Before another man took his place, she ran across the driveway and went into the shed.

Dim overhead security lights shined on long rows of shelves, packed thick with boxes, crates, and plastic-wrapped weapons. Near the back of the shed, behind a stack of empty buckets, there was a workbench. She took two pairs of pliers and a straight-edged screwdriver. Next to the workbench there was a five-gallon gas can. She took it too.

There was no apparent logic to the organization of the

shelves. Near the workbench, there was a row of cardboard boxes from Atlanta Arms & Ammo. She broke a box open and pulled out blue-and-white packages of forty-caliber bullets, fifty rounds to a package. With the pliers, she disassembled twenty rounds, shaking the explosive powder into a pile on the floor.

She separated a pinch of powder from the pile and held the Bic to it. It flared hot. She scooped the rest into the package with the remaining thirty bullets. She repeated the process with a second package.

She put one of the doctored packages in the center of an aisle and stacked more ammunition around it. She carried the other one through the aisles until she found a set of metal shelves loaded tight with blasting caps and other small explosives. She set the gas can in the middle of the aisle. She arranged the contents of the shelves around the can. Then she nested her second doctored package in the middle of it all.

She lit a cigarette. She drew smoke into her mouth and drew in more until the end of the cigarette glowed red. She broke off the filter and stuck the unlit end into a corner of the doctored package.

She went back to the other aisle. She broke a second cigarette in half—making a shorter fuse—and lit it. She tucked the unlit end into the second doctored package. She pushed the other ammunition close to it. She walked to the exit.

A new man stood guard outside the door. Except for a plexiglass window, Missy could tap his shoulder. She eased the door open. Then she stabbed him in the back with the screwdriver.

She ran to the woods at the side of the driveway. She counted silently as the cigarette fuses burned toward the powder. As she mouthed *one hundred thirty-nine*, the ember othe half cigarette burned red against its charge. Hundreds of forty-caliber rounds exploded.

Spotlights, mounted on wooden poles and at the tops of pine trees, flashed on. Men poured from Victoria's house. When they realized the explosions were coming from the shed, most of them turned and ran for the beach. But Victoria shouted at them to move the cars and clear the area.

Missy slid through the trees at the side of the driveway as the men drove vehicles away from the shed, parked them, jumped out, and ran back for others. Missy stepped from the woods onto the driveway and, as headlights shined around her, climbed into a white four-door Jeep. The key was in the ignition. She started the engine and shifted into drive. She pulled toward the road.

When she reached the end of the driveway, she wondered whether the longer cigarette fuse had gone out. If so, men would come after her in the cars and trucks she'd left behind. When they caught her, Victoria would release her worst violence against her.

But as Missy pulled onto the road, a flash lit the night sky. A moment later, an enormous percussion rocked the Jeep. Two more explosions followed. The night sky turned orange. The smear of the Milky Way seemed to evaporate in a mist.

As Missy sped from Victoria's lakeside house, the orange sky fading back to black, she remembered a moment when she was sixteen, her feet tucked into a waterski fighting for a trophy in her final race.

She'd shot through pair after pair of buoys.

Her ponytail had streamed in the wind.

Spray from her ski had lit up the air like a night sky full of stars.

She'd lost herself in speed.

She could have been anywhere.

At that moment, she'd seemed to arrive at the core of herself, where there was heat and joy, and she'd screamed—grinning, laughing—and whipped across the finish line.

A photographer had caught the laughing, grinning, screaming triumph, and the next weekend, the picture of Missy had appeared in the local newspaper.

* * *

Now, as she raced from Victoria Beauvien's house, she didn't laugh or grin or scream. She said, "Dammit." She breathed hard. "Dammit, dammit."

She was a winner, that was all—and winners never looked over their shoulders.

Victoria claimed she saw something of herself in Missy. She said Missy would become brutal.

"No," Missy said to her shadowy reflection on the dark windshield. "No, no, no."

Her reflection gazed back at her.

In the black glass, the gaze looked sickly.

So Missy screamed.

Then she laughed.

She laughed and she grinned and she screamed again.

GONE FISHIN'

Eric Beetner

My father-in-law hated my guts from the first moment I met him, and I can safely say the feeling was mutual. We've been engaged in a cold war standoff ever since.

In fairness to Ol' Chuck, Laura and I got married too quick. We know it now. But we were young and caught up in the romance of it and so it went six weeks from first date to elopement and now, three years later, I think we both wish we'd pumped the brakes a bit. It isn't the six months without sex, or the tiny, bitter arguments that are like foreshocks to the Big One yet to come—it's just that we don't have much in common and we're already out of things to talk about.

Chuck would have been mad at whatever guy came along and took away his Precious Princess. His little P.P. Seriously, that's his nickname for her. It can also stand for Pretty Princess, Perfect Princess and Prize Princess. But I still giggle when I hear it and Laura did not appreciate when I first pointed out that he's calling her Pee-Pee. She told me to grow up.

But I try. With Laura and with Chuck. Because I want it to work. I still see the things that made me fall so hard and so fast for her. And if one way to work my way back into her heart is to make nice with her dad, then I'll do it, damn it. Even if it means spending a weekend at his fishing cabin up in Minnesota.

I'm sure it wasn't his idea to invite me, and I bet he nearly had a heart attack when I said yes. He knows I don't fish. And I suspect Laura has told him how much I hate Minnesota. For an Iowan to go north of the border into enemy territory is like a Yankees fan showing up to Fenway Park in head-to-toe pinstripes.

I'm sure my bringing Laura down to Iowa was another reason Chuck hates me.

But I made the drive up to one of those famous ten thousand lakes. You know what you get with all those lakes? Mosquitos. Millions of them. And what about a bunch of lakes is there to be so proud of? It's one step away from swampland at that point. Might as well be Florida, but with snow.

Don't get me started on that Twin Cities bullshit or why they get to have a baseball team, a football team, and a hockey team—but Iowa gets squat. Just move the Hawkeyes up to the NFL and I bet they beat the Vikings every time.

But I promise to bite my tongue all weekend and talk about pleasant things while stuck in a boat for hours on end with a man who I'm sure would like to use me as bait.

For love, you know.

I pull up to the cabin and it's a simple structure. Nothing fancy for Ol' Chuck. His twenty-year-old Ford Ranger is already parked by the woodpile and there is a wisp of white smoke coming from the chimney. It's dropped thirty degrees from when I left home. This is springtime?

Chuck meets me at the door with an axe in his hand. At first, I'm worried. The idea that this is a ploy to lure me up here into the remote woods so he can kill me doesn't feel like such a stretch. But he shoves the axe forward and says, "Need more wood."

That's the extent of his greeting. He pushes past me and down the steps and around the house. I set my bag inside the front door and go to chop some wood.

Chuck grills steaks and bakes potatoes. Exactly what I expected. Our conversation has improved a little.

"Tomorrow we'll be eating fish," he says. It comes out as a sort of challenge to me to catch my share because if I don't, we'll go hungry.

"Yeah, I guess we will."

His two beers are helping his mood a little. I fully expected alcohol to play a big part in any bonding we might do this weekend, so I go to my suitcase and take out a bottle of bourbon I bought for the trip. Chuck can't help cracking a little smile. It is very good bourbon. I know because I asked the liquor store guy for his best bottle and then when I saw the price tag I said, "Okay, maybe not your best. What's a very good bottle?"

Chuck's a reticent man. Very Midwestern. He likes the sound of the logs on the fire more than my voice, so I don't ruin the atmosphere with any needless chatter.

"Well," he says as he pushes up out of his chair. He tilts his head back and shoots the last of his bourbon. "Got an early morning."

He walks away without a good night. One thing I admire about Chuck is his lack of old man noises. My dad would have grunted and groaned getting up out of that soft leather armchair. Not Chuck.

I go to bed feeling good that bonding has begun.

In the morning he takes me down to a tackle and bait shop to "get me outfitted," which is his way of making a point that I don't own my own fishing gear. He has a rod for me already, but he makes me buy another forty bucks' worth of useless crap while he goes to some special fridge in the back for the good worms. How they are any different from what we could have dug out of the yard, I have no idea. If I'd have brought my own worms from Iowa soil, he'd have chopped me into pieces and added me to the woodpile.

He comes back holding what looks like three takeout containers of Chinese food.

"Gotta have good bait," he says like it's as logical as saying you gotta have air to breathe.

I hold up a bright orange vest. "Do I need life jacket?"

His face pinches like he stepped on a tack. "Life jacket?"

I failed that test. He wants a son-in-law who is a man, not some fraidy-cat scared of drowning in a Minnesota pond that smells like egg salad farts. I fear the ground I gained last night has been lost.

When we turn off the road down the long dirt driveway, we pass the only other house out here that I can see and a woman waves to us from her yard where she is wielding a rake in a futile attempt to stem the tide of debris from the trees. Chuck lifts his hand and waves back.

I have a fleeting thought that Chuck uses this fishing cabin as a love nest for a decades-long affair and if I can prove it maybe I can blackmail him into liking me, or at least acting like he does around Laura. If Chuck gives me a stamp of approval after all this time, Laura might start to love me again.

But if Chuck was going to have an affair, he could do better than rake lady. She is double-wide in her hips, limp graying hair, rosacea on her cheeks. Laura's Mom is still quite attractive. It was one of the things that made me feel good about my choice to marry Laura. Seeing a glimpse of Laura's future had been reassuring. She wasn't destined for gaining a hundred pounds or getting wrinkles as deep as tree bark.

I'd have to find something else to blackmail Chuck with.

"We should've been out an hour ago," Chuck says as he packs store-bought ham sandwiches in a cooler next to a family-size bag of sour cream and onion chips, two cans of Coke, and a six pack of beer.

I'm tempted to remind him that it wasn't my idea to go to the bait shop and force me to buy a bunch of junk I'll never use again or to stop by the sandwich shop because he hasn't made food for himself in fifty years, but instead I nod and lift the cooler to carry down to the water.

There is a short dock, but the boat is on land. It's a flat-bottomed aluminum tub and it sits upside down like a dead animal on the shore. The silver is dull like a dirty nickel.

Chuck hands me two long wooden oars, which are much

heavier than I expect and it makes me drop them. He doesn't say anything but looks at me with all the colossal disappointment of a father whose son just told him he wants to go to art school.

"No motor?" I say.

"Scares the fish." He says it like I should have known that. Like any idiot would have known that. Like I'm the idiot.

Maybe when we get out there he'll start with the beers early and we can get back to the boozy bonding we started last night.

I lift one of the oars in my hands and stand ready as Chuck bends down to flip the boat by himself. He's thick around the middle, but it's a solid thickness, not fatty. Again he doesn't groan or grunt as he lifts, and the boat turns over effortlessly.

I see what I think is a coil of rope where the boat just was, but it moves and it takes me a second to realize it's a snake, startled awake from its shaded sleep. It strikes at Chuck's ankles and he takes one awkward step backward and falls on his backside, then tips over on his shoulder. He's strong and solid, but he's still old.

The snake strikes again and aims for his neck. Later, I'll find out it's a timber rattlesnake, one of only two venomous snakes in Minnesota. The chances of us finding one are about the same as Chuck being struck by lightning, but this is how the weekend is going so far.

It buries its fangs into his neck and I stand there, dumbfounded, watching.

"Hit it. Hit it!" Chuck says in a strangled rasp. I realize I'm holding a weapon and I lift the oar over my head and then I use the same motion I used with the axe to chop wood. Chuck is flailing at the snake and writhing so as I bring the oar down, he twists and the blade of the oar misses the snake and connects with his skull, over his right ear. The sound echoes across the flat lake water.

Chuck is going to be pissed later.

His movements become jerkier, more spasmodic. I lift the oar again and keep my eye on the diamond pattern of the snake as I bring the heavy wooden oar down. Chuck spasms at the last second and again I hit him in the skull. I can feel the bone give and the oar meet a split second of resistance before sinking in.

Chuck stops moving.

I flip the oar and raise it up again as if I am about to plant a flag in a foreign war. I stab the blade down and guillotine the snake in two. Chuck rolls away, with the head of the snake still attached to his neck and about a foot of snake body hanging off and spilling blood.

Somewhere across the lake a bird hoots what would be a beautiful sound, but right then it sounds ominous. Then the silence settles in and that's even worse.

Chuck is still. I'd like to think the venom killed him, but I can see the dent in his head. His hair is thin so it doesn't cover much. There isn't a lot of blood, but the shape of his skull is very, very wrong. His chest is still. His eyes are open and he still looks scared.

I have no idea how to explain this to Laura.

I'm not sure how long I stand there, but I come out of my daze when the oar drops from my hands and lands on my foot. Only falling from waist-high it still hurts and I can't imagine how much force was behind it when I swung it over my head while high on adrenaline and fear of a rattlesnake. It wasn't my brute force that caused the cave-in of Chuck's skull, it was the weight and solid construction of the oar. For all I know Chuck carved them himself out of a solid oak tree.

Nobody can know about this. I'll never get Laura back if she knows I killed her dad, even if it was by accident. My new spouse will be a cellmate as I serve twenty-five-to-life for patricide.

The water beckons. It's flat, dark, deep (I think). I could tell her he fell overboard. No. I could tell her I woke up and he was gone. That's better. If he fell, they'll drag the lake and find him. If he's just gone…

I hear a buzz. Then again. For a second I think it's murder hornets coming for me, because why not add more to this nightmare of a trip? But then I realize it's the phone in his pocket.

I dig it out and he has two new text messages from Laura. In his contacts she is listed as PP.

Is it done yet?

Then I scroll down:

Let me know when that little fucker is gone

I stare at the texts for longer than I stared at Chuck's inert body, trying even harder to make sense of it. I finally decide I need to worry about that later and I need to get rid of Chuck soon. Right now. I decide the axe is a last resort.

I search Chuck's truck for something to help me get rid of his body and I find the perfect thing: two lengths of chain and a tarp. And a cinderblock.

For the third time that morning I stop and think.

That son of a bitch. He was gonna kill me. And Laura knew it.

I reread the texts. She knew. She probably asked him to do it. Oh my God. I accidentally killed him before he could kill me.

I go inside and take a tall slug of the bourbon. He didn't deserve the really good stuff.

It takes me about fifteen minutes to get him wrapped in the tarp and looped with the chains. We went from bonding to bondage in under twenty-four hours. When I finish, I'm sweaty and angry and I hate Minnesota even more.

A car is coming. The engine is old and the dirt road crunches under the tires so I can hear it from a good distance off. I have just enough time to flip the boat back over and cover Chuck. I think I pull a muscle in my back as I do it.

It's the rake lady. She waves at me and I wave back, leaning on one oar for support as the soreness in my back spreads.

She gets out and holds a covered dish in front of her.

"Hey there."

"Hi," I say. I dig the blade of the oar into the dirt to cover the small splash of blood. The snake's or Chuck's or a combo of the two?

"I knew you two were bachelors this weekend, so I brought you a hot dish." She offers it out in front of her like she's showing

195

me a baby she wants me to admire.

Despite the pain in my back, I want to step away from the boat and what is now a crime scene. I drop the oar and take the dish from her and it is indeed hot. I move my hands up to the handles.

"Where's Chuck?"

"Not sure," I say. "He went off into the woods to take care of something to get ready for the fishing. You know how he is."

I don't know and I count on her not knowing either.

"Oh. Well, let him know it's got brats inside and tots on top. His favorite."

I wonder again if he and rake lady ever had an affair.

"Thanks a lot."

"I'm sure you fellas will catch a whole heap, though."

"I don't know. I'm not really a fisherman."

"Oh yeah?"

"I'm from Iowa."

"Oh." She says it as if it explains everything, and also as if I just told her I have six weeks to live.

"Maybe we'll bring you some fish later."

"I love a good lake trout."

"Who doesn't?"

I smile at her, knowing full well that I don't. And that there will be no fish. And that next year's crop will have been feasting on Chuck's bloated body all summer long.

I see rake lady as my first test of whether I can get away with this and I pass. She gets back in her rattling truck and drives away, the hook set with my story. Or alibi, I guess.

Rowing a boat sucks. I can't imagine I'm making less noise and water splash than an engine, so if fish are that easily scared, then I've scared off every fish in this lousy lake. I make it right to the middle. I can't see anyone on shore watching, no other boats. Just bird sounds, mosquitos buzzing constantly and water slapping at the metal hull of the boat.

Getting Chuck up and over the edge, especially after I looped a chain through the cinderblock, almost sends me into the water. I have to crouch low and spread myself wide to calm the rocking after he goes over the side. He sinks fast and just like that, the surface is flat again and I'm there floating on a lake alone with no way back from this. I'll either make it out the other side or I won't. No disguising what I've done, even if the actual killing was an accident, but good luck getting anyone to believe that. Two men who hated each other like we did? Open and shut case.

By the time I row back to shore I'm exhausted, and I sleep for three hours on the couch.

When I wake up I'm starving so I scoop out a serving of hot dish, even though it's gone cold. Still good, though.

My mind refreshed after the sleep, I have a new plan. I kept Chuck's phone. I've reread the texts fifty times now. And I know how to respond. I surprise myself when the idea comes to me. It's not something I ever would have thought of before this weekend. Before learning of their plans for me. But if I can get rid of one body, why not two?

I text Laura back: *It's done. Why don't you come up and see for yourself?*

If I learned anything from Chuck, it's the value of good bait.

THE OPPORTUNIST

Jim Fusilli

Having flown to Grand Forks from Indianapolis, Bob Grayber drove at twilight across the North Dakota border to a Holiday Inn on the outskirts of Westrum, Minnesota, home of Red River Valley Sunflower Inc.

In his room, he kicked off his shoes and emptied his briefcase. Papers strewn around him, he sat cross-legged on the queen-sized bed with his MacBook Air in his lap to review his PowerPoint presentation for the Red River Valley management team. Then he showered and dressed in business casual. At the front desk, he asked the clerk to recommend a restaurant. A steakhouse up the road, she told him, about a mile or so. Fleece zip-up and sweater vest over a collared shirt, Grayber decided to walk.

A gentle wind escorted Grayber along Highway 2, which ran flat to the horizon and was dotted only occasionally with streetlights. Grayber marched on through early October darkness toward Griggs' Roadhouse up ahead. Stars began to flicker in the black sky.

Though not a single car passed him, he found the parking lot peppered with SUVs and pickups, mud-caked due to labor on western Minnesota's cattle farms, crop farms, dairy farms, poultry farms, and so on. Grayber anticipated such company while in Westrum: Red River Valley was the region's largest processor and supplier of confection sunflower seed items including in-shell

199

and kernel products, bird food, and innovative hybrid seed. From three operating facilities in Minnesota, North Dakota, and South Dakota, its distribution network extended across the heartland and into Canada. DVN AG, Grayber's employer, had targeted it for acquisition: based at its U.S. corporate branch, he was appointed point on the early-stage negotiations.

Fast approaching his thirtieth birthday and still as fit as he was when he wrestled in high school, he was full of enthusiasm for his assignment. He felt he had the support of the parent corporation in Germany and at the holding company where he was director, Business Development. His admin aside, he was a one-man department, but he spoke with colleagues in Erfurt almost every day. They thought him brash and cagey, but wasn't that the American way?

The hostess at Griggs' led Grayber to a booth suitable for four. On the journey through the restaurant, which was dressed like a saloon in the Old West, he took note of what the diners were eating. He ordered a sixteen-ounce cowboy steak medium rare, a plain baked potato, and pinto beans. Out of loyalty to his employer's native culture, he added a stein of Spaten Optimator, a double bock that, even with his hearty meal in his stomach, left him a little bit tipsy. He paid the check with the company Amex, then started his trek back along Highway 2 to the Holiday Inn which, when he stepped into the colder-than-chilly Westrum night, seemed a lot further away than the distance he had walked about an hour earlier.

He was about halfway back to the hotel when a white SUV heading west pulled next to him, its tires crunching gravel that had spilled onto the blacktop.

"Bob?" said the passenger. He was about Grayber's age, brown hair, dark eyes, jutting underbite; white dress shirt, no tie, under a suit jacket.

Though the SUV was rolling to keep pace with Grayber, the driver leaned over. Blond, icy blue eyes, broad across the shoulders, big hands on the wheel. A few years older than his

200

passenger. "Erik Magnussen."

Grayber stopped.

"Carl Haugen," said the passenger, who reached out and tapped the Red River Valley Sunflower logo on the door.

"Erik. Carl," said Bob Grayber.

Chief Operating Officer and Vice President, Business Development, respectively.

"Hop in, Bob," Magnussen said.

Grayber cast a casual glance at the Holiday Inn sign above the deserted highway and opened the back door.

The hostess put the three men in the same booth Grayber had occupied only moments ago. Magnussen and Haugen sat side by side, facing Grayber whose back was to the remainder of the room.

"What'll you have, Bob?" asked Haugen when the waitress arrived.

"Another Optimator?" she suggested.

"Optimator," Haugen said to his boss. "Bob here favors high test."

"Better make it coffee," Grayber replied.

"Three," Magnussen said. "So when did you get in, Bob?"

Grayber explained, then said, "How did you know I came here?"

"Where else?" Haugen said, as Magnussen held Grayber in his gaze. "Best steakhouse in town."

Haugen's youngest sister worked reception at the Holiday Inn. As instructed, she directed Grayber to Griggs' and then notified her brother.

"Good ribeye," Grayber allowed.

"You've been to St. Elmo's?" Haugen again, mentioning Indianapolis's landmark notable for its incendiary shrimp-cocktail sauce. "When the Germans visit, is that your go-to?"

In fact, it was. But Grayber replied only with a smile.

"Bob," said COO Magnussen, "what do you need from us to help you through tomorrow?"

Grayber waited as the coffees arrived. "We see it more as a way for you to get to know us. As I understand it, you met with our people at IPM Essen."

The world's leading trade fair for horticulture held annually in Germany.

Nodding, Magnussen said, "Made an impression."

"As did Red River Valley."

Haugen said, "Mind if I ask how wide you're shopping?"

"Well," said Grayber, "if you're at IPM Essen, you know we're seeking to expand our product line and distribution network in North America."

Magnussen circled his spoon in his coffee. "What's the level of ambition?"

"DVN wants to be the next Bayer? BASF?" Haugen asked.

"I think we'd like to expand our product line and distribution network. And add good people who know the North American markets."

"Refresh my memory, Bob," said Magnussen. "Has anyone at DVN spoken to my father-in-law?"

"Was he in Essen?"

"Arne doesn't travel much," Haugen said.

Grayber knew Magnussen was married to the daughter of Red River Valley's president Arne Hebler. He had mentioned it at the trade show; the Germans interpreted his casual remark as an assertion of authority. In his research, Grayber discovered that Magnussen earned his MBA at Northwestern's Kellogg School of Management and had been a regional sales management at ConAgra. Marriage wasn't his only qualification for his job as Red River Valley's number two.

"As far as I know, there's been no contact between AVN and Red River Valley besides my emails with Carl. And our admins, of course."

"You'll want time with Arne?" Haugen asked.

"Won't he be at the meeting?"

"If he's up to it," Magnussen said.

Grayber had to ask. "Is everything all right?"

He already knew the answer: Hebler lost his wife, Agnetha, to COVID-19. According to one of Grayber's contacts at the Indiana Farm Service Agency, Hebler was adrift. Magnussen was running the business—and was looking to sell.

Magnussen leaned in. "Look, Bob, you've done your due diligence. You know our situation. Leave it to me to persuade Arne."

"And the board?"

"The board is Arne, me, and Louise."

"I'm sorry. Louise?"

"My wife."

Louise Hebler Magnussen, with her degree in Art History from Oberlin, had been a curator at the Art Institute of Chicago. Grayber had figured she'd back a sale so she could return to a world of her choosing. Erik Magnussen was born in Scarsdale, New York. Northwest Minnesota wasn't in his blood.

"Where does she stand on our discussions?"

Magnussen said, "She's hands off, Bob."

Haugen said nothing, but let his eyes drift.

Grayber returned to his rental car near the entrance to Red River Valley's long, tidy one-story headquarters. Under a vast gray sky, tall, stout silos stood sentry at the edge of an enormous field that stretched farther than Grayber could see. Pausing for a moment to watch as threshers took down the eye-high sunflowers, clouds of dust in their wake, he reflected on the miracle plant: a self-perpetuating product, every inch of it had a commercial purpose. And it was remarkably profitable. The global sunflower oil market alone topped twenty-one billion dollars in annual sales.

In addition to Magnussen and Haugen, the morning's meeting

had included the vice presidents of the Sales, Finance, and Supply Chain Management departments as well as the Senior Manager of R&D, whose appearance disappointed Grayber: She sat in for Arne Hebler. Though he was Red River Valley's president and CEO, Hebler continued to be deeply involved in research and development. In fact, he was Dr. Arne Hebler, an internationally renowned agronomist who had bred several hybrids that produced an oil rich in linoleic acid the industry preferred.

Magnussen had teed up the meeting as if Grayber had happened to be in Westrum, failing to explain why his guest carried in a carton of DVN annual reports and bound printouts of his presentation. The Finance vice president knew better. "Mr. Grayber, DVN stock is up this morning in Frankfurt and on the NASDAQ on word that you're looking to expand in the U.S.," she said. "Is that why you're here?"

Haugen tried to interject, but Grayber, standing at the head of the table, said, "Yes."

Frowns and quizzical expressions all around. Haugen shifted uncomfortably, but Magnussen didn't move.

Grayber said, "As you suggest, Ellen, it's not a secret that DVN is eager to grow our North American business. But, as Carl knows, in Business Development, we cast a wide net and scale back from there."

"Who else are you meeting with?" the Sales VP asked.

"I'm going to decline to answer that. For obvious reasons."

Soon Magnussen called the meeting to its end. Grayber shook hands with each member of the group as they departed.

Haugen said, "Sorry about that stock market question."

"Not at all," Grayber replied as he unplugged his laptop from the projector. "She was right to ask."

He continued to pack as Magnussen gestured for Haugen to close the conference room door.

"What's your next step, Bob?" Magnussen asked.

"How would you describe your level of interest?"

"Without seeing the numbers? I'd leave it at we're a good fit for DVN."

"I can't disagree," Grayber replied.

"Tell me what you need. I'll facilitate."

Grayber said thanks. "I'll tell Erfurt we should be disposed to continue discussions."

"I can review your draft report. Punch it up, if that helps."

Grayber shook his head. "I'll get back to you asap."

Now Grayber put his computer bag in the rental car's trunk. Rather than return to Highway 2 and the hotel, he turned onto a winding route that ran past the grinding combines toward Red River Valley Sunflower's R&D headquarters. Resembling an aircraft hangar, the humpback facility was home to Hebler Laboratories; thus, Grayber hoped to find Arne Hebler at work, in a lab coat rather than a business suit. Grayber wasn't about to return to Indianapolis without a sense of the company president and employee the Germans valued most.

He was greeted not by a receptionist or one of the dozen or so scientists and technicians on site, but by Louise Hebler Magnussen.

"Hello, Bob," she said, hand outstretched. She was tall and sturdy with short auburn hair beneath a kerchief; a blue down vest over a red flannel shirt, jeans, and mud-stained boots whose untied laces flapped with each step she took. Grayber knew she was forty-four—and thus about ten years older than her husband—but she presented not as the somber, purposeful curator depicted in an old *Art in America* article, but as a farmer full of spark and grit.

"Mrs. Magnussen," Grayber said in return.

"Oh, please. It's Louise. And, you should know that we're not selling. Has anybody told you, Bob? We're not selling."

Louise Magnussen insisted Grayber ride with her to see the farm.

"We have eleven hundred and eighty acres here. Almost two

miles. Golden sunflowers facing east to catch the morning sun."

"I'm sorry I missed it." The remaining sunflowers were brown, desiccated, and ready for surrender.

In his suit and tie, Grayber pressed a hand against the dashboard as the old Jeep bounced him over every rut in the road.

She said, "And since you're the type to go deep so I'll say it before you do. You're thinking I'm here since my mom's death, but can't wait to get back to Chicago. Or that while I'm here I can pretend I'm in Arles in southwest France with Van Gogh, the two of us surrounded by his inspiration."

"No, I didn't—"

"Thing of it is, Bob, I was raised here, among thousands and thousands and thousands of sunflowers, before I saw any of his studies. My parents and Westrum made it possible for me to know and feel what Vincent's art wants us to know and feel. I love this place."

Grayber continued to rattle as the Jeep hurdled toward the processing plants.

"Look around, won't you? A month ago, nothing but big, bright sunflowers. Soon, nothing but rich, raw soil coated in frost. Next spring, nothing but sunflowers under an unimaginably beautiful blue sky. No, we're not selling."

"I hear you," Grayber managed, tie flapping, his bones shaking. "But can you at least slow down?"

"Hell no, Bob."

Eventually, they skidded onto a gravel turnoff to the processing plants. The dust-coated workers paid Louise Magnussen no mind as they guided grain trucks loaded with seeds toward the welcoming bays.

Grayber unsnapped his seat belt. "That," he said, "was invigorating."

She leaped from her seat and met Grayber at the front bumper. "Do you need the 'my father built this' speech?"

He caught his breath. "There seems to be a fundamental misunderstanding between us. DVN sees Red River Valley

Sunflower as your father, the lab, and the sales force."

"Say more, Bob," she said as she tucked a strand of hair behind her ear.

"In Germany, DVN has plenty of management types who can come here and run the business for you." He counted on his fingers. "Graduates of Agricultural Sciences programs at UC Davis, Cornell, Purdue, Texas A&M. DVN isn't looking to big foot Red River Valley. They—*we*—need your father's mind, Louise. His R&D. His reputation. Your people who know FDA and EPA. And the sales force."

She leaned a hip against the Jeep. "And where do you fit in?"

"Not an issue. I'm going home. Indiana born and bred. DVN pulled me out of USDA and I'm sticking with them. Even if Erfurt beckons."

"Why did they pick you? I imagine the Indiana Farm Service Agency has more than a few go-getters."

"They say I know how to size up people."

"Do you?"

"I assess corporate culture and look for a clean fit. We already know what Red River Valley can bring to DVN and we know you know we can bring investment dollars for whatever your father needs for his lab and funds to get your product to markets you can't reach. Given that, Louise, why else am I here?"

"To put an American face on a German multinational."

"All right. And?"

"To see who can stays and who should go."

Grayber smiled. "I can only recommend."

She paused as another grain truck wheezed to a halt near the bay.

"And you're going home? You don't want Carl Haugen's job?"

"Going home to the Hoosiers, St. Elmo's shrimp cocktail, and my mom's sugar-cream pie," said Grayber, whose mother died eleven years ago.

"Before you leave," she said, "you should meet my father."

"I'd like that."

They returned to their seats in the Jeep. Grayber tugged his seat belt tight.

"I won't test you on the drive back, Bob."

"Grateful. But when the Germans come, do it. They love that cowboy stuff."

She shifted into gear and started the trip back to the lab.

Grayber was waiting near the gate for his plane to be prepped for its return to Indianapolis. A half hour, said the agent, but Grayber, an experienced traveler, knew it was likely to be longer. He took out his laptop and began to sketch out his report. Every now and then, he sipped coffee from a Styrofoam cup and popped a piece of a cinnamon roll into his mouth. He might've preferred to return to Griggs' for another ribeye, but he knew it was best if he got out of Grand Forks on the last flight.

Grayber had already prepared an Excel chart with the names and titles of Red River Valley's senior management in a vertical row. He reviewed it now, putting faces to names, recalling comments and body language. During their conversation, Arne Hebler made it plain that whatever were Red River Valley's insufficiencies, they weren't the fault of its personnel. They would all do better with an influx of funding and a sturdier bottom line. If the Germans could prove they could make the fit work, he would listen. As for what DVN had in Indiana, a holding company was a layer of management Hebler and Red River Valley didn't need.

"I'm going to argue with you there, Dr. Hebler," Grayber said.

"Wouldn't expect you not to," he replied. He wasn't wearing a lab coat, but a tattered Red River Valley ball cap over a mess of silver hair and a brown flannel-lined jacket over a shirt and tie. Sighing now and then, he seemed fatigued and perhaps Magnussen was right that he had lost his zeal for the business after his wife Agnetha's death. But Grayber saw that he would fight for his company's survival and several truckloads of euros wasn't going to change his mind.

"Bob doesn't want to come work for us, Dad," Louise Magnussen said.

"No, I suppose not," Hebler replied, inching away. The meeting had continued in a corridor outside a room of technicians at waist-high workbenches. "Man who turns down a second beer to keep his focus has his priorities."

At the airport, his eyes on the laptop screen, Grayber felt someone drop into the seat next to him.

"You knifed me, Bob," said Erik Magnussen in a Red River Valley windbreaker and pressed jeans. "You came out here and you knifed me in the back."

Grayber shut his laptop lid. "How so?"

"You made the deal with Arne. You boxed me out."

"Nope."

"DVN wants the lab and the sales force. You said management is disposable."

"There's no deal yet. And when there is one, DVN will decide who in management is worth keeping."

"You really think the Germans can come here and push me out? With what I know?"

"Yes."

"If you think that, you're just another paper pusher."

"'Paper pusher?' We're all paper pushers. Except the lab techs and the sales force. And your father-in-law. The man who built the thing."

A crowd began to form at the boarding area. The plane was ready. Grayber had gold status. He could board as soon as he was called.

"Never once, Erik, did you ask me about the staff. After IPM Essen, the Germans gave me two instructions. Secure Dr. Hebler and marginalize you, the opportunist. By the way, it's the same word in German. Opportunist. *Der opportunist*? I don't know..."

"You cut me out and I will sue you and your Germans."

"Well, they have a lot of lawyers," Grayber said as he gathered his overnight bag, "but let's be honest. You want a buyout. Now that you know Louise isn't going to sell and move on, you'll take the cash and run. Your only play is to try to make yourself indispensable to due diligence and the closing. But I've a sense Louise and the head of Finance can handle that."

"Louise couldn't read a balance sheet on a bet."

"Not cool, Erik. But she seemed pleased that we're willing to underwrite the Agnetha Hebler Museum of Art downtown. Think DVN can get the Neue Pinakothek in Munich to arrange a loan of Van Gogh's *Sunflowers*?"

"And you think she's all you need. What you don't know."

"She can call on Haugen. He's already let us know he's our guy. Maybe he's a little too 'hail fellow well met' but he'll save me a trip or two out here when it's ten below."

"Good luck relying on that clown."

Grayber backpedaled toward the gate. "You know, it's amazing. The Germans had you pegged all along. 'Arne isn't up to it.' 'Louise can't read a balance sheet.' 'Carl is a clown.'"

"And you're an asshole."

"Could be." Grayber shrugged. "But when this is said and done, I'll have a job. And I won't have tried to sell out my wife, my father-in-law, and my colleagues."

Grayber dumped his coffee and the remains of his bun into the trash can as the gate agent called his row.

THE FAVOR

Raquel V. Reyes

The suitcase in the trunk of my Corolla was giving me mal de ojo. I knew I'd get pulled over for some bullshit mierda and end up in jail for something I had no hand in. *There goes my P.I. license.*

Why did I open my big mouth? *Sorry, I can't help you. I got an out-of-town job.* I should've just left it at that, but no, I say, *I'll be in Chicago.*

That's perfect. St. Paul's close to Chicago.

Ok, so like I was casi seguro, it wasn't drugs.

Listen, mamacita.

Don't call me that I'm not your mama or your girlfriend.

Don't touch the bags. Let the guys on the other end move 'em and keep 'em level.

One of Jefe's bare-knuckle fighters that had taken one too many bell ringers had carried the super-sized luggage and laid it in my trunk. The suspension had squeaked. El Jefe didn't deal in consumables. He was a "people person," exclusively fighters and strippers. How much money does a guy have to owe to end up in a suitcase?

Damn, the smell. This guy's diet must've been pure garlic. Apestoso. I lowered the window. Why couldn't this favor have been in January instead of July?

Near Eau Claire, I took the first exit off I-94 that advertised

211

an independent station. I always paid cash. Leave no electronic trace was my motto. I went into the store, did my business, then grabbed a pop and a water before paying the tired-of-everything Hmong owner for nine gallons.

The guy behind me licked his lips. I was dressed for New Jersey, not Wisconsin. The stars on the back pockets of my cut-offs were getting looks like they'd never seen the Puerto Rican flag or a nice ass. Yo perreo sola, asshole.

A very blonde couple passed by and wrinkled their noses like they were smelling trash. I wanted to flip them the bird, but the breeze changed, and I got a whiff of it, too. I went back inside and bought all the air fresheners they had. I drove down a side road and popped the trunk. The smell of charcoal, grease, and garlic hit me like a sucker punch.

Did they burn this guy? Holy shit. I ripped open the deodorizers and planted a forest. One of the cardboard trees slid off the bulging Samsonite. It landed in a pool of liquid. *Fuck.* The trunk was lined with three mil contractor bags. A dark spot grew on the corner of the big bag. It wasn't blood, but bodies oozed all kinds of gross liquids. I prayed the plastic lining held.

I exited the highway at Lexington Parkway and found my way to Marshall Avenue. Checking the handwritten directions, I looked for the house number.

This feels wrong. Way too nice and across from a park.

Am I being set up? Broad daylight.

I flipped the paper over—no other instructions. What had El Jefe said?

Angel will be waiting for you.

I heard a drum that reminded me of the island. I stepped around the red brick structure and saw a tent and a banner. Three women danced to the bomba rhythm, making waves with the hems of their cotton skirts. A few guys were setting up tables and chairs. I approached the group.

"Estoy buscando a Ángel."

A man in a yellow T-shirt put his hand out. His shirt said

Borikén Center on it.

*This does not feel like the place to dump a body or the guy to
do it.*

"I'm Angel. Are you Ossie?"

"Yeah, I've got a delivery for you."

He whistled, and the other guys came over. They rubbed
their hands together and slapped each other on the backs.

I opened the trunk and got a laugh about the cardboard forest.
Angel unzipped the smaller bag. I looked around for witnesses.
Inside were two large pots with duct-taped lids nestled by
evaporated bags of dry ice.

Fuckin' A. What parts were in there? Hands? The head? Shit.

Angel's muscle took the pots. He told them to hurry back to
help with el puerco.

I was sure that wasn't the dead guy's name but calling him a
pig made me wonder if what he'd done to get dead wasn't
about betting debt. Maybe he stepped over the line at the club.
El Jefe had a rep for protecting "his girls," which didn't make
him a saint because it was all about the Benjamins. But yeah,
certain women exalted him as a protective papa, a family man
even.

Angel moved the big bag closer. He took one end, and his
buddy took the other. As they lifted, the handle broke. The car
bounced from the dropped weight. The guy started to unzip the
suitcase.

"Hey, do you think that's smart? There's a lot of people
here." Cars queued to park.

Angel laughed. "This is why they're here. It's an El Jefe
special."

He flapped the top open. Inside, under layers of tight plastic
wrap and encircled by empty dry ice bags and one melting regular
ice bag, was the fattest porker I'd ever seen.

"Lechon asado!"

*I've been shitting myself for nineteen hours, driving from
Elizabeth, New Jersey thinking I got a dead guy in my car, and*

it's a fucking cooked pig for a party.

"You've never tried Tio's lechon? You got to stay and have some. There's arroz con gandules and pastelón."

"El Jefe is your uncle?"

"Yeah. ¿Quieres una cerveza? We got Medalla."

THE FINAL CURTAIN
Mary Dutta

Prince Charming never could hold his liquor. He stumbled through the choreography, grabbing onto fellow cast mates to keep his balance, always managing to clutch a woman's chest or backside to steady himself.

"The steps haven't changed since Hubert Humphrey's first run for office," one of his targets said. "How hard is it to keep up?"

The cast of fairy tale characters beat a rhythm on the wooden stage. "This isn't amateur hour, people," the director said. "Let's see that again and try not to suck this time." Twenty repetitions later, Prince Charming was not the only one fumbling. The director threw his hands up in surrender and dismissed them. "I want everyone here early tomorrow morning, everyone prepared, everyone doing their damnedest to give The Story Book Playhouse the farewell performance it deserves. It's the final curtain for the Iron Range's most beloved theater, people."

The cast gave him a desultory round of applause then straggled down to grab their belongings from where they were piled in the theater's front rows. A cloud of dust formed as the dirty velvet seats flipped closed.

Bethany was the last to leave the stage. "Nice to see you again," she said to the director. A prolonged pause stretched between them as he looked at her, clearly waiting for a spark of recognition that never ignited. "Nice to see you too, ah…"

"Bethany," she said. "It's okay, I know you've had a lot of chorus members over the years."

"Bethany, of course," said the director. "I remember you. Good to have you back." She knew he was only acting as if he knew her but didn't call him on it. She clattered down the stairs and retrieved her bag.

She caught up with the rest of the actors in the lobby, examining pictures of summer stock casts over the years. The women bemoaned their own lost looks while telling each other how little they had changed. Prince Charming pointed out the stitches on his forehead from the time a scenery flat had fallen on him.

Cinderella leaned in to examine a cast photo. "Who's that blurry person in the last row?" she said.

"Me," said Bethany, insinuating herself into the knot of people. "I always seem to turn my head just when someone takes a picture."

Cinderella looked down at her then back to the photo. "You've changed your hair," she said.

"My hair is the only thing I haven't changed," said her fairy godmother. "I started taking the most amazing weight loss supplements. I'm actually selling them now. I brought some free samples for everyone."

She pulled a handful of plastic packets from her bag and offered them around, extolling the supplements' virtues all the way outside to where the smokers clustered in front of a For Rent sign plastered on the theater's facade. Prince Charming joined them, taking a long drag of his cigarette and exhaling. He squinted through the smoke, his glance flickering past Bethany to focus on Cinderella.

He walked over and slung an arm over her shoulders. "Well, if it isn't our own state fair dairy royalty, Princess Kay of the Milky Way?" he said. "And her faithful companion, Babe the Blue Ox," he added, gesturing at the fairy godmother. "Still packing in the Juicy Lucys, I see." The godmother flushed, and shifted her bag to mask her stomach.

He laughed as Cinderella wriggled out from under his grip. Bethany flinched at the familiar braying sound. "Who needs a drink?" he said, heading for his car. "First round's on Cinderella."

Hurley's hadn't changed. Same sticky floor. Same flat beer. Same scratchy jukebox.

The cast slid into their old booths in the back, a tighter squeeze than twelve years earlier. Bethany couldn't fit in so pulled a chair up to the end of the table.

"Hey," Prince Charming called to Cinderella from the next booth. "We're still here," He pointed at their initials carved into the table. "Interested in a second act?"

Cinderella barely glanced over her shoulder then twisted back around without comment.

"That was quite the showmance, right?" Bethany said to the woman on her right.

"They were hot and heavy that whole summer," the woman said. "We were all so jealous." The beer and reminiscences flowed, the details of long-gone summer romances getting more intimate as the evening progressed.

Bethany laughed along. "I remember that," she said as the pitchers emptied and filled. "That guy from where was it, up north?"

"Right," her neighbor said, "the one with the really big..." she paused dramatically... "pontoon." Her companions tittered. Bethany kept her own stories to herself.

The cast spilled out into the parking lot before last call. Bethany lingered, watching people leave until only Prince Charming and one other actor were left. The prince leaned against his crookedly parked car under the halo of a mercury vapor lamp. Suddenly, he charged at his companion with a wild swing. The other man sidestepped his approach and Prince Charming landed on the pavement. The actor looked down at him and walked away. Bethany watched the prone prince's motionless figure for a while before turning and heading for her car.

Cinderella lifted her skirt for Prince Charming to try on the glass slipper. He ran his hand up her leg until it disappeared. "That's far enough," she said and kicked at him. He fit the slipper onto her extended foot and stood, dropping his script in the process. The pages floated down and fanned across the floor.

"You should be off book, people," the director said. "Let's try not to screw this up, shall we?"

As the prince bent over to pick up the pages a flask fell from his pocket. He managed to kick it into the wings in his stumbling efforts to retrieve his papers then walked after it. The director watched him go, making no attempt to stop him. "They say never to work with children or animals," he said. "They should add has-beens to the list.

"All right, moving on, Steadfast Tin Soldier," the director said, gesturing. "Your fireplace will be stage left, right about here." A slight performer hit his mark and flung his arms wide. Flames leapt from the palms of his hands.

The director hurried toward him, waving both hands. "We are not rehearsing with flash paper," he said. "We barely have enough for the performance."

The theater barely had enough of a lot of things, the cast had noticed. Audience seating, for one, the balcony having been condemned years before. The lighting rig barely had enough functioning fixtures to illuminate the stage. The cast barely had enough costumes to get everyone in character. They had raided the wardrobe room, looking for anything that would suit their roles and fit their current physiques.

Prince Charming sported a plumed hat and a cape, most likely the only elements of his old costume that he could still fit into. Cinderella's fairy godmother kept showing everyone how loose her dress was thanks to the supplements she was peddling from the trunk of her car. Cinderella's old gown, Bethany noted, still looked as though it had been fitted by magic wand. She appeared flawless, as long as you stayed far enough away not to see the stains and tears.

The fairy godmother stopped her running sales pitch. "I smell smoke," she said.

"It's just the flash paper," someone said.

"No, the curtain's on fire." She pointed back to where smoke was now clearly visible in the wing on stage right.

The director ran offstage and returned with a fire extinguisher. Prince Charming, holding a lit cigarette, stood aside as its foam soaked the smoldering curtain behind him.

"Are you insane?" the director said. "You know you can't smoke in here."

"These things are supposed to be flame retardant," Prince Charming said as he ground out his cigarette on the stage floor. "Why is the curtain burning in the first place?"

"We haven't had the money to redo the coating lately. You're lucky the fire extinguisher still worked."

"I'm lucky?" Prince Charming said. "You'll be lucky if I don't report you to the city. They could close you down."

"Well, we'll be closed permanently before city hall opens on Monday morning," said the director, "so good luck with that."

The rest of the cast shifted their weight and exchanged glances as the two men glared at each other.

"Maybe—" the tin soldier started to say.

The director cut him off. "We'll break for fifteen minutes," he said. "Come back ready to work."

The actors scattered. Bethany headed downstairs, eventually wandering into the prop room. She examined the objects on the shelves, picking up a magic mirror and surveying herself. In the mirror's reflection she saw Cinderella come through the door behind her. "Oh," Cinderella said, "I was looking for someone else."

"Prince Charming?" said Bethany.

"Aren't we all?" said Cinderella, and laughed.

Bethany held up the mirror. "I remember this being bigger," she said.

"Remember the woman who ran this place?" Cinderella said. "Sure, she had that..."

"Shih tzu," Cinderella said. "I think it bit everyone in the cast at some point."

"I still have scars from that summer," said Bethany. She put down the mirror and picked up a plastic apple. "Catch," she called, tossing the prop fruit. Cinderella brought her hand up, her bracelet's comedy/tragedy mask charm swinging from the apple's impact. Bethany wondered if she still believed she would make it to the Guthrie Theater.

"Take a bite," said Bethany. "It won't kill you unless you're Snow White."

"I'm many things," said Cinderella, "but Snow White ain't one of them." She looked at her watch. "We'd better get back. After that curtain fire I'm not sure how long the director can hold it together."

The lead cast reassembled to run through a dance sequence. Couples twirled through a waltz as the director clapped time, shedding fragments of lace and sequins as they spun. When the music stopped, Prince Charming and Cinderella stood center stage. He pulled her closer, his hands sinking through layers of tulle to grab her rear. Cinderella broke their embrace and pushed him away. He stumbled back and one leg crashed through the trap door that suddenly opened under him.

"Whoa," the tin soldier shouted and rushed forward. Cast members put their hands under Prince Charming's arms and hauled him out of the hole.

"Why don't you watch what you're doing," the soldier said.

The prince drew himself up and patted the other actor on the head. "And why don't you head back to Dinkytown, little man. You're not needed here."

The director stepped between them. "Who unlocked that

door?" he said, looking around the group. No one answered.

"The place is falling apart," the fairy godmother said. "It probably just gave way."

"Right," the director said, "someone call the carpenter. Everyone else move upstage and stay there." The cast moved to the rear of the stage, undoing the director's carefully planned blocking. Murmurs rose as they crowded together.

"Focus up, people," the director said. "This show goes on tomorrow, stage or no stage. Rapunzel," he called, "do you have your hair?" A woman stepped out onto a balcony above, clutching a yellow mass.

"This wig has had it," she said. "If let down my hair, it's going to fall apart."

"Then Rapunzel, Rapunzel," said Prince Charming, "let down your pants." He laughed his braying laugh. No one joined in.

"This theater now has a zero-tolerance policy for sexual harassment," the director said. "Any more comments like that and you're out of the show." He didn't notice Bethany edging into the wings. She stood there, one hand on her stomach, the other on her chest, taking deep breaths, watching the action on stage until the director called "Chorus."

Bethany stood in a spotlight center stage, taking in the view she had never enjoyed in an actual production. She was ready for her star turn. No Cinderella or Sleeping Beauty for her. She was there to play out a nightmare, not a fairy tale.

She heard the theater's door open on its unoiled hinges and headed for the scaffolding holding the stage's lighting rig. Prince Charming strolled down from the back of the house, right on time for the nonexistent early call Bethany texted him about the previous night. He headed straight for the spotlight and struck a pose.

"Hello," he shouted. "Where is everybody?"

The spotlight went dark, then another light shone down to

his left. He stepped into it and looked up into the darkness, shielding his eyes. The light swept away and he followed it to its new spot.

"Who's up there?" He stepped back to crane his neck further just as a can light crashed down onto the spot where he had been standing.

"Hey!" he shouted. "What the hell are you doing?"

Bethany entered, stage left. "You don't remember me, do you?" she said.

Prince Charming looked her up and down and shook his head. He gestured at the broken light and grinned. "Are you trying to get my attention? Let me guess, we hooked up once upon a time. Is that why you got me here alone? Interested in a second act?"

"You sexually assaulted me," said Bethany.

He dropped the smile.

"Twelve years ago," Bethany said, "right here in this theater." He stared at her, jaw clenched. "I told the director, and the police," said Bethany, "and nobody believed me because your girlfriend said you were with her that night."

"I don't know what you're talking about. I've never assaulted anyone." He stepped closer. "You're the one who attacked me, with that light. And that trap door, I bet." He fingered the faint scar on his forehead. "Were you crazy enough to drop that flat on me back in the day? What the hell is your problem?"

"I've been acting like I was okay all this time," Bethany said, ignoring him. "But I refuse to do that now. You need to pay."

He reached out and grabbed her wrist. "Tell you what. You're not going to tell anyone else about that supposed assault, and as a favor I won't say anything about your lunatic attacks on me."

Bethany twisted free. "You don't control me anymore."

Prince Charming lunged at her, putting a hand over her mouth and pulling her into the wings. She could smell the singed curtain mixed with his sweat and alcohol. "I don't control you?" He laughed as he pinned her down at the base of the stairs to

Rapunzel's tower. Bethany felt the cold metal step cutting into her back.

Summoning every self-defense tactic she'd learned since the summer of her attack, she managed to roll him off. She couldn't get past him and away, so she half crawled up the steps, kicking at him as he grabbed at her ankles. She reached the top of the stairs, and sprinted down the short catwalk to the tower. She looked around the theater, but no one materialized to help her.

Prince Charming appeared at the end of the catwalk. He moved toward her and she backed up against the balcony, her hands in a defensive position. "Skol," he said, taking a long pull from his flask. "Give it up, Bethany, you're out of options."

"She's not Bethany." Cinderella stood at the top of the stairs.

Prince Charming assumed a neutral facial expression and relaxed his shoulders. He turned to face Cinderella.

"What do you mean?" he said.

"I remember Bethany," Cinderella said. "She was as tall as I am. That kept bothering me."

Prince Charming looked between the women.

"Then who is she?" he asked.

"She worked on the tech crew," said Cinderella, walking down the catwalk. "You assaulted her and you don't even remember her name."

"What are you talking about?" Prince Charming said.

Cinderella ignored him. "I believe you now," she said to Bethany. "That summer, he said he didn't do it. He said you lied."

"Shut up," said Prince Charming.

Cinderella kept talking. "That's why I said he was with me the night he attacked you," she said. "Because I believed him. I didn't think he was that good an actor. I'm sorry."

"You're both nuts," Prince Charming said. "What are you doing here, anyway?"

"I got a text about an early call."

"That was me," said Bethany. "I wanted both of you to

answer for what you did to me, and to stop you from hurting anyone else." She began to inch her way from the balcony toward Cinderella.

"You're not going anywhere," said Prince Charming. He grabbed her arm and slammed her against the painted tower wall.

"Don't touch her," Cinderella said. She wrenched his arm away and sent him spinning into the balcony railing. The flask flew from his hand, amber liquid arcing across the space to splatter the plywood set. The railing creaked loudly, swung wide, and detached. He fell twenty feet to the stage below.

Bethany stood immobile, staring down at Prince Charming's lifeless body. She felt a tug on her arm.

"We have to go," said Cinderella. "Come on, before anyone comes." They ran down the stairs and out the theater's fire door to the alley running alongside the building. "Listen," said Cinderella, "we're going to wait for everyone to arrive and we're going to go in the front door of the theater with them. First me, then you. We're going to be as shocked as everyone else when they find his body. It's got to be the performance of a lifetime. Can you do it?"

Bethany nodded.

"Say it," Cinderella said.

"I can do it."

Cinderella gripped both Bethany's arms, her fingers digging white impressions into the skin. "Then Bethany is going to walk out of this theater and disappear, okay?" Cinderella said. "She's going to head out for the Boundary Waters or cruise away down the Mississippi. And you'll go back to your real life and put all of this behind you. Just like you planned. The police will think he was messing around and fell. And if they start to question that, they'll have plenty of suspects. Nobody liked Prince Charming. And they'll never find you because you don't exist."

Bethany nodded again.

Cinderella walked to the mouth of the alley and looked

around the corner. "People are starting to show up," she said. "I'm going in. Wait a few minutes before you follow me."

"What about you?" said Bethany.

"I'm an actress," said Cinderella. "And I already know how to lie to the police."

She started to walk away, then looked back at Bethany. "We're even now," she said and stepped out of the alley.

Bethany stood still, eyes closed, hands on her stomach and chest, breathing deeply. She heard a scream from inside the theater. It was her cue. She had one last scene to play before her final curtain. She stepped into the theater and heard Cinderella say: "He must have been falling down drunk. He never could hold his liquor."

FORLORN LAKE
Edith Maxwell

Geneva Larsen hit the brakes of her old Volvo, peering through the December gloaming at the name of the small store in her hometown of Forlorn Lake.

Ralph's Grocery.

She nearly went into a skid on the icy road. She steered into it, instead. Glad she hadn't lost her Minnesota driving mojo, despite how long she'd lived in balmy southern Indiana.

She shivered at seeing the store sign. Just what she didn't need after having driven for twelve hours like hell itself was chasing her. It kind of was, if hell was embodied in a manipulative, controlling, soon-to-be-ex boyfriend.

Her phone still showed out of range. *Shit.* She didn't need GPS. She could have driven the last two miles to the cabin on Forlorn Lake blindfolded. But she hated not to have a working phone, even though everybody knew there was no reception up here on the north shore of the Land of Ten Thousand Lakes.

Bodies of water in fact dotted the landscape. But Minnesota could also be called the land of ten thousand takes. Shakes. Makes. How many innocents had been taken advantage of? Shaken down? Made to do what they knew was wrong? She did not want to go inside Ralphs's. Too many bad memories lurked there.

Geneva blew out a breath. She had to pee. She desperately

needed caffeine. And she hadn't eaten since a quick Culver's butterburger and custard shake in western Wisconsin. The cabin wouldn't have any food. She girded herself to face the past.

"Welcome to Ralph's Pretty Good Grocery," the tall, now snowy-haired man behind the counter said, looking way too cheerful and rosy-cheeked for such a grim night. "How can I help you, ma'am?"

Or maybe it wasn't grim for him. For over-thirty-five Geneva, being called "ma'am" was grim enough, but there was no denying biology. At least he hadn't recognized her.

"Just grabbing a snack." She glanced around as if she didn't remember where the restroom was. "Ladies room?"

He pointed to the far corner, at the junction of the beer cooler and the deli. "Hope the girls left it clean for you."

She did her business as fast as she could, not thinking, not looking around the small room, not staring at the second door that was always locked—until it wasn't. Still, her stomach roiled remembering the warm breath, the grip on her arm.

Back in the store, she grabbed a basket near the door and prowled the aisles.

"If you can't find it at Ralph's," he called out, "you can get along pretty good without it."

She winced, ignoring him. Her basket filled with quarts of milk and orange juice, a package of cheddar cheese and one of sliced ham, a box of crackers, and a loaf of the least squishy bread they had. At the counter, her eyes widened when she spied the small red and green packages.

"Oh, my gosh. Nut Goodies!" She loaded a dozen packets of her favorite chocolate-and-nut candy, made in Minnesota, into her basket next to the register. "I'm going to grab a coffee, too."

When she returned from the coffee station carrying a large-lidded cup loaded with sugar and cream, the man was leering at her.

"If it isn't Geneva Larsen, all grown up. I'd know that voice anywhere."

"That's me." She lifted her chin. "Hi, Ralph."

"Shit." Geneva lowered her head onto the steering wheel in defeat. Her beloved decades-old car wouldn't start. She could feel Ralph's gaze on her through the store's window. She straightened. One more try. All she got was the futile whining, grinding slower and slower. She gave up, sipping her coffee, wishing she had an IV of it. She couldn't even call AAA.

She grabbed the keys, locked the door, and trudged down the street. She had no choice. She pulled her red Indiana University watch cap farther down over her spiky platinum 'do. Short hair was fine in a warmer climate. Right now she wished she still had the long, dark, shiny mane she'd cultivated in high school two decades earlier.

The yellow and orange flashing lights of Jack's Auto Repair surrounded the name, under which was written, "Complete Satisfaction!" It had been goofy back then, and it was annoying now. This was not fictional Lake Wobegon, but Jack had been an early adopter of the trope, claiming he'd been one of the inspirations for the decades-long public radio show.

Despite the bay doors being closed, light from within pushed out into the increasing darkness of the late afternoon. A bell dinged when Geneva pulled open the door to the office.

"All tracks lead to Jack's," a tired voice from behind a car on a lift called out. "Can I help you?"

The voice wasn't Jack's. *Good.*

"I hope so." Geneva stepped into the closest bay. "My car's down the street, and it won't start. I think it needs a new battery."

A woman in dark blue work pants and a navy sweatshirt stepped out from behind the car, wiping her hands on a red grease-stained rag. A long blond braid fell down her back from under a faded Twins ball cap.

Geneva stared. "Angel? Angel Hagen?"

The woman took two steps closer and squinted. "Son of a

bitch. What in hell are you doing back here, Ginnie Larsen?"

"Heading out to the cabin. You're a mechanic now, it looks like."

"Yeah. It suits me." Angel shoved her hands in her pockets. "I didn't get to escape this hellhole to attend college like you did."

"You know I had to," Geneva murmured. "Escape, that is."

"Yeah. I needed to, too, but I couldn't."

"How is it, working for Jack?" Geneva hated even saying the name.

"Luckily he's almost never here."

Whew.

"I manage the outfit while he's in Florida," Angel went on. "I didn't start working for him until he mostly retired. He didn't even come back last summer. I'm saving up to buy the business from him."

"Sounds like a plan. Did you ever marry? Have a family?"

"Are you kidding?" Her mouth twisted like she'd tasted a mouthful of lutefisk. "All I could land were losers. I stopped looking a long time ago."

"I hear you." Geneva should have stopped looking, too. "Well, I like the sound of Angel's Automotive." She smiled.

"More like Fallen Angel Automotive. But I'll tell you, first thing I'm going to do is take down those damn flashing lights." Angel snorted.

The sound reminded Geneva of their years as besties, back before everything blew up. When one snort could lead to a half hour of uncontrollable, pee-your-pants laughter. "Hey, can we talk about something?"

"I thought you needed a new battery?" Angel cocked her head, but she no longer looked suspicious. "Never mind. We can do both. Where's this dead car of yours?"

"C'mon, goddammit." Geneva fanned the newspaper and kindling in the wood cookstove. Her fire-lighting skills hadn't deserted her either. The newspaper flared up and caught the slivers of wood from the kindling box. She stood, shivering, gradually feeding wood into the hole. The boxy antique stove would be her only source of both heat and coffee. At least the flue hadn't been blocked by a dead squirrel, or worse.

Bless her caretaker. He'd wiped down the place, filled the kindling box, and the wood box next to the door, and gotten the water running to the hand pump in the kitchen sink. This rustic cabin and the twenty acres of woods it sat in were the only property Geneva owned, inherited after her parents died. She hadn't been up in five years, though, not since she'd had new windows and an indoor composting toilet installed. Visiting an outhouse in the woods during winter was too ridiculous.

She hadn't lingered on that visit, though. She'd only made this crazy trip to get away from the latest of her unfortunate choices of men. It was winter break at the university where she taught, so she had time. While Geneva was here, maybe she and Angel could make some changes in Forlorn Lake.

When the fire was roaring, Geneva brought in the rest of her things. Ground coffee, stovetop pot, large bottle of Jim Beam. Electric lantern and flashlight. Down sleeping bag and pillow. Duffle holding warm clothes, TP, essentials of hygiene, books, and snow boots. And her laptop. Its battery would last maybe ten hours. She figured she'd be spending a lot of time in the town library charging devices and using their internet. If she really needed to use her phone, she'd drive the hour south back to Duluth.

She slid the perishables into the cold box, an ingenious feature her father had added many years ago. Accessed by a thick door in the north wall of the cabin, it was an insulated box attached to the outside of the house that stayed naturally cold but didn't freeze.

Once she was settled, Geneva poured whiskey into a chipped mug, grabbed a Nut Goodie, and pulled a chair near the stove to think. As far as she knew, nothing had ever come out about those dark days. It wasn't right. Angel seemed as scarred as Geneva felt, referring to herself as a fallen angel.

Geneva wondered what had happened to skinny Jimmy Berg. Editor of the school paper and president of the National Honor Society, he'd been bullied by the big blond jocks as well as the popular girls. Did the geeky nerd also still have nightmares about the back corner at Ralph's? There had been others, too.

At a scrabbling sound, she froze. Listened. It was at the door. Scratching.

"Fuck," she whispered, her heart thudding. She shot her gaze at the lock. Yes, she had shot the thick dead bolt. It would hold against an intruder. Wouldn't it? She'd also closed the thick insulated curtains over the windows. The only way someone would get in here would be with an axe or a chain saw.

After a minute of silence, she let out a long breath. It had to have been an animal. A hungry racoon. A fierce fisher. Even a bear, late to its den. She was fine. She was safe. Wasn't she?

Geneva stared at her hands, which were clutching the Nut Goodie. She tore open the candy bag. There was no fear that nuts, maple nougat, and chocolate couldn't soothe, washed down with some booze.

Geneva blinked the next morning at the sight of the Forlorn Lake Regional Public Library. They must have razed the shabby brick building that had been a refuge to her as a child. This modern edifice had gone up since the last time she'd been in town, for sure. Inside, she found an empty desk and plugged in her laptop and phone, then went looking for the internet password.

She passed an office labeled *James Berg, Director.* And halted. She peered in the open door. A thin man in glasses sat sideways to the entrance facing a big monitor, his long fingers racing over the keyboard.

"Jimmy?" she asked.

His face whipped toward her. He stared but didn't speak.

She smiled and gave a little wave.

He shook himself. Standing, he came toward her. "Ginnie Larsen. How long has it been?" His voice wobbled, and he kept his hands at his sides.

"Almost twenty years. I go by Geneva now." She gestured around. "And you're the director of this gorgeous new place?"

"Yes. We're proud of it." His voice steadied. "We have all the latest technology, with readiness to pivot to whatever innovations come along. I'm the general director, but I also manage the IT."

"Sounds like the perfect job for you. Did you marry? Have a family?"

He shook his head. "You?"

"Not yet." Who would want damaged goods like her? "Hey, I saw Angel at Jack's yesterday."

"Oh?" He didn't meet her gaze.

"She and I got to talking about the past." Geneva watched him. "Maybe the three of us could have lunch or a drink later."

"I don't drink." His hands fluttered at his sides. "And I'm very busy here. Eat lunch at my desk."

"What time do you get off? We can all grab a burger together."

Jimmy's shoulders slumped, as if defeated.

"Come on," Geneva pressed. "For old time's sake."

"You know as well as I do those old times weren't so great. But, yes, I will meet with you. I finish work at five."

"I'll be here."

Geneva sipped her Imperial stout in the FL Café, with Angel and Jimmy sitting across from her in a booth not far from the door. FL for Forlorn Lake, but who would want to name a restaurant the Forlorn Café?

"This is good." Geneva glanced at the list of beers. "The name Darkness fits it. What did you get?" She pointed her chin toward Angel's glass.

"Axe Man," Angel said. "Surly Brewing likes to go dark in their naming."

Jimmy sipped his ginger ale in silence.

Their young server arrived with two loaded plates. He set down a mushroom cheeseburger for Angel and the meatloaf supper plate in front of Jimmy. A woman carrying Geneva's tater tot hot dish approached. Geneva hadn't been able to resist ordering what some called the state dish.

"What, are we having a class reunion and nobody told me?" Tiff Sheridan set the hot dish plate at Geneva's place. "I heard you were in town, Ginnie."

Geneva gazed into the same stunning green eyes, honey-colored hair, and white, even teeth Tiff had always had. The beauty had been both valedictorian and Homecoming Queen. And now she was waitstaff in a restaurant?

"I am." Geneva might as well give up on asking locals to call her Geneva. "Good to see you."

Tiff cocked her hip and put one fist on her waist as her smile slid away. She narrowed her eyes at the three, lowering her voice. "Or is this a different kind of reunion?"

Geneva checked with Angel, who gave a nod indicating Tiff was also a member of their horrible nightmare of a club. "Can you join us?"

The server still hovered.

"Jason, doll, tell the kitchen I'm on break for twenty minutes, will you, please?" Tiff slid in next to Geneva. "You guys better eat while it's hot."

"We're going to need a lawyer," Geneva said fifteen minutes later, after the four had finally agreed to act. Jimmy had been hard to convince, but he'd come around.

"Tiny's a lawyer," Angel said. "He'll do it."

"Your giant of a baby brother is a lawyer?" Geneva stared.

Angel snorted again. "Hard to believe, but that lunkhead

actually has a pretty sharp brain in there."

"We'll need to get the story out, too." Geneva tapped the table. "Do any of you know a reporter?"

Jimmy pointed at Tiff.

Tiff laughed. "Don't gape, Geneva. I just moonlight as a waitress to make ends meet. I'm the northeast stringer for the *Duluth News Tribune*. I cover Saint Louis, Lake, and Cook counties. All the way to Canada and to the shores of Lake Superior. I'll write up an article and send it around to you all for approval."

"And I have resources for distributing it more widely," Jimmy said.

Tiff pushed up to standing. "I have to get back to work. You have my number."

"Yep." Geneva patted her pants pocket. This afternoon she'd acquired a pay-as-you-go phone connected to the one carrier that offered service in the area.

When Tiff glanced at the door, her nostrils flared.

Geneva twisted to see Ralph staring at them with narrowed eyes.

"Listen, kids," Tiff muttered. "We all need to be careful. Very, very careful."

Geneva knocked on Jimmy's office door at the library the next morning at ten. "Just got a text from Angel. She wants to talk with both of us at the garage. Can you get away for a few minutes?"

"One second." He finished what he was typing. "She what, now?"

"She wants to see us at Jack's. She must be there alone and needs to keep working."

He blew out a breath. "I suppose. I wish this would all disappear, but you ladies clearly aren't going to let it." He stood and shrugged into a coat. "Let's get it over with."

Outside, Geneva sniffed. "Smells like snow." The low, unbroken gray sky looked like it, too.

"That's the forecast. Maybe up to a foot. In fact, here it is now."

Sure enough, white flakes began to descend on them. As they passed Ralph's, Geneva gave the store a quick glance.

"That's strange," she said. "Ralph's is closed. See? The lights are out."

"Maybe he went on vacation and couldn't find anyone to manage it." Jimmy shrugged. "Who wouldn't want to get away from a foot of snow?"

Across the street from Jack's was the Catholic church, Our Lady of the Lakes, the least original name in this state of lakes. Geneva and Angel used to giggle and call it Our Lady of Perpetual Responsibility. Whatever the name, it was closed up tight on this Thursday morning.

At the entrance to the garage parking lot, Geneva nearly tripped on a flapping boot lace. "Go on in," she told Jimmy. "I'll be right there."

He headed inside. She knelt to retie first one boot, then the other. She set her gloved hand on the office door but pulled it back. She couldn't make out the words, but she heard two male voices, one deeper than Jimmy's reedy tone.

She stepped over to the window in the nearest bay door. Her breath rushed in at the sight. Ralph aimed a shotgun at Jimmy. Angel was tied to a chair.

"Shit." Geneva ducked, then hurried around the corner of the building away from the bays in case Ralph came looking for her. Her pulse raced and her breath came fast and furious. She fumbled for the phone in her pocket, tearing her glove off with her teeth, her hands cold and clammy. She poked 9-1-1 but kept going around toward the back of the building.

"Dispatch. What is your emergency?"

The words tumbled out. "Ralph Knutsen has a shotgun pointed at two people inside Jack's. Send someone quickly, please!"

"Are you safe, ma'am?"

"For now. I'm outside at the right side of the shop near the back."

"Do not go inside. Officers are on their way. Get as far away as you can, ma'am."

How could the dispatcher sound so calm?

"Okay." Geneva frantically looked around. Behind the shop was a stand of woods. No way was she heading in there. She'd seen a For Rent sign in the window of the storefront next door, although *Ilsa's Beauty Salon* was still painted on the glass. She wouldn't find shelter there, either. This side of the auto shop had no windows or doors. She'd stay where she was.

At least she hadn't heard any shots. Angel and Jimmy had to be alive. They had to be. Had Ralph tied up Jimmy, too? If Jimmy said Geneva had walked over with him, Ralph would surely come after her. She glanced back along the side of the building, horrified to see her own footprints in the new snow. Except…the snowfall was getting heavier. Her tracks began to vanish.

She had a terrible thought. What if Angel—that is, Ralph—had also asked Tiff to come here? Geneva thumbed a fast text to her.

Ralph has A and J at gunpoint inside Jack's. Do NOT obey Angel's message if you got one.

But why hadn't Geneva heard a siren yet?

"Ma'am?" the dispatcher asked. "Are you still there?"

Geneva startled. "Yes."

"What is your name and address, please?"

"Geneva Larsen. I live in Indiana, but I'm staying at my family's cabin on the lake, on Lost Beach Road. Why aren't the police here yet?"

"They're coming in quietly so as not to alarm the hostage taker."

Ralph. What if he killed Angel or Jimmy or both when the police busted in? Should Geneva have tried to do more than run away and call for help? But what? She didn't have a weapon or even any martial arts skills.

She heard a noise. Whirled toward the street. And let out a breath. Two black-clad officers in helmets and thick vests jogged toward her. One, a woman, slowed.

"Ms. Larsen?" She kept her voice low.

Geneva nodded.

"You all right?"

"Yes."

"Back door?"

"I don't know."

"Stay put, please. We'll let you know when the coast is clear."

"Those are my friends in there, Angel and Jimmy. Please help them." Geneva's last words ended in a sob.

"Yes, ma'am." The officer vanished around the back.

It seemed like forever but probably only five minutes elapsed before the female officer reappeared, again from the front. She beckoned to Geneva, who hurried toward her.

"Are Angel and Jimmy okay?" Geneva asked in a rush.

"They're alive and fine."

Geneva's knees wobbled as the tension flooded out of her. She took in a deep breath to steady herself.

"We have Mr. Knutsen in custody," the officer added. "Your friends would like to see you."

"Thank you." Geneva wanted to hug her. Of course, she didn't. Minnesotans weren't big on hugs, especially from strangers. "Thank you."

Around the front, one of the bay doors had been raised. To get there, Geneva had to pass a cruiser. Ralph sat in the back seat, his face a mask of fury staring out the window. She looked away from the vitriol and hurried into the shop.

Angel and Jimmy stood talking with a Vera Stanhope look-alike in a wrinkled blazer and slacks that might have had an elastic waist. Geneva approached the group.

"Ginnie, I am so, so sorry," Angel began. "He forced me to send that text. He had the shotgun aimed at my head."

"Don't apologize. Are you both okay? Jimmy, did he tie you up, too?"

"Yes," he said. "But it turns out the man is an idiot of the first order."

Vera, or whatever her name was, nodded her agreement.

"Ralph asked where you were," Angel said. "Jimmy said you couldn't make it."

"I love you, Jimmy Berg." Geneva smiled at him.

His cheeks turned as red as his chafed wrists. "Once he got me secured to a chair, he set the gun on its end and ranted to us about how he knew we were going to ruin him and Jack."

"How he couldn't let us do that," Angel added. "Plus more blah, blah, blah."

The woman spoke up. "Such that when the team burst in on all sides, Knutsen wasn't exactly armed and ready to resist nor able to take out his hostages." She extended her hand. "Detective Verena Stanton. You are Geneva Larsen, I assume?"

Geneva shook her hand. "I am." The detective's name was also almost Vera's. All she needed was the hat.

"Thank you for being alert to the situation and for calling it in," Stanton said. "You saved your friends' lives."

Jimmy had certainly saved Geneva's.

"I'm just glad Tiff didn't show up, too," Angel said.

"Tiff didn't do what?" Tiff strode toward them. "Looks like I missed all the fun."

"You didn't get my text?" Geneva asked.

Angel spoke the same words at the same time. She snorted.

"Jinx," they both said, just like they had when they were still-innocent girls.

A week later, the four sat around Geneva's table in the cabin. A bottle of champagne sat mostly empty next to four jelly jars still half full. Even Jimmy was drinking.

Angel held up the *Duluth News Tribune*. "'Victims Expose Small-Town Abusers, by Tiffany Sheridan,'" she read.

"Bravo to Tiff." Geneva raised her glass and clinked it with the reporter's.

Tiff's cheeks pinkened. "Hey, it was all of us working together."

Angel read on. "'Foursome acts to stop long-running pattern of crimes against children. Ralph Knutsen, owner of Ralph's Grocery in Forlorn Lake, is behind bars, arrested on multiple charges, included repeated assaults on minors.'"

"Ralph's Very Bad Grocery is what the sign should have read," Tiff said, arching an eyebrow."

"'Lawyer Timothy Hagen is representing the accusers and other plaintiffs who have since come forward,'" Angel continued.

"Tiny has been great," Geneva murmured.

"'Knutsen's co-accused, John "Jack" Fillmore, collapsed from heart failure when authorities arrived to arrest him,'" Angel read. "'He died hours later in a Venice, Florida, hospital.'"

"Good fucking riddance," Tiff muttered.

"He was sick anyway," Angel said. "He didn't have much longer to live."

"Still, he was a horrible man, him and his buddy Ralph, and I want to put things right." Jimmy gazed around the table at them. "Here's what I'm going to do. I'm single."

Geneva interrupted. "We all are."

"I know, but I make a lot of money with my software consulting on the side. I'm going to buy the grocery and make it a co-op. It'll hire local kids, teach them accounting, provide counseling if they need it, and be a teen center into the bargain."

"You're brilliant, James Berg, you know that?" Tiff asked. "I'll help with publicity, marketing, anything written."

"And if they don't want to work at JB's Grocery, they can be apprentice mechanics at Angel's Automotive, where we don't have to brag about satisfying customers." Angel grinned.

Geneva looked at these old friends. She felt at home for the first time since that awful summer when Jack and Ralph began coercing preteens into the room behind the grocery's restroom, threatening to kill them if they told an adult. An anvil had lifted from her heart.

"You know what?" she began. "Indiana doesn't have all that much going for it. I think I'll move back up here. Get some electricity and winterization into this place. Write that book I've been thinking about. And be part of the new Forlorn Lake."

Nobody should ever feel as forlorn as she had for decades. Or be afraid to go into a pretty good grocery store.

WINDOWS
John M. Floyd

Julie Campbell heard a noise, in the night. Her eyes popped open, her body went rigid, and for a moment she thought she was home in her own bed. Then she realized she was cold. Her little house in south Florida wasn't perfect—far from it. But it also wasn't cold.

Then it came back to her: she was in her uncle's house, just outside Minneapolis. Uncle Rob was in the hospital, and Julie was spending the night here before going back to see him tomorrow. She was in the uncomfortable but bearable bed in Uncle Rob's guest room, looking at the green numbers on a digital clock. Two forty a.m.

The problem was, she was the only one here. And she had heard a toilet flush.

Julie stared up at the dark ceiling, listening to her pulse thudding in her ears. Could it have been a dream? Had she imagined it?

No. It was a unique, unmistakable sound. She had heard it.

Someone else was in the house.

Slowly, breathing hard, she eased out of the bed. There was no way to get help—Uncle Rob had no landline phone, and her cell was in her purse in the living room. *How stupid.* In the dark she fumbled around until she found her coat and pulled it on over her nightgown, then she opened the drawer of the bedside table and with trembling hands groped for some kind of weapon. All she found was a small flashlight.

She clicked it on—the fully awake part of her mind told her to avoid announcing her presence with room lights—and crept barefoot from the bedroom. She didn't know what she'd find but she knew she couldn't just stay still and do nothing. She felt a tear run down her cheek, and wiped it away with the back of her hand. Her thoughts went again to her home near the marshes west of Ft. Lauderdale; how she wished she were there right now. She would not only be warm, she'd be safe. Compared to burglars, snakes and gators were almost welcome.

Julie padded slowly from room to room, shielding the shaky beam of her flashlight with her palm, pausing to listen outside each doorway before entering. She had checked the locks on all the windows and outside doors before heading to bed, but now she made double sure. It was, thank God, a fairly small house, not much bigger than her own. Within minutes she'd covered it all. Kitchen, living room, dining room, two bedrooms, two baths. And, of course, both bathroom lights were off.

No one else was here. *What now?*

Standing in her nightgown and her heavy fleece jacket in the doorway between the kitchen and living room, her bare feet freezing on the hardwood floor, Julie could see her purse there on the couch where she'd left it, still zipped up. She was glad now that she hadn't made a beeline for her phone and called the police. What would she have told them? That she'd heard someone flush the john in an empty house?

Still, she couldn't just go back to bed. Not until she knew what had happened.

At that moment, she heard something else. The unmistakable sound of flowing, splashing water. It was coming from right behind her. Stifling a gasp, she whirled toward the noise—

And found herself looking through her uncle's kitchen window at the next-door neighbor's house. At the next-door neighbor's lighted window, in fact. There couldn't have been more than six feet separating the two buildings. As she watched through the thin curtains, her mouth hanging open, she saw the outline of someone bending over a sink, washing his hands and face. Then the silhouette vanished and the light winked out.

It took her awhile to steady her breathing, and for her heart to slow down. So that was it—the houses here were packed so close together someone else's plumbing noises sounded like your own. Even when the windows were closed tight. A country girl all her life—or at least as country as one could be in the over-populated lower-East Coast—she wondered how people could live in the city.

She also wondered if she'd be able to sleep, after all this. But she didn't have a choice. Tomorrow would be a busy day, and she had to be alert. *Always be alert*, her brother had once told her, *our world needs more lerts*. Smiling to herself and her hyperactive imagination, she trudged back to the guest room, dropped her coat onto the foot of her bed, and then changed her mind and kept it on. Thus insulated, she climbed in underneath the sheets.

Julie sighed. Why be surprised? Everything about this trip had been strange. She had driven down to Miami and then flown to Chicago for a Thursday/Friday conference, and had decided on a whim to take the weekend to visit her elderly uncle in his new house (although "new" in this case just meant smaller and more affordable). She'd called his cell phone night before last to get his street address and after the final conference session yesterday, she'd driven up through Milwaukee and Madison and up I-94 to the outskirts of Minneapolis. She found no one home when she got here, and calls to other relatives revealed that Robert Campbell had fallen ill that afternoon. When she located the hospital and navigated her way to his room, he had apologized for not calling her and given her a hug and a house key and told her to go get some sleep. It was only a flare-up of his kidney stones, he said. The doc would probably let him out tomorrow. Actually later today, she reminded herself; it was already tomorrow.

But be careful on the way to the house, Uncle Rob had said. *The neighborhood's usually safe, but one never knows.* There'd been two recent murders not far away, and everyone here recalled the not-too-distant and not-too-long-ago riots.

Remembering all that, right now, didn't exactly help her feelings.

At least she was warm now. She burrowed her face into the unfamiliar pillow and forced herself to close her eyes, made herself relax. Sure, she was stressed, but she'd also worked until noon the day before and driven two hundred miles, and was dead tired. Besides, all was well. The house was secure and this city and state had always had a reputation for being safe, and she was indeed alone and all right and out of harm's way. After several minutes she began to drift into sleep—

And heard a window break.

She sat straight up in bed, her heart in her throat. What she'd heard wasn't just glass breaking. It was the crash and tinkle of *window* glass. She was sure of it. And she *still* didn't have her damn phone.

Once again Julie grabbed the tiny flashlight and crept from the bedroom (she stopped only long enough to make sure *its* window was intact) into the hallway. She knew already that the house didn't have many windows. Much like her own place, in its little shaded lot on the east edge of the Glades. But something was bothering her, a tiny fact that she could almost see but couldn't. She vaguely remembered that something about houses here was almost always different from those in the deep south— something Uncle Rob had told her—but she couldn't recall what it was. Not that it mattered. It seemed important somehow, but it wasn't. The only important thing at this moment, the only thing that mattered, was what she had heard just now, and making sure no bad guys had broken in.

One by one, holding her breath most of the way, she rechecked every window. All were still closed, locked, and intact—just the way she wanted it.

After three minutes she wound up once again in the kitchen, and even glanced out its window at the neighboring residence as she'd done earlier. This time there were no lights on over there, and when she pressed her nose to the cold windowpane, she could see the entire side of the other house. The moonlight's glow showed her that no windows there were broken.

Julie hurried down the hall to the other bedroom and looked out that window too, to the house on the opposite side. Nothing wrong there, folks. She sighed, retraced her steps, turned on the kitchen light, clicked off her flashlight, and sagged into a chair at the table. She felt exhausted. What in God's name had caused the noise she'd heard? Could it have been a window she couldn't see, on one of the other sides of the neighboring houses? Could she have been wrong, and some other kind of glass had broken? A dish, or a bottle? That didn't seem likely, at three in the morning. A toilet flushing is one thing; lots of people get up to use the bathroom during the night. But glass breaking?

Oh well. She'd done all she could do. Everything was okay here. If she could only think of what it was that was bothering her, hiding just out of sight in the back of her mind...

Then it hit her. The main difference between houses up north and her own, down south.

This house had a basement. The houses at home didn't. The water table there was too high.

And the basement here had a window. She'd seen it from the side yard the previous afternoon, low to the ground, when she had arrived to find the front door locked and had gone around to try the back.

Now, sitting here at the kitchen table, the soles of her bare feet cold against the kitchen floor, Julie Campbell turned and looked for the first time at the closed door beside the fridge, the door that she assumed led down to the basement. She focused on it, her mouth dry, her eyes wide, her heart pounding.

And watched the doorknob turn...

RAGE BEAT

Bryon Quertermous

Any other night, the scene would have been beautiful. The snow fell in thick, wet flakes and the bent headlights illuminated the sky in all directions. It wasn't particularly cold, and I stood in the middle of the road in only my jeans and the T-shirt I'd been wearing under my suit at the gig earlier that evening. The silence would have been welcome another night.

Tonight wasn't that night.

Tonight the silence gave me more space to think about my failed set—my embarrassing performance on stage and off, and most importantly, it made it easier to obsess over how much I wanted to kill Kurt Smalls.

I'd hit a deer with my minivan an hour outside of Minneapolis on my way to some stupid casino on the border with Wisconsin hoping to get to the gig I'd been booked to play at before word of my performance made its way south.

The van was still running, and I thought about getting right back in and continuing my trip, hoping the van didn't crap out on me somewhere else along the way. But I was too shaken up and tweaked on adrenaline to get behind the wheel. I wasn't sure how much of that was because of the crash and how much of it was because what had happened at the Smooth Note Supper Club, but either way, I needed to calm down before I tried to drive again.

I got back in the car and laid my head back against the seat. When I opened my eyes again, there were red and blue lights flashing behind me. My initial instinct was to panic, but I quickly realized I had nothing to hide, and panicking would only make things worse. I rolled my window down as the cop approached with his flashlight in my face.

"How are you doing this evening, sir?"

"Not great," I said. "Goddamn deer jumped out in front of me."

"Have you had anything to drink tonight?"

"No, sir. Just coming from a gig in Minneapolis and on my way to another gig at the Treasure Island casino."

"You some kind of musician?"

"Drummer," I said. "Jazz mostly. Some blues and classical when the mood and the paycheck strike, if you know what I mean."

He flashed his light inside the car and waved it around, then he made his way around the rest of the van.

"You want to tell me what happened?"

I gave him the full version of what happened and felt better when I was done.

"Did anyone else hit the deer after me?" I asked. "It flew out in front of me after I hit it and then I ran over it. I worried I tore something up underneath."

The cop turned back toward where the deer was in the street then walked away. A few seconds later I heard two pops. When he came back, the cop brought a smell with him that was a mix of skunk and the venison sausage my uncle used to make during deer season.

"Dumb thing kept trying to get up, so I had to put it out of its misery," he said.

The smell and the sound of the gunshots hung in my head like a gooey nightmare I wouldn't be able to easily shake.

"I...uh...I mean what happens next?"

"Doesn't seem to be anything hissing or smoking, so you're

probably good to drive. Just keep an eye out for anything that sounds weird with the vehicle. You need a report for your insurance company?"

"Shit. Yeah. I'm going to have to pay to get this fixed, aren't I?"

The officer seemed to be ignoring me as he typed on something that looked like an old school mobile phone with a small printer attached to the top. When he was done typing, the little printer spit out a form roughly the size of a large receipt, and the officer handed it to me.

"Case number's at the bottom. Give that to the insurance company and you should be all set."

I thanked him and he hung around awkwardly for a few seconds afterward, but he eventually went back to his car. When he finally did a U-turn out onto the street and drove away, I let out a huge pent-up sigh and screamed. I kept the radio off the rest of the drive so I could listen for any sounds that indicated the car was about to fall apart on me, but I made the rest of the drive without incident.

The hotel looked mostly deserted, which seemed about right for the middle of the night during the middle of the week in the middle of winter. I wondered briefly if they would cancel my set because of lack of attendance. I also wondered if that would be better for me than having to explain myself and what happened to keep the set I'd been hired for.

Long term, it would be better for me to have the gig canceled and let the dust settle on the supper club mess before I tried to get booked again. Short term I needed money. My rent was three months past due, my van note was two months past due, and my bank account was a day or two away from being shut down due to excessive insufficient funds penalties. The money from this gig would catch me up on two of the three, maybe more if the crowd turned out to be the type that liked to buy merchandise or throw extra money in my tip jar and not make me hand over a T-shirt or CD for it.

I thought about grabbing my duffel bag and heading up to the room they'd reserved for me first and maybe catching a nap before talking to the manager, but I wanted to get that conversation over as quickly as possible. I locked the van and as I walked toward the hotel entrance, I got the first glance of the front of the van in the full light.

Cosmetically, it looked much worse than I'd expected. There was a huge crack in the driver's side of the front bumper and the entire front grate was gone. There were other mid-sized cracks spread across the front of the van with chunks of hair and flesh stuck between them. I felt sick to my stomach and had to hold back a wave of nausea as I stepped backward.

Operationally, looking inside, everything else was intact. If there was such a thing as luck with an accident like this, I'd been lucky to hit the deer in a way that did far more damage to the deer than to my van. I'd lived in the Midwest my entire life and knew that was rarely the case.

I grabbed the copy of the police report the cop had left with me and crammed it into my pocket, so that I could call the insurance company as soon as I checked into my room. Again, I was tempted to go straight to my room and call the insurance agent and order room service and go right to bed hoping the next day would bring a reset and better luck, but I knew that was just hiding from the problem and I needed to get in front of it instead.

I could tell things were going to go south almost immediately when I entered the lobby and everybody avoided making eye contact with me. I'd never been in this casino or hotel before so that meant the only way they recognized me was from the video from the last gig. I was already committed though so I quickly moved past the hotel staff and moved into the casino floor area where I had a brief reprieve from the sad looks because everybody was focused on their slot machines or their cards. A sign indicated the theater was on the far side of the casino floor and I suspected the office where I needed to go was at the back of the theater.

If I hadn't been suspicious before, trying to open the theater doors and finding them locked would have done it for me. The fact that three security guards appeared almost immediately afterward only made it worse. A smarter man would have left right then and moved on to the next gig or taken a break for a while and waited for it all to blow over.

I'm not a smarter man.

"Hey, glad to see you guys," I said. "I'm supposed to be performing in a bit and was hoping to—"

"You're going to have to leave, sir."

"I think maybe you have me mistaken for someone else because—"

"We know who you are, sir. Don't make us…"

I lost track of what he said after that. The man who put me in this situation was striding across the casino floor without a care in the world and I wanted to beat him to death with the craps rake.

I looked back at the security guards and gave them the friendliest smile I had to offer and said, "I'll be right back, and we can finish sorting this out. I see a friend of mine over there."

Before they could argue with me or put their hands on me, I was halfway across the casino floor heading toward Kurt Smalls. That's how I'd been referring to him in my head since I first found out he'd been added to the trio by the sax player who'd hired me for the gig. They were both university pricks, Kurt a full professor, and his bio only ever referred to him by his full name. That carried over in how he asked to be referred to in person too and it was irritating.

In my head though, I genuinely thought I would be able to approach him and work with him to make things right. I'd convinced myself it really was a misunderstanding and that he would be the perfect voice to vouch for me with everyone here.

That lasted until I saw his smarmy mug and clocked him as hard as I could.

The security guards had also made their way across the casino floor as quickly as I had and were on top of me the second my fist recoiled back from Kurt Smalls's slobbery, bearded face. They were needlessly violent as they handcuffed me and dragged me to my feet.

"We were going to just dump you out front," the lead security guard said, "but now you pissed us off and I think we'll head out the back way where the security cameras don't work anymore."

I was saved by a giant of a woman, both in height and in girth, dressed like a mother of the bride. I assumed she was Macy Griggs, the one who managed the theater and booked me for the gig. She mumbled something to one of the guards who unlocked the theater doors then unlocked my handcuffs. For a brief second, there was a flicker of optimism that maybe everything was going to be all right, and this would be a story I could tell at gigs in the future to warm up the crowd.

"Go," she said, pointing to the office at the other end of the theater.

The tone in her voice dissipated my optimism, and I trudged across the theater like a prisoner on his way to an execution. I was getting angrier with every step. Why was it necessary to humiliate me like this? Was she going to lecture me before shafting me on the money she owed me? Why not just throw me out and get it over with?

The office was nice, but sparsely furnished. It could have easily been a storage room with a fancy desk if you didn't know any better. She sat behind the desk, and I stood where I was because there were no other chairs. She typed something in her computer while I valiantly kept my mouth shut even though every part of me wanted to scream and plead my case.

After a few minutes of silence though, my nerve started to crack. I was about to say something when I felt a presence over my shoulder and turned to see Kurt Smalls smiling at me. I rushed him again and had my hands around his neck before Macy was able to pull me away from him and fling me to the floor.

"Enough," she said.

Kurt Smalls knew enough not to say anything. I did not.

"If you just give me a chance to explain—"

"En*ough*," she said again. "There is no explanation."

"Then why not just throw me out?"

"Ask the man you almost strangled to death," she said.

"I wasn't going to strangle him," I said, at first completely missing the point of what she was saying. "Oh, wait. What?"

"If it was up to me, you wouldn't have made it past the front desk. But Kurt Smalls here and I go way back. He asked me to keep you on for tomorrow's show."

Be grateful, I thought to myself. Don't be an ass.

Be grateful, don't be an—

"How did you get here so quickly?" I asked Kurt Smalls. "We left at the same time and—"

"These back roads are great for opening up the full power of the 'Vette," he said. "It was almost warm enough for me to think about putting the top down. Global warming might not be the worst thing this time of year, you know what I mean?"

"But the thing tomorrow, that's supposed to be just me. Nobody mentioned anything about—"

"I asked him to come," Macy said. "After what happened down in Minneapolis, I needed someone to fill in for you. Kurt Smalls is always ready to go."

"If you saw the video, then you also saw that he...wait, is this why you want me to play with you tomorrow? Steal half my check and get another shot at embarrassing me?"

Kurt didn't say anything, he just shook his head slightly and gave me a condescending look.

"Listen, we've both had a rough night," he said. "Why don't you go to your room—I made sure they kept your reservation intact—go get something to eat from room service and get a good night's sleep. We can regroup in the morning."

I was running the numbers through my head while he talked. Splitting the fee with Kurt would barely cover one of the bills I was behind on. Sharing the stage with him again was an even worse thought. I had no idea what he was planning, but I knew for sure it wasn't a warm and fuzzy reunion. He probably hoped getting both of us back on stage so soon after the incident would get even more attention, giving him a bigger stage for embarrassing me and making his own performance go viral. There was no way I was going to let that happen. I wasn't going to give up either. I'd go back to my room like he suggested, and then after a good night's rest, I'd get up early and get to Macy before the show and plead my case in a better head space for why I should do the show solo.

"You're right," I said. "Thank you. Both of you. We'll catch up again tomorrow."

I left and expected Kurt Smalls to follow, but he stayed behind with Macy. All the way back to my car I fumed and wondered if I should even wait until morning to try and plead my case again with Macy. Maybe I should give it a bit and try again that night before she could think any more about whatever nonsense Kurt Smalls was putting in her head about me.

When I got back to my van, the back door wouldn't open for me to get my stuff and I considered once again just getting back on the road and going home to pretend this never happened. I'd made money before doing things other than music and I could do it again. In fact, the few times I took jobs other than music to pay the bills, I ended up making much more money with more stability and less stress. So that was it. I was done with music. I was finally going to grow up and get a real job.

I went back around to the driver's side and got in and was about to drive away when I saw Kurt Smalls and Macy walking across the lot with each other, chatting like they were the best of friends. My heart started beating faster than I'd ever felt, then the beat in my chest went to my head then my eyes and I could hear a rhythm developing. It was a rage beat.

The only formal training I ever had in music was during a two-year stint at community college in the jazz band. I had a partial scholarship and dreams of being a session musician, but this one teacher of mine put bigger dreams in my head that I would never forgive him for. He tried to help me control my beats and find a voice in the off beats where he said true genius lived. All I was ever able to find in the off beats was rage. Ugly beats I chased desperately before some pianist or trumpet player would bring me back around to a generic melody we'd finish out with.

After two years without any meaningful progress and a diminished music department budget, my scholarship was cut. I left school shortly after. A kid I played with started a trio at an Italian restaurant that doubled as a comedy club, and I found something else I'd end up chasing even more desperately than rage beats: the spotlight.

I couldn't go back to office work, no matter how much money it offered. I couldn't take the mundane small talk, the forced friendliness, the monotony, and worst of all, the lack of a spotlight. The lack of danger. As much as I hated messing up or bombing a set, the fear that it could happen gave me a thrill I'd never been able to replicate. I needed music to be my job and that wasn't going to happen with Kurt Smalls around.

I let my mind wander as I sat in the van wondering what to do next. Getting a gun was out of the question because I knew there was no way to do it without it being traced back to me. Every method I thought of eventually led back to me because I wasn't a criminal. I was a good guy getting screwed over by a bad system. Eventually my mind stopped generating murder ideas and I decided it was time to go. Then I saw Kurt Smalls walking back across the parking lot toward the casino. I revved the engine in the van, hoping he'd look over at me and maybe come to confront me and we could fight it out. Maybe he'd hit his head on the pavement and I could say it was an accident. But he didn't notice me. He veered away from the front of the casino and headed toward the back. Probably going in some secret entrance for hotshots.

Where the security cameras weren't working.

I revved the van again.

If I hit him at the right angle, the van would be the perfect weapon and I already had a good story for why it was damaged. A story with an official police report and everything. But I had to do it right without damaging the van so much I totaled it and couldn't drive away.

I floored the gas and tried to remember exactly what I'd done when I hit the deer. Instead of slamming on the brakes, I took my foot off the gas right before impact. Kurt Smalls's body flew out in front of the van just like the deer had. I ran over him with a thud and then backed over his head again with a wet, prolonged *thunk*.

Then I drove back to the same spot I'd been parked, grabbed my luggage, and went inside. I called the insurance company hotline and arranged to drop the van off early the next morning before I performed.

My alarm went off at five a.m. and I could see police cars swarming the spot where I'd left Kurt Smalls's body. Nobody stopped me as I left.

The shop owner's brother drove me back to the casino in his wife's minivan and I went right to Macy's office when he dropped me off. She was behind her desk crying with a bottle of rum in front of her.

"Is everything okay?" I asked.

"You didn't hear about Kurt?"

"I had to drop my van off at the shop this morning. What happened?"

"He was hit by a car and killed last night."

"Jesus," I said.

"I know you and he didn't get along, but—"

"No. That was just some silliness with egos. That's why I came here this morning to talk to you and I hoped he'd be here too. I wanted to say thank you for the second chance. He's a great partner on stage and—"

"We're going to cancel the show tonight and go dark in his

honor. I've got your check here though if you don't mind not playing. Is that okay?"

I bit down hard on my tongue and tried to keep my face as solemn as I could manage.

"Of course," I said. "It's what he'd want. I'll even donate his half of the fee to his family for final costs."

"That's sweet of you, but unnecessary. The casino will be covering his funeral expenses. But thank you."

"No. Sure. I get it."

"I have a friend who books for a casino about an hour from here if you were still interested in playing somewhere tonight. I can give her a call if you'd like."

"Yeah. That'd be great. Thank you. Really."

"Now if you don't mind, I'd like to be alone for a while."

I went back to my room and packed my stuff then ordered an Uber to take me to the other casino. The show went great and every time I hit the high tom, I heard the van hitting Kurt Smalls. Every time I hit the bass drum, I heard the final thump of my tire on his head. It was invigorating, and I was finally able to navigate the rage beats and find a path through the off beats to the genius I'd been searching for.

When the set was done, the audience exploded in applause. I sold enough merchandise that night alone to catch up on all of my back bills and that was before they cut me a bonus check.

My car was in the shop for five days, and I was invited to play at the casino every one of those nights. On the sixth night, I returned to the Treasure Island for a show in honor of Kurt Smalls. One woman in the audience stared at me the entire time. I wondered if she was a groupie wannabe or if she recognized me from the other video. It didn't matter to me. I was on top of the world.

Even when she introduced herself as Detective Monday.

Even when she mentioned one of the employees that worked on my van had called with concerns about blood and other matter that didn't match what they'd seen before in deer crashes.

Even when she put me under arrest.

I knew it wouldn't stick. I'd follow the beat to the end, and it would all work out.

SOMETHING STRANGE

Bev Vincent

SPPD Officer Amanda Hodges didn't put much stock in ghost stories or tales of things that go bump in the night. In her many years on patrol, she'd seen just about everything. There were incidents she couldn't explain because she didn't have all the facts, or because people lied, but she'd never encountered anything she considered inexplicable. Which is why she was skeptical about the perp who accused a ghost of committing assault.

Then she met Libby.

Her shift started with a domestic abuse call. By the time Amanda arrived on the scene, the abusive boyfriend had already fled, so all she could do was take a report. It wasn't Amanda's first call to this address. She was familiar with both the victim, Viv, and the accused, Ian. They argued over everything. How she prepared dinner. Why he couldn't find a job. Why the place looked like a pigsty. Where they were going to find the money for the crap he insisted on buying. The way she looked at some guy. The way he looked at some woman. Their arguments were usually fueled by alcohol and drugs.

On this occasion, Ian had attempted to strangle Viv. When she grabbed her phone to dial 911, he punched her in the face. Her nose was still bleeding when Amanda arrived, but Viv—who looked like she was around Amanda's age (thirty-five) when she was, in fact, only twenty-three—refused Amanda's offer to call paramedics.

While Amanda was recording the details, a Code 1 call came over her radio about an incident in progress a block away. Amanda told Viv she'd be right back and proceeded to the new location on foot.

This assault victim was sitting on the curb in an apartment complex parking lot, blood streaming from his face. The unknown assailant, who had stolen the man's wallet and phone, was long gone. Amanda held the scene while waiting for other officers to respond. Once they arrived, she returned to finish the original complaint. Viv's demeanor had changed in the interim. She was even less cooperative and had become fidgety. Amanda suspected Ian had returned to the apartment while she was out.

She called for backup, unsnapped her sidearm, and yelled, "If anyone's in there, come out, with your hands in plain view."

Ian emerged from the bedroom. He was unarmed, but his appearance worried Amanda. His eyes were wide, his hair in disarray, his face unshaved. His clothes looked like he'd been wearing them for weeks and he reeked something awful. He was jittery and talking a mile a minute. He was on something, no doubt about it. Amanda made him sit on the couch while she waited for her cover to arrive.

When he did, Officer Scotty Williams took Ian aside to get his statement. Once finished, he and Amanda compared notes.

"She says he hit her," Amanda said, "but she's not sure she wants to press charges."

"Let me guess," Williams said. "She said something to set him off, so it was partly her fault."

"Pretty much," Amanda said. It was a familiar refrain. "What's he saying?"

"The usual. She fell down a couple of times and hurt herself."

"What about the marks on her neck? She didn't get those in a fall."

"That's where it gets interesting," Williams said. "When asked about that, his story suddenly changed."

"Oh?"

"Yep. Get this. He says she was attacked by a ghost."

"He...What?"

"He didn't even blink. In fact, I don't think he's blinked the whole time I've been here. The apartment is haunted, he says, and the ghost has a nasty temper. Sounds like projection to me."

"Or the drugs talking," Amanda said. "We can't leave them both here. Do you want to take him in?"

"Will she sign the complaint?"

"I think I can get her to do that."

"Okay, I'll take him in."

Amanda got out a pair of latex gloves, a precaution she always took when there was a chance she'd have to put her hands on a citizen. The minute Ian saw Williams reaching for his cuffs, he was out the front door like a gazelle.

"Son of a bitch," Williams said, taking off after him.

"Let him go," Amanda said, but it was too late. The other officer was gone. A few seconds later, Amanda heard him requesting backup over the radio. He provided frequent and increasingly breathless updates on his location.

She shook her head at the cop's gung-ho behavior. Over the years, she'd learned she didn't have to chase every perp who ran. They knew where Ian lived. Sooner or later, he'd show up here again. All they had to do was get a probable cause warrant and the warrant squad would pick him up. Not that it would do much good. Viv had only reluctantly signed the complaint and her lack of cooperation was likely to increase if the time ever came to go to court, assuming the DA agreed to take the charge and didn't find some reason to drop the case.

Five minutes later, she heard a call go out for "officer down," something that sent shivers through anyone wearing a badge. The "assailant" in this case, though, was a tree root. Williams had tripped while in pursuit, possibly breaking his right arm in the process. That was why cops shouldn't chase someone they could pick up later, she mused with a mental shrug. Now Williams was going to be off work for weeks, on light duty after that, and he'd messed up his shooting hand. All over a lowlife who'd gotten away anyway.

She convinced Viv to spend the night with a friend in case Ian showed up again. Then she drove to the parking lot at the police substation on Hamline, where she completed her paperwork on the skirmish. She always used a secure location when she was going to be focused on her computer for a while; otherwise, someone might catch her off guard. There were plenty of people who hated cops enough to kill one on sight, given the opportunity. She debated over whether she should include the bit about the ghost, then decided to use it. It would help her remember the incident if the case ever came to trial.

Before heading back on patrol, Amanda decided to refuel her cruiser. Technically, she was supposed to use the city pumps at Central, but that would take her out of circulation for nearly thirty minutes. She'd received special dispensation to use the pumps at the fire station on Snelling Avenue. She liked maintaining a good relationship with the local firemen, despite the natural enmity between the two departments. If she ever got an open chest wound while on duty, these would be her first responders and she wanted them to care about her.

In addition to availing herself of their gas pumps, Amanda also routinely stopped at the station to use the restroom. There were a limited number of places she could go—bathrooms were another place where cops were vulnerable. She couldn't go behind a tree like male officers did, and she wasn't about to hang her belt on the back of a restaurant or gas station restroom door. In addition to her sidearm, she was packing a stun gun, a baton, a flashlight, two knives, and three extended magazines, giving her a total of nearly sixty bullets, which might seem like a lot given that she'd never had to shoot anyone, but some of her colleagues had been involved in a shootout recently where over 150 rounds were exchanged, so you never knew. It added up to over twenty pounds, and she wasn't going to get caught with her pants down without it.

Back on patrol, heading west toward Tangletown, Amanda chit-chatted with the dispatcher. She knew the dangers of making a dispatcher mad from when she had worked in dispatch while on light duty during her pregnancy. They decided when she could take a break, when she could eat, and what kind of calls she got. Tonight's dispatcher was an acquaintance who had come to her baby shower and had even joined her for a ride-along a year or so back. She was a friendly soul to talk with during the long slow hours of her shift.

She scanned the computer display. On nights when there were numerous calls, she could pick the ones she wanted to handle. She chose a report of a disturbance at a nearby residence and keyed in the code that showed her responding.

When she arrived, the street was quiet. She climbed out of her squad car and approached the front door. Disturbance calls were among her least favorite because she never knew what she was going to find, even in a good neighborhood like this one.

It looked like every light in the house was on. She rapped on the front door and announced herself as a police officer. It took nearly a full minute for someone to answer—an elderly woman, over eighty if Amanda had to guess. Even though it was well after midnight, she was wearing an elegant dress, a white apron, and had a string of pearls around her neck. She looked perplexed. "I saw you through the parlor window," she said. "Did you knock?" Her hand went to her right ear. "Oh my. I don't have my hearing aids in." She plucked two small buds from her apron pocket and placed one in each ear.

"You called the police, ma'am?" Amanda asked.

"Did I?" The woman rested a finger on her cheek. "Why, yes. I suppose I did. Please come in."

"You reported a disturbance," Amanda said, hoping to prod the woman's memory.

"There are people everywhere," the woman said. "I want them all to leave."

The house was silent. "Are they here now, ma'am?"

The woman stepped away from the door.

Amanda followed. "What's your name, ma'am?"

"Elizabeth Passmore," the woman said. "But you can call me Libby. Everyone does. My, you remind me of my grand-daughter..." She paused. "It'll come to me. What's your name?"

"Amanda. My mom calls me Mandy." She wasn't sure why she added that.

"No, that's not it." The woman stopped in the middle of the hallway, apparently lost in thought.

"Ma'am. The people?"

"What people?"

"You said there were people."

The woman looked around the room. "Well, there are. And I can't get them to leave."

"In there?" Amanda asked, nodding toward a room she assumed was the parlor.

"They're *everywhere*," the woman said, sounding distraught. "Him and her and her." She pointed randomly around her.

Amanda looked, half expecting to see something, at least photographs on the walls.

"And in here, too," the woman said. She marched into the living room and threw up her arms in exasperation. "They talk and talk and talk, and they never leave."

The room was cozy enough, but quite empty of people. "Ma'am? Libby? Is there someone I can call? A relative? A friend?"

"No," she said in a faraway voice. "There's no one."

"Well, I'm here now," Amanda said.

"And who were you again?"

During Crisis Intervention Training, a psychiatrist had dispensed this pearl of wisdom: never argue with a crazy person. Amanda had taken that advice to heart. "I'm Amanda. I'm going to help you."

She was reminded of an episode from a reality television

show where an elderly man complained that his house was full of cats and dogs. His adult son was there when the police responded, explaining that his father suffered from dementia. The officers came up with a solution—they rounded up all the "cats" and "dogs," which the man happily pointed out to them. Once they were all in custody, the man relaxed. It was a stopgap measure—no doubt another delusion would arise—but it served for the moment.

"Do recognize any of these people?" she asked.

The woman paused, as if the question hadn't occurred to her before. "Noooo...I don't think so." She peered into the void. "Well, now that you mention it, this one might be my husband."

"And what's his name, Libby?"

After a brief hesitation, she said, "Earl. His name is Earl."

"Do you want Earl to leave?" Amanda asked. "I can arrest him if you'd like. Get him to leave you alone."

"Why would you do that?" Libby asked. "He's my husband. He hasn't done anything wrong."

Amanda nodded. She wanted to put a hand on the woman's shoulder to reassure her, but she held back. "That's all right, Libby." She paused. "What about the others?"

"Well, there's our daughter, Donna. She got married and moved away, but I'm sure that's her."

"So, she can stay, right?"

"Of course. And this must be her husband. I can't remember his name. There was an accident, I seem to recall, but it was a long time ago. He looks fine now, don't you think? Such a handsome young man."

"They make a nice couple," Amanda said.

"Don't you go making eyes at him, young lady. He's taken."

"I wouldn't dream of it. Your daughter is a lucky woman." Amanda took a deep breath, trying to hold the illusion together.

Libby nodded. "There were children, too."

"Maybe they're playing somewhere."

"They were so young," Libby said.

Amanda sensed a sad story, but she didn't want to pry and risk bursting the bubble. "Do you recognize anyone else?"

Libby's hand flew to her mouth. "I don't know why I didn't realize it before. There's my sister and my brother—and our parents. Oh my, it's been so long since I saw them. And I do believe that's Helen, my oldest friend. She had cancer and was so bad for a while, but she looks fine now. It's a miracle, don't you think?"

"A miracle," Amanda agreed. "Are you sure I can't call someone for you?" She saw a stack of mail on the coffee table and browsed through the return addresses. One caught her attention. "What about your pastor? Reverend Booth?"

"I don't know him," Libby said.

"He's at the Presbyterian church."

"Yes, that's my church. Earl and I were married there after he got back from Korea. Weren't we, honey?" she said, speaking to the wall.

"Do you mind if I call him? Reverend Booth?"

"Oh, I'm not sure," Libby said. "There such a crowd here already."

"What's one more, then?" Amanda said, pulling out her phone. "I'm sure he won't mind."

Libby settled into an easy chair next to the fireplace. It was well worn and looked comfortable. Amanda imagined the woman spending a lot of time there. Knitting, perhaps, if her rheumatism wasn't too bad. Reading or watching TV if she still had her eyesight.

Given the late hour, it took her a while to get through to someone at the church. The answering machine helpfully supplied an emergency contact number. The woman who responded eventually said she was familiar with Mrs. Passmore, although no one had seen her for some time and their home visitation team hadn't been able to get her to answer the door in over a year.

"She's a little deaf and doesn't always wear her hearing aids," Amanda said. "Probably didn't hear the knock. Does she have family nearby?"

The woman on the other end of the line was silent for a few seconds. "No, it's so sad. All her relatives are dead. She lost her husband—"

"Earl," Amanda said.

"That's right. Earl. Must be twelve years ago, now. And there was a terrible accident. It was before my time here, of course…"

"Donna. Her daughter," Amanda said.

"The whole family," the woman said. "Terrible."

Amanda glanced at Libby. "She seems calmer now, but it would be good if someone could check in on her."

"I know just the person. Can you wait a while?"

Amanda glanced at her watch. "How long?"

"Not long. I promise."

The woman was true to her word. Twenty minutes later there was a knock on the door. Libby didn't appear to notice.

"Libby? Someone's here. You mind if I let them in?"

Libby smiled. "That's nice, dear."

Amanda greeted an elderly lady who said her name was Winnifred and that she was with the Ladies Auxiliary. She lived nearby and had been going to the Presbyterian church since Nixon was president, she said proudly.

Amanda explained the situation. Winnifred nodded. "So sad when they lose their faculties. I used to be a nurse, back when I still had my figure." She winked. She said she knew Mrs. Passmore, although not well. "It's a huge congregation," she said.

Amanda led her into the living room. "Libby, someone to see you." She explained who Winnifred was. Libby frowned for a few seconds, as if trying to remember where she knew her visitor from. "We've met before, haven't we?"

"Yes, Mrs. Passmore. I'm Winnie."

"Oh, call me Libby. Everyone does. This is…" She frowned at Amanda.

"Mandy. My name is Mandy."

"And why are you here again? Are you one of the nieces?"

"No, Libby. Just a passing acquaintance. Can I leave you to it?" she asked Winnifred.

"We'll be just fine, young lady. Won't we, Libby?"

Libby smiled and relaxed into her chair.

"I'll make us some tea. Would you like that, Libby?"

"That would be lovely. Be sure to make a big pot, enough for everyone."

"Of course," Winnifred said.

Once the kettle was on, Amanda gave Winnifred her card. "Call if you need help," she said. "I can get social services involved."

"She seems pretty self-sufficient," Winnifred said. "There's plenty of food in the cupboards. The fridge is full. The house is in tip-top shape."

Amanda nodded. "And everyone she loves is here. It would be a shame to take her away from it all."

"I'm so glad you understand." Winnie tucked the business card into a pocket. "Now let me finish making the tea."

Amanda let herself out and drove back to the substation parking lot, wiping a tear from her eye as she completed her report. When she was done, she pulled out her cell phone and pushed "1."

"Hi, Mom. I know you're asleep. I'm at work. Just wanted to call and say I'm thinking about you. See you Sunday."

She tucked the phone into her vest pocket, put the sedan in gear, and headed back out on patrol, attentive to everything around her, alert for trouble spots while scanning her computer display for calls. There were six pending, none urgent, and not a single one mentioned ghosts.

Amanda found herself humming an old song by Ray Parker, Jr. as she punched in the code that showed her responding to the next complaint on the list.

ILLEGAL CATCH

Marcie R. Rendon

Cristine paused at the door to the Bigfoot Lodge to stomp the snow off her Sorrel snow boots. A paper flyer, curled at the corners, was taped to the glass display case that usually held a cheap photo of whichever local band was playing in the bar that weekend. #*MMIW*, in large red lettering, followed underneath by *Have You Seen Tonya?*, was printed above a grainy photo of a young Native woman. The minus-fifteen-degree windchill was making Cristine's fingers numb. Still, she thought to herself, the freezing cold was a welcome reprieve from the heat and sand of the overseas desert where she had been deployed just a few short months ago. Every morning she put out her tobacco, giving thanks for being back in the north woods.

As Cristine read the rest of the flyer, she blew warm air into her cupped hands. Tonya Bullhead, age seventeen, had been missing from her aunt's house in Bemidji since the week after New Year's. She was last seen leaving the high school gym wearing black Nike tennis shoes, black jogging pants, and a Lumberjack hoodie. In the photo Tonya smiled and her hair was in neat French braids that hung down over both shoulders. She wore elaborate earrings with a bear paw in the center of a swirl of beads. A starter on the girls' basketball team and a jingle dress dancer at summer pow-wows, she was not a runaway. Her family begged for any leads to find her. Their number was listed as well as numbers to the Bemidji Police and the Minnesota Bureau of Criminal Apprehension.

Poor kid's been gone over a month, thought Cristine. She blew warm breath on her hands one more time, stomped her feet again, and opened the door to the lodge. Through the steam created when the warm air collided with the cold air from outside, Cristine surveyed the room. It was filled with a host of indeterminate gendered bodies, all wearing thick, padded snowmobile suits, stocking caps, and insulated boots.

Thousands of anglers had migrated to this lake, this week in February, for the largest ice fishing tournament of the year. Over one hundred thousand dollars in cash and prizes was up for grabs with twenty thousand dollars alone going to the angler who caught the largest fish. Most fishers were men, with a handful of women sprinkled throughout, Cristine being one of the handful.

Some of the women had taken off their headgear. Scandinavian-blonde ponytails were flipping around as women flirted with the men, many who sported full beards, their snow goggles pushed up on the tops of their heads, cold beers in hand. Business accountants and low-level lawyers pretending to be lumberjacks for the season. Cristine shook her head.

She surveyed the bar area. A four-piece band was crowded onto a corner stage and three couples, snowsuits unzipped, two-stepped around a four-by-four wood dance floor. There were booths filled with couples while a group of heavy drinkers stood at the bar drinking shots. She heard snippets of conversation: *drilled five holes, one for each son-in-law; been jigging red wax worms; hand-lined in a big one-perch, not a winner though.*

Cristine had driven the three hours from Nett Lake Reservation to hand-drill a hole through the two-foot-thick lake ice. Her shelter from the elements was a low-budget Walmart fishing tent. She sat on an overturned paint bucket and dropped a line in hoping for the big nibble. Even with her tribal ID she couldn't afford a room at the casino hotel; instead, she slept at a local mom-and-pop motel on a bed with threadbare sheets and the threat of bedbugs.

Cristine didn't like to think of herself as judgmental but the folks wearing brand-new snowmobile suits told her which anglers owned luxury ice fishing houses. She overheard one conversation where a guy was bragging to a young woman, his free arm around her waist, his other one holding a beer, that inside his "shack" he had his own hot tub. "Why don't you come by for a midnight soak?" He pulled the woman closer. Cristine could hear nylon rubbing against nylon.

She shook her head as the woman laughed and flipped her ponytail. Cristine looked around the room; it was safe to bet who the partygoers were, those willing to pretend to freeze for a weekend; their bragging rights would be who they had snagged rather than the fish they had caught.

Cristine squeezed into an open spot at the bar and ordered a hamburger basket with fries and a Coke. She ate standing. An older man to her left acknowledged her presence with a nod of his head. On her right, a guy with a grenade tattooed on his left hand eyed her, then made a racial slur under his breath followed by a derogatory slur about the women of her tribe. He looked her face on. His eyes had the dead metallic sheen she had seen many times overseas. She finished her meal, caught the bartender's eye before she left a twenty under the saltshaker.

As she turned to leave, the guy with the grenade tattoo said, loud enough for her to know she was meant to hear it, "Hey guys, I got some fresh meat back at my little hotel on the ice. Come on over for a taste. And I'm not talkin' any tough ol' deer meat." The small crowd of men around him laughed loudly and chugged their beer.

Cristine didn't even bother to throw them a dirty look. She just left.

The next day she drove out on the ice when the sun came up. She had a thermos of hot coffee, a chicken sandwich from a local gas station, a tin can of wax worms and another of frozen corn kernels. With the windchill at minus seventeen, she rotated between the shelter of her tent and the warmth of the car. She caught two small northern pike and an eelpout with corn kernels, all of which she released back into the water.

Midafternoon she sat in her car, looking out over the lake, contemplating quitting for the day. Her chances of winning the big prize were slim. The fishing tournament had turned the lake into a small city on ice. As far as she could see, fish houses dotted the lake. Pickup trucks and snowmobiles were parked outside each building. There was a large ice mansion half a football field away from her cheap tent from which she could hear occasional whoops of laughter.

They must be catching all the big ones before they ever get to me, she thought, cupping her hands tightly around the warm cup of coffee she had just poured. *With all the snowmobiles and trucks revving around that place I don't know how they can be catching anything,* was her next thought as she watched another snowmobile glide up to the house. A guy swung his leg off the machine, knocked, then entered the doorway, wisps of steam billowing out into the cold air.

She checked her phone. Another couple hours of sunlight. *May as well try one more time. With a wax worm this go 'round.* She shut off the car and went back into the tent. Sat on the cold plastic bucket and dropped the line into the cold water. Silence.

She thought back to the noise of the desert, the constant presence of other humans, in a tent, in a Humvee. A group, armed, sitting around outside looking up at the vast stars of the night, always conscious of other people somewhere out there in the darkness not wanting them on their land. Inside this tent, on this lake, here, back in the land of her people, was peace, was quiet. Stillness. She heard another burst of raucous laughter from the ice mansion. *Well, except for them,* she thought.

Just then she felt a nibble on her line. She gave it the slightest tug and felt the nibble again. She waited. Another nibble. She gave a quick jerk and felt the fish move away. She looked down into the water as she slowly pulled the line in. Before the hook even reached the surface, she saw a glint of something in the water. She pulled the line slowly in. On her hook was an elaborate beaded earring with a bear paw in the center.

Her whole body froze as she stared at the earring hanging on the fishhook. *Where have I seen this before?* she asked herself even as her mind's eye visualized the flyer on the wall outside the lodge. Tonya Bullhead, beautiful face framed by dark French braids, with this earring hanging from her ear. Cristine looked down into the water, half expecting to see a face, a body. Expecting to see Tonya Bullhead.

She put the earring in her jacket pocket. Grabbed the fishing pole and put it into the water. Moved it around. Tried to feel if there was a body down there. She tried to think. *If a body was put in freezing water, did it float? Did it sink?* Not feeling the pole catch on anything, she brought it up out of the water. She sat, immobile, on the plastic bucket. Staring into the hole in the ice.

She didn't know how long she just sat there. Finally, she took her gloves off and retrieved the earring from her pocket. She wanted to believe it wasn't the same earring from the #missing and murdered Indian women's flyer at the lodge but she knew with every fiber of her being that it was. She used her fishing pole one more time to feel around in the water before packing up her gear and getting in the car. *Guess I better find the tribal cop's office,* she said out loud as she turned the key in the ignition.

As she drove past the ice mansion, the guy she had seen arrive earlier exited the building. He was grinning broadly as he gave a farmer's wave to another man standing in the doorway. Through the cloud of steam Cristine recognized him as the man with the grenade tattoo. She shivered, and it wasn't from the cold.

The rest of the afternoon passed in a blur. The tribal cops took a statement from her. They compared the earring in her pocket to the one on the #mmiw flyer. Had her drive with them out to her fishing tent where they used a high beam flashlight to look down into the water. Stood around and shook their heads. Reached down into the water with a long pole that had a metal hook on the end. They walked to the nearest fish houses and asked the people still fishing if they had caught anything suspicious during the day. Stood around some more shaking their heads.

Cristine sat in the warmth of the tribal cop car and waited while they investigated. Finished, with nothing more to show for their effort, they dropped her back at her car. They kept the earring. Dismissed her.

She drove to the lodge and stood outside in the cold, staring at the picture of Tonya. She pulled out her cell phone and dialed. "Hey, Jayne, it's me Cristine." And she relayed the events of the day.

Cristine and Jayne had served together two years before Jayne was sent home with an honorable discharge and half of one leg gone. Jayne had gotten rehab and now lived in a small town on the border of Minnesota and North Dakota near the Canadian border. When the numbers first surfaced that there were five thousand-plus missing or murdered Indian women across the upper part of the continent, Jayne, a wild Anishinaabe-Lakota woman warrior, started her own grassroots organization. She used her yearly per cap earnings to get two rez dogs and herself trained in the search and rescue of missing humans. She was like the female version of the television bounty hunter without having the same national recognition. Most folks didn't even know that Indians still existed, let alone that their women were being trafficked in alarming numbers.

"I'm at the Bluebird Inn, room 115. I'll wait there for you," Cristine said before hanging up. It would be a good four hours before Jayne reached the lake. Cristine had another hamburger at the bar with the same scene as the night before. Back at the motel she watched a Las Vegas poker tournament, the action was almost as slow as ice fishing. She must have dozed because she jumped a little at the sound of a soft knock on the door. She rolled off the bed and opened the door to a blast of artic air; two German shepherd-pit bull mixes, leashed and harnessed, entered, followed by a bundled-up Jayne.

"Hey, girl, good to see you," Jayne said and gave Cristine a hug. "We got some work to do huh?" she added. Jayne was never one to waste time. She threw a duffle bag on the bed and put some dog food and water into bowls she pulled out of her jacket pockets.

They rehashed the earring story again. "Damn, wish you had been able to keep the earring. We could have had the dogs smell it," Jayne said. She sat looking at her dogs. "You had the earring in your pocket? Let's try that." She grabbed Cristine's jacket off the end of the bed, pulled the pockets inside out, and had the dogs sniff them. "Worth a try," she added. "Come on. Let's go see what we can find."

Both women bundled up with extra layers against the cold. They rode in Jayne's vehicle back to Cristine's fish tent. The lake looked like a deserted ghost town dotted with shanties, tents, and ice mansions. Some of the fancier ones had windows and you could see light from the windows. Those with heaters had smoke trails coming up out of thin metal chimneys on the roofs. The one Cristine called the ice mansion was lit up like a regular trailer house. It even had curtains over the windows.

At Cristine's tent, Jayne had her dogs sniff the pockets of Cristine's jacket once again and gave them the command to search. The dogs went directly to the tent, came out, circled the tent, circled the tent again, more slowly the second time. Cristine, already chilled in the night air, was doubtful that given the cold and ice that the dogs would be able to sense anything. She just prayed there wasn't a body under the ice.

The dogs, noses to the ice, headed away from the tent. The two women followed, their boots crunching on the snow on top of the ice. The dogs were headed directly to the ice mansion, which was really nothing but a glorified corrugated steel fish house. Cristine tugged Jayne's coat arm and whispered. "I don't think the guys in there are too friendly."

Jayne pulled her dogs to a stop, knelt, and talked to them in a low voice, so low Cristine couldn't hear what she was saying.

Jayne stood and flicked the leash and the dogs continued walking. About five feet from the ice mansion, on the distant side of a dark pickup truck, which was parked alongside five snowmobiles and an SUV, the dogs stopped and sat. Ears on alert, they gave a low throat growl while looking up at Jayne. "You stay here," Jayne said to Cristine. "We're going to go up a bit closer. Just stay behind the truck." And she and the dogs kept walking. Cristine could hear the soft crunch of Jayne's boots on the snow. Over the bed of the pickup, she watched the trio quietly circle the trailer.

They circled the trailer twice, then returned to where Cristine stood. "I think she's in there. Alive," said Jayne quietly, both dogs sitting silently at her feet.

"What?"

"The dogs are signaling that she's in there and alive."

"No fucking way?"

"Listen, you have an event like this, a couple thousand guys, there is always going to be trafficking going on."

"Are you kidding me? It's too damn cold to be having sex out here."

"Don't matter. Look at that building. It's like one of those expensive tiny houses. They probably got everything they need in there. Heat, water, toilet."

Cristine pulled out her phone, "I'll call the cops."

Jayne pushed her arm down. "No, they can't go in without a search warrant. I've been in this situation before. Some guys have a girl or a couple women locked up in a private residence. It's just me, a private citizen, with my dogs saying there's a woman in there in danger. Cops can't do anything. And if the cops go to the door, the guys refuse entrance and by the time the cops come back with a search warrant, that's if they bother to at all, the guys have moved the victim to a different location."

"We can't leave her in there."

Just then the door opened. The two women ducked down behind the truck's oversized tires. Music and laughter wafted out across the cold air. A single man exited, jumped on a snowmobile. His headlights swept across the truck as he turned and headed to the shoreline.

"Four snowmobiles, a vehicle, and this truck. There could still be at least six guys in there. You think it's just one girl?" asked Cristine.

"I don't know. Let me think." Jayne, still crouched down by her dogs, swiveled around, and surveyed the scene. It was cold and what noise there was on the lake was muffled by the snow and cold, dense air. There was the occasional sound of a snowmobile engine. A burst of laughter. The dull thud of a car door closing. A thin plume of smoke rose from the fish house chimney.

Finally, she spoke. "Get the car, don't turn on the headlights. Park by the house over there that looks empty. Keep the car running, headlights off. Doors unlocked. Then come help me."

"What are we going to do?"

"Fuck up their machines so they can't chase us. Go."

Cristine did as she was told. With the car mostly out of sight, engine quietly running, the two women slashed the tires of the pickup truck and SUV. Jayne crawled under them both and punched a hole in the radiators. She retrieved a red gas can from the back seat of her car and poured gasoline around the three snowmobiles. She handed Cristine a box of wooden farmer's matches. No one had exited the building or looked out the windows.

"What now?" asked Cristine.

"I'm going to walk up with the dogs and knock on the door. As soon as they open it, throw a match on the gasoline, and run like hell to the car. Drive to the back. With any luck, I'll meet you there." She pulled a black balaclava over her face. Told Cristine to cover her face with a scarf.

"Are you fucking serious?"

"Dead serious." And Jayne and the dogs walked to the door of the trailer.

As soon as the door opened, Cristine threw a lighted match onto the gasoline and flames flew into the air. She ran like hell to the car. Jumped in and drove wildly to the back of the building, the car sliding on the ice.

She could hear men yelling and see flames shooting into the air. Car doors slammed. Engines turned over. No sound of vehicles moving. Swearing. A gunshot.

"Go. Go. Go," screamed Jayne as she opened the back passenger door and pushed two people in. She and two dogs jumped in the front passenger seat. Cristine stepped on the gas. The car spun out. She turned into the skid. Got the car going straight to the shoreline. Jayne looked out the back window. "They're fucking shooting at us," she yelled as she ducked down. Cristine slid down until she could barely see over the dash. Jayne peeked back up. "Think we're in the clear," she said.

Cristine didn't turn on the car lights until they were three miles away on the highway. Two firetrucks passed them in the opposite direction headed to the lake. She parked the car by the black garbage bins behind the motel. They all crowded into the tiny motel room. Tonya and a girl named Layla, both drugged and physically hurt, sat shell shocked on the sagging mattress, wrapped in thin blankets from the bed. They were shivering, more from shock than from the cold.

"I don't think we can call the cops for any help," Cristine said quietly. She too was shaking.

"No, I don't think so either," answered Jayne. "Let me think."

In the end, they put the two young women in Cristine's car, filled the tanks of both cars at the casino gas station, and drove, in tandem, the two hours and forty-five minutes to the edge of Bemidji. At a Cenex station, Jayne called Tonya's family and told her to tell them where to come find her. Cristine gave both women some cash, enough to get a cup of hot coffee and something to eat. Told them to sit in the deli until Tonya's family got there.

Cristine and Jayne parked in the shadows in their respective cars, engines running, lights off, until they saw a beat-up pickup with Red Lake license plates pull into the station. Before the vehicle even came to a complete stop, a woman jumped from the truck and ran to deli door. The man driving quickly jumped out and followed her in.

The women watched as Tonya was scooped into the woman's arms. Then the man's. They talked briefly. It looked like everyone was crying. Then the older woman quickly turned to the other young woman and pulled her in for a hug.

Cristine gave a light tap on her car horn and motioned for Jayne to follow her. They got gas at a Holiday station, then drove two more hours to Cristine's home on the Nett Lake Reservation. While Cristine cranked up the heat in her HUD house and put a stack of quilts and a pillow on the couch, Jayne set out bowls of food and water for her dogs. Without talking both women fell asleep.

The next day they scoured the news on social media. A few lines in the local paper mentioned a fire at the fishing tournament, possibly caused by a faulty gas heater. The fire was quickly put out by the local fire department. After a breakfast of eggs and bacon, Jayne got her dogs in the car and drove west.

Later that week, Cristine shared a social media post with Jayne. It was a picture Tonya's aunt posted of their family. Everyone was smiling. Tonya sat in the middle. Her eyes were sad but she was smiling. The post read, "Safe."

ABOUT THE EDITOR

GREG HERREN is the award-winning author of over forty novels and editor of twenty-five anthologies. His most recent novel, *#shedeservedit,* was released in January; his next, *A Streetcar Named Murder,* is forthcoming in December 2022.

ABOUT THE CONTRIBUTORS

ERIC BECKSTROM is a writer and photographer from Minnesota, now based in Bloomington, Indiana. His stories have been published in the Bouchercon anthology and *Black Cat Weekly*, and his one-act, "A Terribly Sophisticated Party," was produced by Indiana's only professional theater, the Bloomington Playwrights Project.

ERIC BEETNER is the author of more than twenty-five novels including *All the Way Down, Rumrunners* and *Two in the Head*. He's been nominated for three Anthony awards, an ITW, a Shamus, and a Derringer along with six Emmys—and won none of them. When not writing, he works as a TV editor and producer in Los Angeles. For more info visit EricBeetner.com.

MARK BERGIN spent four years as a newspaper reporter, winning the Virginia Press Association Award for general news reporting, before joining the Alexandria, Virginia, Police Department in 1986. Twice named Police Officer of the Year for narcotics and robbery investigations, he served in most of the posts described in his 2019 debut novel *Apprehension*, a finalist for the 2020 Silver Falchion Award from Killer Nashville. Bergin is a member of Mystery Writers of America, Sisters in Crime, and International Thriller Writers. Retired, he and his wife divide their time between Alexandria, Virginia and Kitty Hawk, North Carolina. MarkBerginWriter.com.

SUSANNA CALKINS, a historian and educator, writes the award-winning Lucy Campion historical mysteries set in seventeenth century London and the Speakeasy Murders set in 1920s Chicago. Her fiction has been nominated for the Mary Higgins Clark Award, as well as the Agatha, Anthony, and the Lefty awards, and she received the Sue Feder Historical Mystery Award (Macavity). She holds a Ph.D. in early modern English history and once served as a "living history specialist" (a.k.a. "pirate") aboard the *Golden Hinde*. Born and raised in Philadelphia, she lives in the Chicago area now, with her husband, two sons, and a cat.

L.A. CHANDLAR is the award-winning author of the Art Deco Mystery Series, nominated for the Agatha, Lefty, Macavity, and Anthony awards, winner of *Suspense Magazine*'s Crimson Pen 2019. Laurie has been living and writing in New York City for twenty years and has been speaking for a variety of audiences including a group with the United Nations. Laurie has worked in PR for General Motors, is the mother of two boys, has toured the nation managing a rock band, and is a fierce advocate for women's rights. She loves coffee and wine; and hates thwarted love and raisins.

MEREDITH DOENCH is the author of the Luce Hansen crime thriller series and *Whereabouts Unknown* from Bold Strokes Books. Her writing has also appeared in many literary journals, and she is a board member of Mystery Writers of America, Midwest Chapter. Doench is also a senior lecturer of creative writing, literature, and composition at the University of Dayton in Ohio. For more information about this author, visit MeredithDoench.com.

MARY DUTTA is the winner of the New England Crime Bake Al Blanchard Award for her short story "The Wonderworker," which appears in *Masthead: Best New England Crime Stories*.

Her work can also be found in the anthologies *Mystery Most Diabolical, Murder by the Glass, The Fish That Got Away, The Best Laid Plans*, and the forthcoming *Hook, Line, and Sinker*. She is a member of Sisters in Crime and the Short Mystery Fiction Society. Visit her at MaryDutta.com and follow her on Twitter @Mary_Dutta.

JOHN M. FLOYD's work has appeared in more than 350 different publications, including AHMM, EQMM, Strand Magazine, The Saturday Evening Post, three editions of Best American Mystery Stories, Best Mystery Stories of the Year 2021, and Best Crime Stories of the Year 2021. A former Air Force captain and IBM systems engineer, John is an Edgar finalist, a 2021 Shamus Award winner, a five-time Derringer Award winner, a three-time Pushcart Prize nominee, and the author of nine books. He is also the 2018 recipient of the Edward D. Hoch Memorial Golden Derringer Award for lifetime achievement.

JIM FUSILLI is the author of nine novels including *The Mayor of Polk Street* and its predecessor *Narrows Gate*, which George Pelecanos called "equal parts Ellroy, Puzo and Scorsese" and *Mystery Scene* magazine said "must be ranked among the half-dozen most memorable novels about the Mob." The *Narrows Gate* setting is based loosely on Hoboken, New Jersey, where Jim was born. The former Rock & Pop Critic of *The Wall Street Journal*, Jim is the author of *Pet Sounds,* his tribute to Brian Wilson and the Beach Boys' classic album. It was translated to Japanese by Haruki Murakami.

BARB GOFFMAN specializes in writing short stories and has won the Agatha Award twice and the Macavity, Silver Falchion, and Ellery Queen's Mystery Magazine Readers Award one time each. She's been a finalist for major short story crime awards thirty-six times, including sixteen Agatha nominations (a category record) and multiple nominations for the Anthony, Derringer, and Macavity awards. She's an associate editor of *Black Cat Weekly* and works as a freelance editor, focusing on cozy and traditional mysteries. In 2023, she'll be toastmaster at Malice Domestic. Learn more at BarbGoffman.com.

R. FRANKLIN JAMES grew up in the San Francisco Bay Area. A UC Berkeley graduate, she cultivated a different type of writing—legislation and public policy. After a career of political advocacy, she returned to her love of writing. Her debut novel, *The Fallen Angels Book Club*, was the first of six books in her Hollis Morgan Mysteries. The books have been made into Lifetime movies. Her latest series, the Johanna Hudson Mysteries, opens with book one—*The Inheritance*, which has already received a *Publisher's Weekly* "must read" review. James resides in Northern California.

JESSICA LAINE writes contemporary crime fiction with a Latinx twist. Her work has been published in the Anthony-nominated anthologies *Trouble No More, Murder-A-Go-Go's,* and *Pa' Que Tu Lo Sepas*. Jessica is also a past recipient of the Sisters in Crime Eleanor Taylor Bland award. A proud member of the Crime Writers of Color, she tweets @msjessicalaine. Learn more at JessicaLaineBooks.com.

BV LAWSON's short stories have been nominated for the Pushcart Prize, honored by Derringer, Golden Fedora, and Gemini Magazine awards, and BV was also a contributor to the Anthony Award-winning *Blood on the Bayou*. BV's poetry has appeared in *Noir Riot, International Poetry Forum, Midwest Poetry Review,* and more. BV's Scott Drayco crime novels have also been named Best Mystery in the Next Generation Indie Book Awards, chosen as a Featured *Library Journal* Pick, and been finalists for Shamus, Silver Falchion, Daphne, and Foreword Book Reviews awards. Visit BV's website at BVLawson.com.

Agatha Award-winning author **EDITH MAXWELL** writes the Quaker Midwife Mysteries and short stories of murderous revenge. As Maddie Day she pens the Country Store Mysteries, the Cozy Capers Book Group Mysteries, and the new Cece Barton Wine Country Mysteries. A lifetime member of Sisters in Crime and a member of Mystery Writers of America, Maxwell was a decades-long listener to *Prairie Home Companion*. She lives with her beau north of Boston, where she writes, gardens, cooks, and wastes time on Facebook. Find Edith/Maddie at EdithMaxwell.com and on social media.

MINDY MEJIA's internationally acclaimed thrillers have been translated into over twenty languages. Her books have been picked for People's Best New Books and listed in *The Wall Street Journal*'s Best New Mysteries. A CPA and graduate of the Hamline University MFA program, she lives and works in the Twin Cities. Her next book, *To Catch a Storm*, is forthcoming from Grove Atlantic. Find out more at MindyMejia.com.

RICHIE NARVAEZ is author of the collection *Roachkiller and Other Stories* and the thriller *Hipster Death Rattle*. His most recent novel is the historical YA mystery *Holly Hernandez and the Death of Disco*, which won an Agatha Award and an Anthony Award. His latest book is the collection *Noiryorican*, which was nominated for an Anthony. He lives in the Bronx.

ERICA RUTH NEUBAUER is the Agatha Award-winning author of the Jane Wunderly mysteries. She spent eleven years in the military, nearly two as a Maryland police officer and one as a high school English teacher before finding her way as a writer. She has been a reviewer of mysteries and crime fiction for publications such as *Publishers Weekly* and *Mystery Scene Magazine*, and she's a member of Sisters in Crime and Mystery Writers of America. Erica Ruth lives in Milwaukee, WI.

BRYON QUERTERMOUS is the *New York Times* bestselling author of the Dominick Prince trilogy and *Jackpot*, co-written with Stuart Woods. His short stories have appeared in many print and online journals of varying repute. Visit him online at BryonQuertermous.com and on Twitter @bryonq.

MARCIE R. RENDON, White Earth Ojibwe. *Oprah Magazine* 2020 listed Rendon as one of thirty-one Native American authors to read. Rendon received Minnesota's 2020 McKnight Distinguished Artist Award. *Sinister Graves,* the third Cash Blackbear, will be available October 2022. *Girl Gone Missing,* Rendon's second Cash Blackbear novel, was nominated for the Sue Grafton Memorial Award 2020. *Murder on the Red* River received the Pinckley Women's Crime Novel Award 2018, all available from Soho Press. Rendon's children's book, *Stitches of Tradition*, will be published by Heartdrum in 2024. Diego Vazquez and Rendon received the Loft's 2017 Spoken Word Immersion Fellowship for work with incarcerated women.

RAQUEL V. REYES writes Latina protagonists. Her Cuban-American heritage, Miami, and Spanglish feature prominently in her work. *Mango, Mambo, and Murder,* the first in the Caribbean Kitchen Mystery series, won a Lefty for Best Humorous Mystery. *The New York Times Book Review* wrote, "it executes its mission—with panache." Raquel's short stories appear in various anthologies, including *The Best American Mystery and Suspense 2022.* Find her across social media platforms as @LatinaSleuths and on her website LatinaSleuths.com.

BEV VINCENT is the author of several non-fiction books, including *The Road to the Dark Tower* and *Stephen King: A Complete Exploration of His Work, Life and Influences.* He co-edited the anthology *Flight or Fright* with Stephen King and has published over 120 stories, with appearances in *Ellery Queen Mystery Magazine, Alfred Hitchcock Mystery Magazine,* and *Black Cat Weekly*. His work has been published in twenty languages and nominated for the Stoker (twice), Edgar, Ignotus, and ITW Thriller awards. Recent works include "The Ogilvy Affair" and "The Dead of Winter," the latter in *Dissonant Harmonies* with Brian Keene. To learn more, visit BevVincent.com.

TESSA WEGERT is the author of the Shana Merchant series of mysteries, which includes *Death in the Family*, *The Dead Season*, and *Dead Wind*. A former freelance journalist, Tessa's work has appeared in *Forbes*, *The Huffington Post*, *The Economist*, and *The Globe and Mail*. Tessa grew up in Quebec and now lives with her husband and children in Coastal Connecticut. She is co-president of Sisters in Crime Connecticut (SinC-CT), and is currently working on her next novel.

MICHAEL WILEY's most recent novel is *Head Case*, the third in a series featuring the deeply disinhibited Chicago P.I. Sam Kelson. He also writes the Daniel Turner and Franky Dast thrillers and the Shamus Award-winning Joe Kozmarski mysteries. Michael grew up in Chicago and lived and worked in the neighborhoods where he sets his Kelson and Kozmarski books. He teaches literature and creative writing at the University of North Florida in Jacksonville, Florida—the setting of the Daniel Turner and Franky Dast stories. Missy Denners, in "Spinout," is based loosely on one of Michael's friends and neighbors.

SANDRA SG WONG (she/her) writes fiction across genres, including the cross-genre Lola Starke novels and Crescent City short stories. A Crime Writers of Canada Awards of Excellence finalist and Whistler Independent Book Awards nominee, as well as a speaker, mentor, and hybrid (indie/trad) author, Sandra is Immediate Past President of Sisters in Crime and a proud member of Crime Writers of Color. A standalone suspense, *In the Dark We Forget,* is her most recent release. Connect with her on

Twitter @S_G_Wong, Instagram @sgwong8, and via SGWong.com.

On the following pages are a few
more great titles from the
Down & Out Books publishing family.

For a complete list of books and to
sign up for our newsletter,
go to DownAndOutBooks.com.

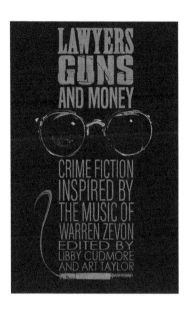

Lawyers, Guns, and Money
Crime Fiction Inspired by the Music of Warren Zevon
Edited by Libby Cudmore and Art Taylor

Down & Out Books
June 2022
978-1-64396-266-5

The songs of Warren Zevon are rich with crime and intrigue and suspense—guns and gunners, assassins and drug dealers, a supernatural serial killer, and a heap of hapless losers along the way too. And Zevon himself was a fan of crime fiction.

15 fantastic writers offer fresh spins on his discography with tales that span the mystery genre: caper, espionage, noir, paranormal, private eye, and more. Contributors include Gray Basnight, William Boyle, Dana Cameron, Libby Cudmore, Hilary Davidson, Steve Liskow, Nick Mamatas, Paul D. Marks, matthew quinn martin, Josh Pachter, Charles Salzberg, Laura Ellen Scott, Alex Segura, Kevin Burton Smith, and Brian Thornton.

Swing Gang
A Vince McNulty Thriller
Colin Campbell

Down & Out Books
June 2022
978-1-64396-268-9

Titanic Productions has moved to Hollywood but the producer's problems don't stop with the cost of location services.

When McNulty finds a runaway girl hiding at the Hollywood Boulevard location during a night shoot e takes the girl under his wing but she runs away again.

Between the drug cartel that wants her back and a hitman who wants her dead, McNulty must find her again before California wildfires race towards her hiding place.

NEW YORK TIMES BESTSELLING AUTHOR

Moonlight Gets Schooled
A Dick Moonlight PI Thriller
Vincent Zandri

Down & Out Books
August 2022
978-1-64396-284-9

When Dick Moonlight PI is called in by the APD to look into a beautiful blond woman by the name of Virginia Gamble who teaches English at a prestigious private boy's school and who's allegedly sleeping with her underage students, he finds himself snared in a trap of illicit sex and violence.

He also comes face to face with Gamble's angry Mexican Cartel drug dealing boyfriend who's vowed to kill every man and boy the teacher has slept with. Including Moonlight.

Like Whitewashed Tombs
Ryan Sayles

Down & Out Books
August 2022
978-1-64396-272-6

A bloody liquor store robbery.

Two diverging police partners. One is haunted by the pain of being widowed and God's request of him. The other is stalked by adversaries both spectral and all-too real.

Their already messy lives become further entangled together as redemption slips farther away.

CPSIA information can be obtained
at www.ICGtesting.com
Printed in the USA
JSHW051939240822
29585JS00003B/13